THE BIG WEEKEND - LARGE PRINT EDITION

A STELLA REYNOLDS MYSTERY

LIBBY KIRSCH

Sunnyside Press

Sunnyside Press
PO Box 2476
Ann Arbor, MI. 48106

www.LibbyKirschBooks.com

Publisher's Note: This is a work of fiction. Names, characters, places, and incidents are a product of the author's imagination. Locales and public names are sometimes used for atmospheric purposes. Any resemblance to actual people, living or dead, or to businesses, companies, events, institutions, or locales is completely coincidental.

The Big Weekend/ Libby Kirsch -- 1st ed., large print

ISBN 978-1-7337003-7-5

❋ Created with Vellum

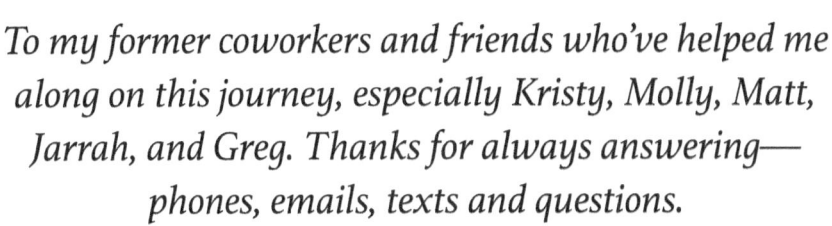

To my former coworkers and friends who've helped me along on this journey, especially Kristy, Molly, Matt, Jarrah, and Greg. Thanks for always answering— phones, emails, texts and questions.

1

Stella shivered at a gust of cold wind. Disgusted with her umbrella, she set it down by her feet, pulled the drawstring of her hood tighter around her face, and shoved her hands deep into her pockets. Her fingers, red and chapped, were glad to find a tiny bit of relief, but it was too late for her hair. Auburn locks plastered uncomfortably against her cheek and neck as the rain not only drove down from the sky in sheets, but also came at her sideways in the wind and bounced up from the sidewalk, soaking her legs.

Five degrees colder and she'd be covering a blizzard, instead of a murder.

Her eyes followed the water, rushing down the

street-turned-river, toward the crime scene. The front lawn was brown and stunted after a long winter, and a pair of legs stuck out from under a light blue baby blanket someone had hastily thrown over the body. The victim's face was covered, but Stella couldn't stop staring at his feet. One foot was covered by a black sneaker, but the other was bare, the missing shoe balancing on the top step of the nearby porch. She could only imagine it had fallen off the victim's foot when he stumbled to the ground as the first bullet struck.

Click, click, click. She turned toward the sound to see Devi press the igniter on his lighter four more times in rapid succession before it finally worked. The photographer sucked in a breath and the tip of his cigarette glowed red.

"You weren't here, yet, but there was a riot at the bus stop around the corner about five years ago," he said, the cigarette bouncing on his lips as he spoke. Although his pants looked just as soaked as Stella's felt, his umbrella, protecting not only himself, but the camera perched on the tripod, didn't waver in the storm. Devi was in his mid-fifties with graying, black hair, and Stella had only seen him in his work uniform: khakis, a Polo shirt embroidered with the station call letters, and a ball cap he only took off in court. Today, a quilted parka topped off the outfit. Early spring in Columbus, Ohio, wasn't much different from winter.

She looked in the direction he pointed and nodded, and they both fell silent, listening to the relentless rain. She shifted her weight from one foot to the other with an audible squash, and her thoughts turned longingly to her rain boots tucked neatly under her desk in the newsroom. She'd been on her way to cover a zoning board meeting when the scanner on the dash of the live truck had crackled to life. *Shots fired. Man down.* Now, an hour later, her toes were frozen, her hands were numb, and her patience was running out.

Stella and Devi had gotten to the scene only minutes after the police, but every time new officers arrived, they pushed the media farther away. Now, the live truck was parked across the street from the crime scene, and they were stuck almost a block away with nowhere to shelter from the storm.

After half an hour, Stella squinted up at the sky. The rain seemed to be letting up—it was less like a downpour with each passing minute. Sure enough, another ten minutes later, it had settled to a bare drizzle.

"Can't believe we didn't W3 it," Devi said sarcastically from the side of his mouth.

W3, or Wall-to-Wall Weather, was what Harry, their news director, called his plan to "own" weather coverage in the market. When severe weather struck, he wanted their NBC affiliate to be the first to interrupt regular programming with live weather coverage and the last to go back to regular programming when the threat had passed.

"It's just a rainstorm," Stella said, looking up at the sky again. It was still gray, but it looked lighter to the north and west.

"Doesn't seem to matter, though, does it?" Devi said, not taking his eyes off the crime scene.

With the break in the weather, people came pouring out of nearby homes to get the latest. A particularly chatty neighbor carrying on a noisy conversation on her cell phone caught Stella's attention. "Let's go."

Devi ditched his umbrella, heaved the giant news camera onto his shoulder, and then took the stick microphone out of an inside coat pocket and handed it to Stella as they hurried over.

"Excuse me, miss?" Stella bit her lip, realizing as they stepped closer that the woman was probably twice Stella's age. Ma'am might have been more appropriate. "Do you mind if we ask you a few questions?"

The woman looked Stella up and down before raising her cell phone to her lips and saying, "Imma have to call you back, DeeDee. Don't go anywhere, Imma call you right back." Her short, spiky, black hair had a red streak on the right that clashed shockingly with her electric pink jeans and three-inch heels. Her top was as colorful as a tropical bird, and even flapped like wings on either side of her thin frame with a sudden gust of wind.

Stella shook herself, realizing she'd been staring. "Can you say and spell your name for me, please?" The woman frowned, and Stella nodded encouragingly. "It helps us make sure the microphone levels are okay."

The woman shrugged and said, "Sure, sure. My name is Valerie Osmola. Spell that, V-A-L-E-R-I-E-O-S-M-O-L-A."

"Okay, great, Valerie. What can you tell me about the people who live there?" Stella nodded toward the crime scene.

"Sure, sure. You got Tabby-Cat and Bobby. It was a bad divorce, that much I *know*," Valerie nodded hard as she said it. "They fought like cats and dogs."

"I'm sorry," Stella interrupted, "did you say 'Tabby cat?'"

"Tabitha, you know, she look like a cat. She act like a cat, too, always sneaking around. Anyway, they always yelling out in the neighborhood, causing all kind of trouble. I wasn't one speck surprised when he left. To be honest, I'm not one bit surprised she shot him."

"Well," Stella clarified, "police haven't yet identified a suspect in the shooting."

"She killed him. I saw the whole thing from my living room."

Stella stared at her witness for a beat before hastily pulling her closer to the nearest porch, away from the street. If this woman was telling the truth, Stella didn't want any of the other stations honing in on her exclusive. She lowered her voice. "Tell me exactly what you saw, Valerie."

"Sure, sure. I saw that crazy, blond woman open the door, raise a gun at Bobby's face, and pull the trigger. No warning at all."

"You say they were divorced. Any idea why Bobby was here today?"

"I suspect to pick up the kids."

"They have kids?" Stella asked, a feeling of despair tamping down her excitement at the exclusive.

"Three. They young, too. Youngest is just outta diapers." Valerie wiped a raindrop off her nose and chewed her lip for a moment before continuing with new fervor. "Yup, she just fired the shot off, like *bang! Pow!* He went 'Argh!' and then he grunted," she demonstrated with a commendable sound "and just bounced down the steps. *Boom!* Hit the ground like a bag of concrete, and then nothing—silence. She stood there and watched him to make sure he was dead, and then she slammed the door like she just turned away the Jehovah's Witness ladies."

Stella, taken aback by the unexpected dramatic display, stared at Valerie for a moment, collecting her thoughts. "What did you say her name was? The shooter, I mean."

"Tabitha Herbert."

Stella looked down at her notes, thinking. This woman was colorful in more than just her outfit choice, and as much as she hated to admit it, Valerie would make a great live interview. Did she want to risk it, though? She chanced a glance at Devi, who was already nodding, and then turned back to the eyewitness.

"Valerie, can I interview you live on the news tonight?"

The woman's eyes sparkled. She dialed a number on her cell phone as she said, "Sure, sure, I can make that happen." As she walked away, she whooped into the phone, "You ain't never gonna believe this! I'm gonna be on the *news* tonight, girl..."

"I'll need you back here at quarter 'til!" Stella called to the retreating figure.

"Sure, sure," Valerie called back.

Devi cleared his throat. "Just make sure—"

"I know, I'll tell her she can't name the shooter —at least not until police confirm it," Stella said to her photographer.

Just then, she saw movement at the crime scene. The commanding officer walked out of the house and down the front steps, stopped to look at the body one last time, and then headed their way. He walked with the gait of a former military man, and the rest of him matched. His brown hair was shaved close in a buzz-cut, his uniform looked crisply-pressed, even though it was just as soaked as everything else outside, and finally, his per-fectly-manicured mustache dripped water down his chin.

It had started to drizzle again, and Stella picked up her umbrella. As she and Devi walked up the sidewalk, a patrol officer got out of his car and met them at the yellow caution tape blocking the way.

"Sergeant Coyne says you can go through, now," he said, holding the tape up so they could duck under. He waved the other news crews through, as well, and they formed a line as they headed toward the dead body. Stella looked at her watch: it was just after four. Her first deadline was fast approaching for a live tease at 4:55.

Before they got to Coyne, another officer stepped in their path and asked everyone to lower their cameras. A social worker was leaving the crime scene with three kids in tow. The youngest held onto a blanket and burst into tears as they stepped off the back porch. Stella saw the tallest child quickly crouch to pick up a small, green pacifier, which he wiped off on his shirt before handing it back to the baby. They got into an unmarked Escalade and drove away.

"Let's make this quick, guys. I'm soaked," Sergeant Coyne said as he walked up. He slicked water off his head before slapping on his police-issued hat.

The cameramen gathered around, and three microphones pointed toward him.

Stella kicked off the impromptu press conference. "Sergeant Coyne, what happened out here today?"

"We were called out to 144 Journey Street on reports of shots fired. When crews arrived, they discovered a male victim already deceased on the front lawn. One person of interest is being questioned. Homicide detectives are on scene, collecting evidence."

"Can you give us a name on the suspect?" a reporter from the FOX affiliate asked.

"Right now, we're not releasing any names. It's still very early in the investigation."

"Is Tabitha Herbert under arrest?" Stella asked.

"No."

She doubled down. "Did the shooting happen outside Tabitha Herbert's home?"

Sergeant Coyne hesitated for a fraction of a second and then said, "Yes."

"Was she home at the time of the shooting?"

"No comment."

"You're saying she's not under arrest?"

"That's correct," Sergeant Coyne said with a

resigned sigh, "but she is accompanying us down-town to answer some questions."

"What is her relationship to the deceased?" the other reporter asked.

"They were married," Sergeant Coyne said. He then held out his hands, as if to hold down the barrage of questions that came exploding from the gathered reporters. He spoke over them all. "From what we can tell, the victim was coming to this house to pick up his kids. He had weekend visita-tion rights. It looks like he was ambushed."

"What's the motive?"

"Could be anything, because this investigation is ongoing." He said the last part deliberately, and everyone knew the interview was over.

Once the microphones were turned off and the photographers and other reporters had moved away, Stella said, "You look like a Canadian Mountie in that hat."

He took it off and looked at it. "Nah. Mine's more stylish."

Stella smiled. She and Coyne both served on the board for a victim and witness organization. *Stop Crime Now* was a group of law enforcement officers, judges, and media representatives who came together to help publicize unsolved crimes and raise money for victim services.

She felt like she knew him well enough to say, "Brandon, I'm going to interview a neighbor live at five. The woman says she saw the murder happen. Do you see a problem with that?"

"Valerie Osmola?"

Stella looked over in surprise. "Oh. Yes, it is."

"My detectives already interviewed her. She's very..."

"Chatty?"

He barked out a laugh. "Sure. No, I think that's fine. I'm not worried about another crime—"

"Because you have a suspect in custody?" Stella watched Coyne's face as she asked the leading question.

His eyes narrowed. "Nice try. Off the record, Stella?" She nodded. "I'm not sure what we have here. By most accounts, the woman and her ex got along beautifully. She says she didn't shoot him, but can't say where she was when he was shot. The kids are acting weird, too, and then you've got the neighbor's testimony... and, well..."

"Are you saying the suspect is unknown?"

"I'm saying we still have a lot of work to do on this case."

Stella nodded, looking at the sergeant thoughtfully. "Will you call me if Tabitha gets booked in?"

"Sure."

"Thanks. Where are the kids headed? Do they have family in town who can take them?"

"Yeah, the grandma's right here on the block, but they'll have to spend the night in FCCS custody. It's protocol."

Stella blew out a noisy breath. Franklin County Children Services had a good reputation, but still. "That's gonna be a tough night for the little one, especially."

"Agreed. The youngest is just two-and-a-half. His first night without mom or dad will be with strangers at a foster home." He shook his head.

The sound of a long zipper pierced the monotony of raindrops hitting the sidewalk. The coroner's office had finally been cleared to take the body away from the crime scene, and two men struggled to get the limp, heavy, wet body from the ground and into a body bag. Stella looked away, not wanting to see where the bullet had entered or exited the victim.

"You think you'll get used to it," Sergeant Coyne said, watching Stella focus on her notebook, "but you never do."

She looked up to watch them load the body bag onto a gurney and roll it down the sidewalk into a waiting ambulance.

Coyne headed to his car just as her phone rang. It was Joy, the assignment editor back in the newsroom. "What do you have out there, Stella? We're trying to decide if we lead with you or with weather."

"It's not an open and shut case, if that's what you're asking. Anyway, I've got a live interview that I think will knock Harry's socks off," Stella said.

"So, what, you've got cop sound again?" Joy grumbled.

"Not a cop—a neighbor. She seems pretty... hmm, what's the right word? Outgoing?"

"All right, we'll put you at the top. I hope she keeps it interesting."

Stella stifled a laugh as she disconnected the call—she didn't think Valerie would have trouble holding the viewers' attention.

2

S tella stared at the camera and pressed her IFB earpiece into her ear with the hand that wasn't holding the microphone.

"Who is that?" Beatrice asked. The producer back at the station must have been looking at Stella's live feed.

"I've got Valerie Osmola here with me; she's our live interview. Do you have the package that Devi and I sent back?"

"We've got it. I've got you down for two minutes total, so keep your live interview quick."

Valerie had earbuds in and swayed to a song with her eyes closed, occasionally belting out a line.

"Is that *Salt-N-Peppa*?" Beatrice asked. "Is she singing *Shoop*?"

Stella nodded and had to bite her lip hard to keep the smile off her face. She looked down at her notebook, but Valerie was still undulating in her peripheral vision. The neighbor had spent the last forty-five minutes getting ready for her live television debut, and she was now wearing full-makeup, as well as what Stella could only guess was her best, most colorful outfit. Her hair—short and spiky before—now hung in soft, perfect curls around her face—a wig?—and an aura of excitement wafted from her like the smell of warm cookies from a bakery.

"Live tease is in thirty," Devi said, adjusting the camera.

Stella looked at Valerie. "I'll do this live tease, and then you'll join me for the five o'clock hit in about five minutes."

Valerie wrinkled her nose. "I'm not going to be live?"

"In five," Devi called.

Stella didn't answer Valerie because she heard her cue.

Stella: A gunshot rings out in East Columbus. A father of three dead on the front steps of his former home. I'll have the latest on the investigation into his murder in just a few minutes.

"Clear."

Valerie had moved behind her while she was talking.

"Yup, she did," Devi said before she could ask.

Stella bit her lip again, although this time, she didn't find anything funny. "Valerie, don't worry, you'll be live with me during our next hit. It's literally minutes away, okay?"

Valerie grinned. "Sure, sure."

Stella blew out a sigh and looked over her notes one last time. Soon, Devi said, "Standby. Show open starts in twenty seconds."

She nodded and heard the pre-recorded teases play over the airwaves, plugging stories that would air throughout the newscast. A two-shot of the anchors back at the station came up on the small playback screen Devi had set up by his feet.

Mark: Good evening, everyone. I'm Mark Markus.

Vera: And I'm Vera Evans. We begin tonight with a shocking shooting in East Columbus. Police say a man was killed as he picked up his kids for weekend visitation. Stella Reynolds is live at the scene with the very latest. Stella?

Stella: Mark, Vera, a terrible scene out here on Journey Street. One man gunned down in cold blood just feet away from his three children. Tonight, investigators still have a lot of questions. Police are interviewing a person of interest, and the victim's children are with FCCS for the night. Joining us live now, a neighbor who actually saw the shooting. Valerie, thanks for being with us tonight.

Stella only noticed then that Valerie was still clutching her cell phone in one hand. She jiggled it nervously when Stella said her name and bounced up and down on her toes as she started speaking.

"I seen it all. I seen the whole thing go down right in front of my face."

The volume was so unexpectedly loud that

Stella took an involuntary step backward. Valerie's last word echoed in the silence of the neighborhood, but the eyewitness was just getting started.

"It ain't unusual to see Bobby come to his ex's house to pick up the kids, and that's just what I seen today and I thought it was just a normal day, but then, *BAM!*"

It was like she'd rehearsed her lines from her earlier interview with Stella; Valerie added arm gestures, along with wild facial contortions as she talked of watching Tabitha shoot her ex-husband in cold blood. It was awful and riveting at the same time.

As she went through her frenzied description of the crime, two people sidled into the live shot from behind and started dancing. It wasn't just a subtle two-step, either, but as if the pair had started an intense, choreographed show. Stella glanced up at her photographer for direction. Devi was waving the pair away, but they didn't move. Valerie noticed and interrupted herself.

"Ooh, I have some backup dancers. I'm like, legit official now. What do you think about that, Sally?"

Stella's eyebrows drew down and she said, "Uhh... who—"

"You just like that Sally Jessy Raphael lady, you know?" Valerie said.

"Jesus, Stella, wrap it up when you can," Beatrice said through her earpiece.

Valerie stopped talking to regroup, and out of the corner of her eye, Stella saw a third person slip behind the live shot. It was too much, and she was just preparing to tell the entire group to move aside when she noticed the third person was a little girl. No more than ten years old, her hair was in untidy French braids, and even though it wasn't quite dinnertime, she appeared to have on pajamas, already.

The little girl took in the scene in front of her and shook her head. The gesture, coupled with a wary facial expression, pulled Stella up short. She looked back at Valerie and cleared her throat.

"Valerie, thanks so much for your time." Stella turned toward the camera and took two steps closer effectively blocking Valerie and her friends from view. "That's all we have from the scene for now. Reporting Live, I'm Stella Reynolds. Mark and Vera, I'll send it back to you."

Valerie immediately pivoted and took off to congratulate her friends. The girl was still eyeing

Stella, but before she could call her over, Devi tapped her on the shoulder.

"The station wants you to call in. I guess Harry wants more of that live interview at six."

Stella nodded, never taking her eyes off the girl. When Devi headed back to the live truck, the girl marched forward with a sure and steady step.

"Ms. Valerie told all of us to watch the news tonight and that we would have quite a show. As soon as I heard what she was saying, though, I thought I needed to set the record straight."

Again, Stella was taken aback. This was not your usual ten-year-old. She seemed wise beyond her years, and maybe she was. This was the kind of neighborhood in which a child might see more than they should.

"What do you mean?" Stella asked.

"Tabby didn't shoot that man."

Stella frowned. "What are you saying? Did you see something?" The girl nodded, her arms crossed defensively across her chest. "Have you talked to police?"

The little girl scowled. "It's complicated."

"Complicated? Why?"

She opened her mouth to answer, but then she

shut it again. "It just is, okay?" She shook her head and started to walk away.

Stella's brow wrinkled. This old soul knew something, but didn't want to tell her or police about it. She wondered if it was important.

3

S tella stared at the small TV screen on her desk, watching a makeover session on the ABC affiliate with interest. Edie Hawthorne hosted a weekly style show, and she had devoted the entire half-hour to *eye* makeup. Stella could have summed up the entire program in twenty short seconds: pick a color, put it on.

The stay-at-home-mom Edie was working on, however, appeared to be completely enthralled in the multi-step process, and Stella was completely enthralled by that fact.

"Stella, can you order the rundown today?"

She scrunched her eyes and looked up at the weekend producer, Amanda, with a smile plas-

tered on her face. The staff was small on the weekends, so everyone who worked the shift had to
wear multiple hats. Stella anchored and usually
wrote and voiced a story for the news. Amanda
Shaker should have been Stella's closest ally—
after all, they worked together all day Saturday
and Sunday.

"No problem, Amanda. What's going on?" She
looked at the pale, blond, gloomy woman with interest. She had just arrived at work ten minutes
earlier without even a hello and was now asking
Stella to do her job for her.

Amanda threw her hands up. "Always the
Spanish Inquisition with you people," she said angrily. "It's like we're all supposed to be a team, until
someone asks you to do something."

Stella glanced around the deserted newsroom,
confused. "What?"

With that, Amanda's hands came crashing
down onto her legs and she pushed herself up and
sucked in a deep breath. Before she could get going, though, Stella held out her hands and said,
"Amanda, I'm happy to do the rundown. No need
to get so upset."

The woman stalked out of the newsroom; a

few moments later, Stella heard the door to the parking lot slam.

She blew out a sigh. Amanda had made it clear from Stella's first day at the station that she wasn't a fan. After Harry had introduced her during a staff meeting, she'd overheard Amanda complain that they didn't need a weekend co-anchor. Things only got worse from there. Snarky comments, bad cues during the newscast, and even a clear preference for Stella's co-anchor—Amanda's husband—to read the stories usually resulted in Stella having nearly a third fewer stories to read. It was so bad that her boss had once asked her if she was trying to save her voice.

She closed her eyes and twisted her hair into a loose bun on top of her head as she muttered, "That woman is—"

"Crazy?"

Her head swung around sharply toward the voice, but she smiled when she saw who it was. During the week, Parker Sharpe was the makeup artist who worked on the main anchors at the station. Stella occasionally ran into him in the makeup room if she happened to have a live shot in the studio. He had dark, smooth skin, and just then, his chocolate-brown eyes smiled wickedly at her.

"I've said it before and I will say it again: that woman is crazy. I don't know how she and Spenser stay married."

Stella bit her lip, but couldn't stop a laugh from bubbling out. "Well, my co-anchor is a mystery in many ways," Stella finally said, making Parker chuckle. "What are you doing here today? I thought you had weekends off?"

"There aren't days off when you're self-employed, mmkay?" He studied her from head to toe and finally clucked his tongue disapprovingly.

Stella wrinkled her nose. "What?"

"Is that what you're wearing tonight?"

She looked down at her outfit—a black suit with a lilac shell underneath and a delicate, silver necklace—and then looked back up at Parker. "Well... it was *going* to be."

Parker shook his head. "That necklace would be perfect for a funeral, but unfortunately no one will be able to see it at home."

"Huh?"

"You need more color by your face—something chunkier. Oh, and lilac ain't your color,

Stella. Maybe on your feet, but not by your face and *not* by that hair."

"Just last week, I heard someone say red and purple are great colors together."

"Who said that?" he asked skeptically.

She nodded at the screen on her desk, "Edie Hawthorn." The stay-at-home mom stood gleefully next to Edie, all done up in a cocktail dress, with a new, bob haircut and honey-blond highlights framing her now-dramatic eyes.

"Edie Hawthorn?" he said incredulously. "You're going to take Edie Hawthorn's word over mine?"

Stella smiled innocently. "Not now, obviously."

His lips were pursed as he stared disapprovingly at the TV screen. "A woman with dark brown hair doesn't need blond highlights that will grow out in about two weeks." He turned his attention back to Stella. "Okay, open up."

She looked at him quizzically and he motioned to her half-open desk drawer. She grinned and pulled out the bag of mini Snickers, offering them to the tall, lanky stylist. "I never would have pegged you for a chocolate bar kind of guy—more like green tea and raw almonds."

Parker brushed the bag aside with a wrinkled

nose and reached into her drawer for her makeup bag.

"Oh," she laughed as she watched him unzip the case and gingerly pick through her makeup supplies, occasionally opening a tube to look at a color, and clucking under his breath.

"I'm gonna be here, doing paperwork, for a couple of hours. Meet me in the makeup room at twenty to six. They don't pay me to do the weekend anchor's makeup, so this is a one-time job—mmkay?—but it's obvious that you need help."

Stella's nose wrinkled, unaccustomed to Parker's candor. She opened her mouth to politely decline his offer, but he was already halfway across the newsroom. He called over his shoulder, "Five-forty. Don't be late."

Stella shook her head and crossed the newsroom to the assignment desk. Now that Amanda was gone, and since her co-anchor wasn't in yet, apparently Stella would be sitting at the assignment desk, listening to the scanners, rewriting scripts, and organizing the rundown of stories for the six o'clock newscast that night.

Despite the extra work, she couldn't help thinking that anchoring was kind of a breeze. No matter the weather, the studio was always dry and climate-controlled. There was no soaking rain or bitter cold, and a bathroom was always just a few steps away, as well as the coffee machine, the vending machine, and even the mini Snickers she kept in her desk drawer.

The only problem, of course, was that her weekend coworkers didn't like her. If Amanda's irritation was easy to identify, her husband's was covert. Spenser wouldn't greet her when he arrived, only deigning to talk to her when they were live on camera.

Her ears perked up when a tone rang out from one of the scanners. When the dispatcher only asked for a roll call, however, Stella went back to her computer. The stories were stacked haphazardly in the rundown, and she moved them around, hoping to improve the flow of the newscast. Next, Stella assigned the reads evenly, and she finally started reading through scripts, making minor changes to wording and updating information.

The editor was hidden away in one of the editing suites, working on getting the video clips ready for the newscast. Meanwhile, the blond head of the newscast director, Randy, was buried behind his computer three desks away. He was busy entering the correct computer codes into the rundown to dictate which cameras in the studio would move and when.

Her new station was pretty cutting edge, and the entire studio was controlled by computers.

When one of the college interns showed up, Stella gleefully gave up her seat behind the scanners and asked him to make beat calls to all the local police departments and fire stations while she proofread the last few scripts in the show.

Soon, the only sound, apart from the usual beeping and clanking of the scanners, was his dispirited voice as he asked the same question over and over. "Hi, this is Russ from NBC News 5. Anything going on today?"

Eventually, Spenser cruised into the newsroom, barely inclining his head in greeting before heading to his desk to get ready for the newscast.

"No worries, Spense, I'll take care of the show," Stella muttered under her breath.

Russ cleared his throat. "Man, it's so quiet this afternoon."

The director groaned from his spot a few desks away.

"What did he say, Randy?" Stella covered her head with her hands in mock horror.

"Kid, you're killing me!" Randy called.

The twenty-year-old looked around, his eyes as wide as saucers. "What?"

Stella smiled kindly at him. "Russ, you should never say something like that in the newsroom; it almost guarantees that a fatal fire, a highway shooting, and a drowning will happen all at the same time. It's an unwritten rule." As if to prove her point, a tone rang out across the scanner, and everyone—even Spenser—stared silently at Russ as they waited to hear what emergency would be announced.

"10-24, repeat, 10-24 near Spring and Cleveland."

"They're asking for an ambulance. Better keep listening." Stella reached over him to pick up the microphone to the two-way radio.

"Lou, did you hear that?"

The weekend photographer answered from the live truck, "Yup. Hope and I are close. We'll check it out."

Amanda breezed into the space, clutching a twenty-ounce latte in one hand and her sunglasses in the other. With no explanation for where she'd been or thanks to Stella for filling in, she said, "I've got this, Stella. Move."

Stella barked out a laugh before she could clamp her lips. This woman was too much. Nevertheless, she obediently gathered her things and went back to her desk only to realize it was five-thirty. Happy for the distraction, she grabbed her makeup kit and headed to the dressing room next to the studio.

She opened the door and found the lights already glowing along the mirrored wall. Parker was just tying an apron around his hips; on further inspection, Stella noticed it was a kind of makeup artist apron with easily accessible pockets for two-dozen small brushes. Parker's game face was on, and he motioned for Stella to take a seat in front of him. She held out her makeup bag, which he took and tossed onto the countertop behind him without a second glance. He then clipped her hair back from her face.

"Sit back, close your eyes, and don't talk. I'm gonna need about fifteen minutes."

Stella felt her shoulders tighten. The makeup, the hair, and the constant critiques of what she looked like and how she dressed wasn't her favorite part of the job. She knew it came with the territory, but it still made her feel defensive. Parker put his hands on her shoulders and pushed them down.

"This is supposed to be *fun,* Stella, so just relax, mmkay?"

She did her best and soon felt various brushes, pencils, lotions, and creams being applied to her face. Parker had a light touch, and after a few minutes, she felt herself getting drowsy. Once, she pried her left eye open a smidge to try to see what was going on, but she was rewarded by Parker spinning her chair away from the mirror.

"Uh-uh!" he admonished, applying yet more eyeshadow. "No peeking."

Finally, after one last swath of blush across her cheekbones, she felt him step back and heard the brushes go back into his apron pockets.

"All right, Stella. What do you think about this?"

He spun the chair toward the mirror and she slowly opened her eyes. It was like staring at a stranger, the change was so remarkable. Her eyes seemed to have grown to twice their usual size, and her cheekbones stood out, thanks to several layers of darker and lighter blush. The result was a thinner-looking face with a dark fringe of eyelashes framing enormous eyes that looked greener than they ever had.

"Is that... purple eyeshadow? Didn't you just tell me—"

"It's the shade of purple that's so important, Stella. See how this one works with your coloring?"

"Wow." It was all she could say for the next minute.

Parker nodded with satisfaction. "I'll say," he said with a smile. "Wow."

"How did you do that to my eyes?" She turned her head one way and then the other to see how enormous they looked from all angles.

"A lot of makeup," he said. "Like, *a lot* a lot." Stella turned from her own reflection to Parker, who was barely containing a laugh. "That's why I'm called a makeup artist, Stella. It's all about layering, contouring, and fading the colors in and out in the right places on your face. You're a knockout —you always have been. You just haven't always known how to look like yourself on TV."

"I'll never be able to do this myself."

"I'll put a list of everything I used on your desk."

"This was so nice of you. How can I repay you? Is there anything I can do for you?"

Just then, the loudspeakers came to life. "Stella Reynolds to the studio, please."

Parker grimaced. "You can stop listening to Edie Hawthorne, the hack. Listen to me. *I* know what I'm doing."

His oddly irritated tone caught her attention, and as Stella hurried to the studio she wondered if there was history between the two of them to elicit such a reaction.

Spenser was already sitting behind the anchor desk, and Stella smiled at him when he looked up. He didn't smile back. "Amanda needs a mic check," he said. His eyes lingered on her newly made-up face before he looked back down at his scripts.

Stella stared grimly at his bowed head for a moment as she clipped her microphone onto the lapel of her jacket and plugged her IFB cord into the box under the desk. "Mic check, one-two."

"That's fine," Amanda said through the earpiece. "We are about two minutes away."

Stella did a double take when she saw her copy of the rundown on the desk. "So the ambulance call was news-worthy? What do we know?" she asked, holding up the paper up to see it better.

"Amanda saved us after you disappeared. Shots fired. Hope and Lou just got set up; we think they'll make the top of the newscast."

"I didn't disappear, I—never mind." She blew out a breath and tried to reign in her irritation. "The call said near Spring and Cleveland. Where exactly are they?" Stella asked.

"Journey Street."

The name jolted Stella. She'd just been on Journey Street the day before. "Are you sure?"

"More sure than you, Stella," Spenser answered airily, "since I've been holding down the fort with Amanda for the last half-hour. I guess you'll find out all the details, along with everyone else, live on the news tonight."

Stella stared, open-mouthed, at Spenser before deciding she didn't have time to deal with his pompous attitude. She grabbed the phone on a small table hidden under the desk, which rang through to the director's booth next door. Amanda picked up, irritated. "What, Stella? I'm kinda busy in here."

"I just want to make sure you all know that Hope is on the same street—"

"I don't have time for your stories right now!" Amanda hung up the phone and Stella banged hers down in frustration.

It was a big part of the story *today,* if Hope was covering a shooting on the same block as a different shooting *yesterday.* One shooting on the street was definitely news, but two shootings two days in a row on the same street? That changed the story. Hope needed that information before her live shot, but apparently no one else cared. Before she could pick up the phone and argue her case with Amanda, however, the music that opened the newscast rang through the studio.

She guessed they were all going to learn something that night.

4

The studio was tense. Not only was there late breaking news, which automatically put everyone on edge, but Stella was also doing her best not to snap at the husband-wife duo that spent most of their free time making her life more difficult.

"Your chair is too high," Amanda said through the earpiece. Stella bit back a snarky retort, and instead pulled the lever on the side of her seat. "More," Amanda said, and Stella pulled the lever again.

At 5'9", Stella was the same height or taller than many of her coworkers. It only became a problem when she had to co-anchor the newscast with Spenser, who was noticeably shorter than her at 5'2".

Right after she'd started, Spenser complained to their news director about the height discrepancy. Harry agreed that Spenser should appear taller than Stella when they were on set together, so now Spenser's entire lap was visible over the news desk and Stella looked like a child sitting at an adult table with half her torso hidden.

The cold open—the very beginning of the newscast, which contained a number of teases for what viewers could expect in the show ahead —began with a live shot from Hope out in the field.

Hope: A shooting on Journey Street has residents on edge. We're live with the latest from the scene, next.

Stella breathed a sigh of relief as the live tease went off without a hitch. The next two elements of the cold open were pre-recorded, so Stella took a moment to check her scripts one last time before the red light on top of the camera in front of her lit up.

Spenser: Good evening, everyone. I'm Spenser Shaker.

Stella: And I'm Stella Reynolds. We begin this evening with breaking news on the city's east side.

Spenser: That's where we find Hope Ballard live with the latest.

In the waning daylight, you could see the police caution tape spinning off behind Hope, along with several police officers and evidence techs moving officially around the crime scene. As Hope started her report, Stella exclaimed, "That's the same house I reported from yesterday! I can't believe there was another shooting there today!"

Stella's microphone wasn't hot, so her comment was only heard by Spencer, who completely ignored her, and they watched the end of Hope's live shot in silence. The reporter didn't mention anything about yesterday's crime, and Stella resolved to call her during the first commercial break—bypassing Amanda completely—to let her know the important angle to the story.

Stella had the next read, an update on the

murder from the day before. The camera came back to her on a one-shot, but before she could open her mouth, Spenser broke in.

Spenser: Hope, I understand the area behind you is no stranger to crime. What can you tell us about other recent police activity there at the scene?

It was all Stella could do to keep her eyes on the camera in front of her, her expression neutral. After an unusually long pause in which only Stella's face was on camera, the director was finally able to pull up Hope's live shot again.

Hope: I'm sorry, what was that?

Spenser: I said: is today's crime related to yesterday's shooting?

Hope's blank expression quickly morphed to panic, and it was clear that she didn't know anything about yesterday's shooting. The problem with breaking news was you were often forced to go live on TV before you could gather all the facts. Stella imagined Hope had gotten to the scene minutes before the live shot and had spent the whole time getting the live truck ready, the microphone out, and some small bit of information about the active crime scene while the photographer got the camera connected.

After a moment of stunned silence, Stella jumped in.

> **Stella:** Hope, I was out on Journey Street yesterday—it looks like at the same house —where a man was shot and killed. I wonder if police are considering a possible link between the two crimes?

Hope latched onto the new information in Stella's question and recovered nicely. "Stella, as you can see, the scene behind me is still very active, and we don't expect to get any updates from police until later. That is certainly something we'll dig into for our viewers, though, and plan to bring you the latest before the end of this half-hour newscast. Back to you."

Stella nodded, glad Hope was able to salvage an awkward on-air exchange, and started reading the next story in the rundown. She could feel anger radiating from her co-anchor, though. He took the opportunity to unload as soon as he tossed to a network package moments later. They had two minutes before they would be live again in the studio, and his face turned from red to purple as he turned to face Stella.

"I can't believe you interrupted me."

Stella took a deep, calming breath before she spoke. "I didn't interrupt you, Spenser—I was trying to help Hope out. She'd obviously just gotten to the scene and didn't have much information, yet."

Amanda piped into their earpieces, "Yes Stella, that was Busch league."

Stella's reply died on her lips. That was at least the third NASCAR reference Amanda had made to her over her few months at the station. Most people knew Stella's boyfriend was Lucky Haskins, a top NASCAR driver, but it didn't usually create tension or inspire ridicule.

"Is there a problem here, Amanda? Is there something you need to get off your chest?"

Amanda had apparently been waiting for just the opportunity. "I just think you never would've gotten this job if you weren't dating Lucky Haskins."

There it was. The feeling Stella had since she

started at the station wasn't just her imagination. She looked at her co-anchor. "You feel that way, too?" Spenser nodded.

"Standby," Amanda snarled seconds before the network package ended and Stella and Spenser were back on air.

When they finished the block, Stella tore out her earpiece and stormed out of the studio to the bathroom, needing the ninety-second commercial break to calm down. She stared at herself in the mirror, her cheeks flushed under the new streaks of blush. "I got this job because I'm good at what I do. I work harder than other people, I'm a good reporter, and I'm becoming a better anchor," she said to her reflection.

She then barked out a laugh at the absurdity of talking to herself. But she needed to get this out, and it was better to talk to herself than to say something she might regret to Spenser or Amanda. Things were already tense on the weekends, and she didn't want or need an all-out war with her coworkers. The simmering anger at Spenser's unfair words boiled over, though, and she made a face at herself in the mirror.

"By the way, Spense, I'm the one who was there yesterday! Don't take credit on air for my knowledge about a crime and then *mansplain* my own story back to me!"

She blew out a breath and realized she needed to hustle back to the studio—the commercial break was surely almost over.

She walked back into the dark, quiet space—it was even quieter than usual—and sat next to Spenser without making eye contact. She plugged the cord to her earpiece back into the box and then rolled her neck and straightened her hair.

"Standby," Amanda said tersely through the earpiece.

"Mansplain?" Spenser was looking at Stella with a mean grin. "You know the old saying, Stella: every mic's a hot mic."

She felt her cheeks flush again, realizing she'd been wearing her wireless microphone during her bathroom pep talk. Had everyone heard her Stuart Smalley-esque moment? She might as well have ended with, "Doggone it, people like you."

The commercial break ended and somehow Stella managed to stay collected throughout the rest of the newscast, but she couldn't wait to get out of the studio. After the weather segment and sports, they went back for one last live hit with

Hope. She was ready with much more information, this time.

> **Hope:** We are back here at the scene on Journey Street. Police are telling us the victim is in critical condition at County Hospital. A big question for police is why the victim was here in the first place. The woman who lives here was booked into jail early this morning on charges of murder after her ex-husband was shot and killed on the front lawn yesterday. Now, another shot of violence with a second victim. So far, no suspects have been named in this case. Reporting live, I'm Hope Ballard. Back to you.

After she and Spenser closed out the newscast, Stella raced out of the studio to lean against the wall in the back hallway, glad to be alone with her thoughts for a moment.

So what if they'd overheard her in the bathroom? She didn't say anything she couldn't have said in front of her boss. She pushed off the wall, passing the vending machines on her way to the newsroom.

Stella ran a hand across the huge, old-school coffee machine that sat between the vending machine and refrigerator. She did love having it just a few steps away, but in truth, Stella couldn't wait to get back to dealing with real life and death problems, instead of the manufactured angst of the studio. She would start first thing Monday morning with the murders on Journey Street.

5

Minutes after she walked into the newsroom from the studio, the phone rang. Amanda answered, and after a few quick words, she put the call on hold. Only because Stella happened to look up did she see a small smile of satisfaction flash across Amanda's face before she arranged her features into a more serious expression.

"Harry is on the line for you, Stella."

She took a bracing breath, sat down at her desk, and looked at the flashing red light next to Line One on her phone console. A call from the news director immediately after the newscast ended was rarely a good thing. She rolled the tension out of her neck and then picked up the phone. "Hello, Harry."

"Stella, I don't know what to say."

"Uhh," was all she could manage in response.

"You finally did your makeup! I love it! Honestly, I didn't think you had it in you," he added with a bit of a laugh. "Jerry didn't understand why you wouldn't glam it up—and don't get me started on your clothing choices, he just didn't understand the hire. I told him, 'she's a diamond in the rough,' though."

Jerry was the general manager at the station— someone Stella had seen once or twice in passing over the last several months of working there. She was struck speechless for the second time that night. "A diamond in the rough?" she finally choked out.

"No offense, but you know what I mean. Your reporting has always been great. Like last night out at the murder scene—that was great stuff with that live interview. With your new look tonight, though, it just totally proves my case. You *were* a diamond in the rough. Now you're just a diamond. Well, you will be when we fix your hair. Keep it up, okay, kid?"

"My hair?"

"You need highlights. Big time."

Stella let out a shaky breath. "Okay," she said, drawing out the last syllable. "Well, uh, thanks."

"Oh, one more thing. Vera is going to be off covering some meetings later this week for a sweeps piece she's working on. Can you fill in on the main shows while she's gone?"

"You need me to anchor the main newscasts later this week? Like, during prime time?"

"That'd be great, thanks Stella. Keep doing what you're doing."

Stella held the phone to her ear long after her boss had hung up. A slow grin spread across her face. Doggone it, people *did* like her! She almost laughed at the absurdity of having her coworkers be so disrespectful while, at the same time, her boss decided to give her a new opportunity.

She slowly lowered the phone to her desk and glanced up to find Amanda staring at her with a contemplative look on her face. Spenser was standing just over her shoulder, muttering into her ear.

Stella grimaced and turned away, not wanting them to sense her happiness. She typed a name into the virtual Rolodex on her computer and picked the phone back up to dial Hope.

"I wanted to touch base before your next live shot. Since I was out there yesterday, I thought you might have some questions."

"Thanks. I don't want to be caught off guard again, so I appreciate it."

Stella let the dig at Spenser pass. "Do you have a name on the victim, yet?"

"Police won't confirm, but neighbors around here say the victim is the brother of the woman who lives here."

"Tabitha Herbert's brother?"

"Mmhmm, her brother." Hope sounded distracted, and soon, Stella knew why.

Through the phone and a bit muffled, she heard someone call out, "Is that my girl, Stella? Hey, Stella!"

Hope added a bit irritably, "I've got a woman here named Valerie who wants to talk to you."

After a moment of muffled sounds, Valerie came on the line. "It's like the durn Wild West out here, Stella."

"Valerie, what happened? Did you see anything?"

"I ain't got time to talk, but would you tell this fool reporter to stop asking so many questions? She's gonna get us killed is what she's gonna do."

"Valerie, did you see something?" Stella repeated.

"I ain't saying nothing. I ain't saying nothing to nobody—not when murders are happening every damn day out here!"

Before Stella could ask another question, Hope came back on. "That was so weird. She made a point of coming to find me just to tell me she wouldn't talk to me. What is *up* with her?"

Stella ignored the question and asked one of her own. "Who is in charge out there for police?"

She heard Hope flipping back through the pages of her notebook. After a moment, she said, "Sergeant Coyne. Never met him until tonight, but he's not very chatty, I'll tell you that."

"I'll give him a call to see if he can confirm the victim's identity. I'll get back to you as soon as I can."

Stella hung up the phone, but before she could place another call, she felt Amanda's hot, coffee-scented breath on the back of her neck.

"What did Harry say?"

"He asked me to fill in for Vera this week." Stella stared at her computer, afraid that, if she looked up, her producer might correctly read her expression of glee.

Amanda didn't say anything, but Stella could tell she was trying to come up with words. She cut her off at the pass. "Hope should have some great new stuff for us tonight at eleven. Is there anything else you need, or am I free to take my dinner break?"

Stella looked up in time to see Amanda clamp her mouth shut, pivot, and march back up to the producer pod in the front of the newsroom. Stella smiled grimly to herself and then picked up her cell phone. She scrolled through her contacts and tapped a button to place the call as she walked out to the parking lot.

"I'm busy."

Stella smiled. "I know you're busy, and so is my reporter out there. She needs information for her story for the late news." The cool, frosty temperature made her think winter wasn't ready to give over to spring just yet, and she tightened the ties on her coat and picked up her pace.

"Yeah, yeah, all you reporters want the same thing: information. It's ridiculous."

Stella unlocked her car and jumped in, slamming the door shut behind her to block out the wicked wind. "Can you confirm that the victim is Tabitha Herbert's brother?"

Sergeant Coyne tsked into the phone. "I swear you get information faster than my guys do out on the street." He blew out a sigh. "Yes, the coroner's office has confirmed the identity, and we've notified next of kin. Your reporter can use that tonight."

"The coroner's office? He died?"

"He succumbed to his injuries about an hour ago."

"Suspects?"

"It's an ongoing investigation."

"This has to be related to yesterday's murder."

"Was there a question in there?"

Stella grinned in the dark car. "Is this related to yesterday's murder?"

"No comment."

"Will you walk over and give Hope a new sound bite?" Sergeant Coyne groaned. He sounded like an irritated kindergartner, and it made Stella chuckle. "Or you could be live with her tonight at eleven, if that sounds like more fun?"

"I'll go find her. I'm not going live, that's for darn sure."

They hung up, and Stella smiled again as she started up her car. Some parts of her job she loved, and bantering with Sergeant Coyne was one of them. Two murders at one address in two days deserved more attention, though. Why was the man at his sister's house that day? Why was he killed there one day after Tabitha's ex-husband was gunned down? Police would be working hard on this case and so would Stella. She loved digging around to see what might turn up.

Stella's headlights swept across the building as she drove out of the parking lot, illuminating Spenser as he headed to his car. She grimaced. Nobody loved everything about their job, right?

6

Stella lived in the Short North, a very cool, artsy area just north of downtown Columbus with cozy restaurants, shops, and art galleries sprinkled throughout the neighborhood. Her apartment had a slightly awkward entrance just a few feet down from a stationary store on Pearl Street called *Just Write*. There was just enough room for one person to stand inside the entryway before heading up a steep staircase to her actual front door door on the second floor.

"Hey, Jones," she called to a burly, bald man who was signing a FedEx delivery receipt. Ed Jones was the long-time boyfriend of Yvonne, the woman who owned the store. He was always impeccably dressed, and Stella nodded in silent approval of his tan dress pants, white button-down, pale pink sweater vest, and matching tie.

"Evening, Stella!" He grinned before disappearing into the store with a box of paper under each arm, wielding the fifty-pound boxes like feather pillows. He was a probation officer for the county, and she had no doubt he kept his charges in line with little difficulty.

A bit breathless at the top of the stairs, she unlocked the door and grimaced as she crossed the threshold. The loft had potential, but it looked like she was still in the process of moving in nearly three months after she'd unpacked her last box.

The apartment was small and tidy, and Stella spent as little time as possible there. When she'd taken the job in Ohio, she'd left behind her old friend and former roommate, Janet Black, who'd decided to stay in Knoxville, along with their dog, Ole Boy. Stella hadn't been surprised; it was time for her friend to set down roots and make a life for herself. That didn't mean she didn't miss the friendship, though.

A pass-through counter from the kitchen to the family room was where she usually stood to eat her meals, and her single investment since moving to town, an expensive European coffee maker, gleamed on the concrete countertop. From the front door, she could see her queen-size mattress on the floor of the bedroom, along with a dresser her brother had brought down from Cleveland shortly after she'd moved in.

A balcony barely big enough for one camp chair off the back of her apartment overlooked a small park. Well, it actually overlooked the Dumpster in the parking lot for the park, but she could definitely see trees.

Her other camp chair was perched across from the flat-screen television, which was currently set to ESPN.

"That's odd," she said, walking into the main room to turn off the set. "I wasn't watching..." her eyes opened wide. "Lucky?" she called, spinning around to face the open apartment. "Lucky?" she called again, quickly scanning the empty space. Movement on the balcony caught her eye, and a grin stretched across her face as she saw her boyfriend stand from the camp chair, toss his phone into the now empty seat, and slide the glass door open.

"Hey, you." He stepped into the room and Stella swore the lighting changed to a soft, hazy, golden hue. His tousled, blond hair was tucked behind his ears, and light from the street lamp outside shone a halo around his head. His shirt was rumpled from a day of driving, but his tired eyes lit up when they met Stella's. He crossed the floor between them in two steps and swept her into a bear hug.

"You smell good," he mumbled into her hair. She pulled back a fraction and put one hand on either side of his face.

"You sneak! You told me you had meetings all day and couldn't talk!"

"I was driving here and didn't want you to figure out I was in the car," he said with a grin as he started carrying her toward the bedroom.

"Oh, no, no," she laughed, watching the floor beneath her feet move. "I'm only on my dinner break. There's no time for—"

"How long have you got?" His eyebrows lifted suggestively.

She threw her head back and laughed again at his playful mood. "Lucky, I'm serious! I have less than an hour!"

"Plenty of time," he said, taking the last three steps into the bedroom and kicking the door closed with his foot.

~

WHEN SHE GOT BACK to the newsroom an hour-and-a-*half* later, she found a long list from Parker of the different colors of eyeshadows, blushes, foundations, primers, lipsticks, liners, and brushes she would need to recreate her new look. There were a few tubes on her desk for touch-ups before the eleven o'clock show, and he'd also added a note to the bottom of the list: *Makeup lesson, my house tomorrow, two o'clock. Get your supplies first.*

She bit her lip. How much was this going to cost? She flipped the paper over and chuckled. He'd written: *A lot. It's going to cost a lot.*

The sound of her laugh caught Amanda's attention, and Stella bit back a groan when the other woman stood from the producer's pod and headed her way. She had a grim look on her face, and Stella had no interest in hearing what the other woman had to say. She'd already come to terms with the fact that the eleven o'clock newscast was going to be brutal.

Luck was on her side that night, though, and when Amanda was halfway to Stella's desk, the lights inside the news director's office turned on.

Harry stepped out into the newsroom and raised a hand, beckoning them over.

As they walked closer, Harry said, "Great job with the six o'clock tonight, ladies. Amanda, that was probably the best-ordered rundown I've seen from you in years. Well done." He led them into his office and closed the door.

Amanda glared at Stella, but both remained quiet about their roles in organizing the rundown that afternoon.

"Stella, since you'll be anchoring Thursday and Friday, why don't you take next weekend off? We'll have Spenser solo anchor while you get some down time." He pointed to the open seats and walked around his desk, finally sitting after both Stella and Amanda were settled. He then narrowed his eyes and said, "Does anyone know how the clip got online?"

Stella looked blankly back at Harry. His piercing gaze moved slowly from Amanda to Stella and back again.

"What—what are you talking about?"

"Someone posted an audio clip and added still shots of you, Stella. You didn't know?" He glared at Amanda.

"I tried to call her on her dinner break, but she didn't answer," the producer said defensively.

"I was... it was a busy..." Stella felt her cheeks flush, but she plowed ahead. "Where? Where did someone post the clip?"

Harry took a minute to log onto his computer, launch his internet browser, and tap a few keys before he turned the monitor toward his employees.

The audio had been lifted directly from her microphone during her bathroom pep talk, and the pictures were shots of her, easily accessible from the station's website. Stella's mortification grew by the minute. She sounded like a bad beauty queen contestant. She'd actually told herself she was good at her job—it was so embarrassing.

"That literally just happened two hours ago." Stella's eyebrows drew together as she stared at the computer screen, and then she turned to Amanda in a flash. "Did you do this?"

Amanda's mouth opened and closed silently like a fish out of water, and she took a few steps back until she finally managed to produce words. "I am... I would never—"

"Why was my mic hot in the first place? We were in a commercial break!"

"Ladies, ladies, I agree that we need to do some investigating. Right now, though, we have nothing to worry about. This clip only has a few views. It might fade away into nothing, or it might explode. We just don't know at this point." Stella looked up sharply at his tone. He sounded excited at the thought of thousands of views. Before she could clarify which way they were hoping it would go, he said, "I just wanted everyone aware of the situation. Now, back to work." He spun around in his chair and opened a file drawer behind his desk. "Amanda, be back here in twenty, please, to look over the rundown."

Stella stalked out of Harry's office, fuming. She avoided looking at a curious Spenser and headed for her corner of the newsroom, where she threw herself down at her computer and started going through scripts.

"Knock, knock," Parker said, walking over with a cheerful smile. It faded, however, as he took in her scowl. "Who died?"

She grunted and continued savagely attacking her keyboard. "Why doesn't anybody," she glared at Amanda over her computer monitor, "know the difference between *their, there,* and *they're,* anymore?" She aggressively deleted the word *their* and replaced it with *they're*. "I mean, *they're* completely different words *there*, you know? *They're* not inter-changeable!"

Parker slowly lowered himself into the seat at the empty desk next to her. "I came over to offer to touch up your makeup," he said, raising an eye-brow. "Did you run a marathon on your dinner break?" He clucked. "Never mind, but I'm happy to listen, if you need to get something off your chest."

"Oh, it's just that... that... *woman!*" She nodded dismissively at the producers' area. "I think she's trying to get me fired!"

Parker nodded. "Probably."

"What? You think so, too?"

Parker leaned in and lowered his voice. "She got Lindsay fired. That's why there was a job opening when they hired you."

"What happened?" Stella breathed, some of her anger replaced with surprise.

"Spenser and Lindsay might have been doing more than anchoring the show together."

"Ew," she said, now swinging her gaze across the newsroom at Spenser. "He's so... just... ew."

"Apparently Lindsay didn't think so. Amanda got wind of it, and two months later, Lindsay was gone."

"Well, I'm not doing that!" she said, disgusted at the thought.

"I think she doesn't want to take any chances."

"Take any chances?" she parroted back. "That's outrageous! She can't—"

"She can try. You can't let her, though, and that probably means your new look is important. Let's not lose it after only one newscast," he added, collecting the few supplies he'd left out. "Makeup room, quarter to eleven. I'll fix... this," he gestured to her face with a frown.

"Fine," Stella said moodily, staring at her screen again.

"What was that? Thank you, Parker, for making my work-life bearable? *You're* welcome," he sang out as he walked away. Stella smiled in spite of her foul mood.

The rest of her shift passed in an angry blur of editing, rewriting, glaring, and more layers of makeup. Finally, she was in the studio, waiting for the newscast to begin. Harry was in the booth with Amanda, so Stella knew she didn't have to worry about any more shenanigans that night, although she wondered how long it would be before the woman tried to exact revenge.

Her only distraction was that Hope was live off

the top of the newscast again with even more of an update than Stella had gotten before her dinner break.

> **Hope:** Police confirming, once again, they now have a homicide investigation on their hands tonight, the second in as many nights here at this address. The latest victim was the brother of the woman arrested after yesterday's killing. Detectives suspect tonight's murder might be a crime of retaliation, although they caution that their investigation has just begun. Neighbors say it caps off a series of terrible events that will stay with them for years. Reporting live, I'm Hope Ballard. Back to you.

During Hope's live tag, Stella saw the same little girl she'd talked to the day before. This time, she was standing on the porch behind Hope, staring right into the camera. Her piercing look was unsettling, and Stella was glad when Hope's live shot ended.

As she headed to her car after the newscast, she couldn't get the kid out of her mind. The ten-year-old girl's words at the murder on Journey

Street from the day before came roaring back to her. "It's complicated."

The girl was convinced Tabitha didn't shoot anyone, and now another shooting at the same house meant another gunman was on the loose— or was the child right and Tabitha was innocent? If police had the wrong person in custody, a killer was popping off members of Tabitha's family at a rapid clip. Who would be next?

7

The next morning, after getting in a strenuous workout without leaving the bedroom, Stella and Lucky were finally standing in the kitchen, waiting for the coffee machine to warm up. "Top-of-the-line, European machine—you'd think it wouldn't take five minutes to heat up!" He shot Stella a sly smile.

She only glared in response.

"Is something wrong?" Lucky asked. "You seem... subdued, or, I don't know, maybe reflective?" She screwed up her face and he added, "I'd like to think it's because you're going to miss me when I leave, but I've known you long enough to know it's not that."

Stella blew out a breath and ignored the subtext of his last statement. "It's just this... thing at work."

At his curious expression, she opened her laptop and showed him the clip online. So far, it had fourteen views—at least five of them were hers.

"Can't somebody make the clip disappear?" he asked, his eyes shifting to the highlight reel playing on ESPN behind her.

"Hello? This is the internet—the great Wild West. No one can control anything. Plus, the person who posted the clip is anonymous."

"Yes!" Lucky breathed after an outfielder for the Atlanta Braves made a diving catch.

"Really? Can't you focus on this—on me—for one minute?"

"Stella, all I'm saying is what's the worst that can come of this?"

"I could get fired! What if the number of views on this video explodes? I might have to resign!"

"First of all, you didn't swear and you didn't really even disrespect your colleague. Even if that *did* happen, though, you can just come back to Tennessee," he said with a smile.

"What? That's—that's just—" she spluttered,

unable to come up with words. She took a deep breath and finally said, "How can you treat the imminent demise of my career with such calm?"

"Okay, now, let's not get so dramatic!" he said, suddenly reading her mood correctly. He pulled her in close for a hug, but she pushed away.

"Then let's not act like my problems at work are small and insignificant!" The light on the coffee machine finally blinked, and she marched past Lucky to press a button. A burst of steam pierced the silence in the apartment and she watched the line of deep, dark coffee stream into the mug with feigned concentration. She flinched when Lucky touched her arm.

"I didn't mean that. You know I didn't," he said in a conciliatory tone. "I just miss you. Twelve hours every other week isn't enough Stella-time for me."

Her stiff shoulders relaxed a fraction. "I know. Me neither. I'm sorry, too." She motioned to her computer. "I just hate thinking about people laughing at me."

He stepped back and pressed a button on the remote. The TV went black. "Darlin', you can't control other people—only yourself."

Stella nodded, handed him the first cup of coffee, and then set about making one for herself. "Are you heading back today?" she asked, ready to change the subject.

He nodded. "Only two more days until you come to see me in Knoxville. I can handle two days," he added with a boyish grin.

"Oh..." she hesitated and he frowned.

"What?"

"It's just that my boss asked me to fill in on the main shows, which is a great opportunity..."

"So you don't have any days off at all?"

"Well, I'll have the weekend off, instead."

"But I'll be in D.C. for a press tour by then," he said, his tone accusatory.

"I know," Stella said, avoiding eye contact. "It's just this really amazing opportunity, and I didn't feel like I could say no." Lucky looked at her for a long moment. She added, "It's just a great—"

"Opportunity, yeah, I heard you the first time," he interrupted before pivoting away from Stella and deliberately turning the TV back on. He increased the volume and sat to watch.

Stella felt her temper start to rise again and excused herself, not wanting to get into another fight. "I'm going to get ready for work."

Lucky didn't answer.

~

AN HOUR LATER, she couldn't stop thinking about the cold goodbye she and Lucky had at her apartment as she left for work: a stiff hug and a promise to call soon. She felt like they were at a turning point in their relationship. She'd always known long-distance was going to be hard, but frankly, she had assumed that, with Lucky's resources and her own odd schedule, they'd be able to make it work. Now it was clear, however, that she'd overestimated what their relationship could withstand—perhaps what any relationship could withstand.

Stella was still burned by the thought that Lucky didn't respect her career. If she was being honest, he was probably burned that she didn't make the same effort he did to visit. She didn't know what to do. Her job was important to her, she felt like she was helping people, and she still had so much to learn and prove.

She got the first good piece of news of the day when she walked into the newsroom: both Amanda and Spencer had called off sick. Beatrice, one of the weekday producers, was filling in, and Stella would solo anchor the newscasts. It was like a giant weight had been lifted from her shoulders.

Beatrice's brown hair was pulled back into a sleek ponytail, and stylish glasses and a trendy scarf around her neck completed her professional look. She was all business, but she sent a friendly wave Stella's way as she chatted on the phone at her desk.

Stella pulled up the rundown on her computer and saw her initials next to several scripts she was expected to proofread and approve for air that evening. Stella did her work quickly and efficiently and had enough time before the newscast to start setting up stories for the following day. She left a voicemail for Sergeant Coyne, asking for an update on the murders, and then switched tactics and lucked out when a source with the public defender's office answered at home.

"Do you know who'll be assigned to Tabitha Herbert's case?" she asked.

Monica let out a gentle laugh. "Stella, our office is so overrun and understaffed that I can't begin to imagine who'll get stuck with it. Besides, she might decide to hire her own lawyer."

"No way will she have the funds for that. When will we know for sure, though? During her arraignment?"

"Yup. She has to fill out a form if she's requesting public assistance. We usually have someone there to help with the initial paperwork, and then our office manager assigns the lawyers based on their current workload and experience."

"What about her kids? Does she have a say in where they go?"

"No, but the preference is always to settle them with family. I heard—from you, actually, on the news—that her parents live here in town. FCCS will probably try to place the kids today—get them out of the system as soon as possible."

"Thanks, Monica. See you at spinning class?"

"Yeah, I might be there Wednesday morning."

Stella hung up feeling oddly unsettled. Before she could get back to work, though, her cell phone rang.

"Do you ever have a day off?" Sergeant Coyne asked.

Stella barked out a laugh. "I guess as many as you!"

"Fair enough. What's up?"

"Just looking for info on the murders. Do you have a name on the victim for me?"

"Victim identified as Darren Lambern, brother to Tabitha Herbert."

"Can you tell me anything about him?"

"Sure. He delivers flowers for a small company out in Westerville. He wasn't married, had no kids, and had no friends—at least that we can find."

"Anything else?"

"No. Detectives are working overtime, though. It's not often we have back-to-back shootings at the same house."

"Still think the brother was killed in retaliation?"

He blew out a long sigh. "That's the official theory, but off the record, nobody saw or heard anything."

"Do you know why the victim was at Tabitha's house yesterday?"

"Best we can tell, he was picking up stuff to bring to her kids. We found a plastic bag with a teddy bear, some changes of clothes, and toothbrushes at the scene."

Stella's mouth went dry. She couldn't think of anything to say. How terrible. After a moment, she cleared her throat. "So, no news on suspects? We'd love to update the story with new information today, if it's out there."

"We have less than nothing on this one, Stella. Unless some witnesses come forward, the case is stalled."

They disconnected and Stella stared at her computer screen. She felt an increasing sense of duty to Tabitha's parents. Although they'd never met, in the span of forty-eight hours, the couple had, in effect, lost a daughter, a son, and now grown their household by three children!

The weekend wasn't even over, but Stella knew where her next week would begin. Her star witness from the first murder had made a point of telling her she wouldn't talk about the second murder. Valerie Osmola knew something; Stella just had to find out what.

8

Arraignments were typically held first thing in the morning. It was a brutal turn-around to go from anchoring the news Sunday until nearly midnight, to covering a court case at eight Monday morning, but Stella felt the familiar thrum of adrenaline pumping through her veins. She had a feeling this story was going to be big.

Lou stood next to the tripod between her and the hard plastic and metal chairs in the lobby of the jail. His expression was grim. The two had started at the station on the same day, she from Tennessee and he from a smaller TV market in Ohio.

"How's your fiancée?" she asked, looking at Haylee's picture, which he'd taped to the side of his camera.

"She's great," he said, smiling for the first time that day. "Just passed her M-CAT."

"Wow. You said her first choice for med school is OSU?"

"Of course, but she'd take Michigan, too."

"Shh," Stella said with a grin, "not so loud." He made a face. The competitiveness between the universities didn't stop on the football field—even uttering the word "Michigan" could elicit jeers and taunting from those in Ohio.

Lou adjusted his thin, red, metal-framed glasses. While Stella stood quietly between sips of coffee from her travel mug, Lou was in perpetual motion, bouncing around the camera, checking switches and dials, wiping down the lens with a soft cloth, and then checking the level on the tripod. He wore green skinny-jeans and a beige and black, plaid, flannel shirt unbuttoned over a black *Smashing Pumpkins* T-shirt.

"Why do we even cover these things?" he asked, looking disgruntled.

Stella shot him a sympathetic look. This proceeding was happening via a video conference link between the judge in a closed courtroom and a holding cell in the jail. The local news stations were allowed to watch and record the proceeding, but only from the TV screen hanging on the white, cinderblock wall in the lobby of the jail, which was already busy. Some people sat in chairs, others waited to walk through the metal detectors, and a long line of impatient people snaked back from the information window.

A surly man bumped into Stella and he only stopped to avoid getting splashed by the coffee that slopped out of her mug onto the tile floor at his feet. Before she could even react, Lou jumped in front of her.

"Careful there," he said to the man. His tone was pleasant, but there was a steely glint in his eye.

The stranger made a face, but stepped back. "Sorry," he mumbled as he walked away.

"People ought to pay more attention," Lou said, moving back to his camera and adjusting some dials. Stella shook herself after realizing she'd been staring at her photographer. He had a slight frame and seemed artsy and aloof—in fact, until that very moment, she would have described him as more butter knife than dagger—but just then, he'd impressed her. It was nice to think he was ready to stand up for her. She couldn't say that about everyone at the station.

The proceedings finally got underway on the TV monitor. After watching nearly a dozen women step forward, facing charges from drunk and disorderly conduct to public urination, the inmate Stella had been waiting for finally walked up to the podium.

The court bailiff spoke from off-camera, "Your Honor, this is case number OH-567731, the State of Ohio versus Tabitha Herbert. The charge is second degree murder in the death of Robert Herbert."

The video was overexposed and everything looked washed out, but Stella devoured her first look at the murder suspect.

Tabitha Herbert had limp, blond hair that hung down past her shoulders. Though she had now spent nearly three days in jail, she walked with a swagger that was visible from the lobby.

Judge Ryan Rohr, in his early thirties and newly elected to the position, looked bored. His wavy, brown hair flopped over his right eye as he picked up his gavel and banged it once. "Ms. Herbert, do you have a lawyer, or do you need to have one provided for you?"

With one hand on her hip and her head

cocked at an irritated angle, she addressed the judge as if she was talking to a naughty child. "I guess you have to give me a lawyer, because I sure ain't got the means to get one."

"You'll need to fill out form 504C. If you qualify, an attorney will be provided for you. The bailiff will give you the form, and a lawyer will be assigned to you by the end of the week." Judge Rohr picked up his gavel and banged it again, then closed a file and put it at the bottom of the stack. Another inmate started walking toward the podium, prepared to take Tabitha's place, but Tabitha wasn't ready to leave.

"Is my brother dead?" she asked, gripping the sides of the podium. "Last I heard, he was rushed to the hospital, but nobody will tell me what's going on. It seems to me that, if somebody's brother has been shot, they should be told what's going on—and not tomorrow. I mean today."

The judge looked up in surprise. "I don't know anything about your brother. What's his name?"

"Darren Lambern the Third."

A man leaned into the camera frame and whispered into the judge's ear. Recognition seemed to dawn slowly across his face, and finally he nodded, taking a moment to shuffle some papers before speaking. "I have just been informed, Ms. Herbert, that your brother passed away from his injuries. I suspect police will be in to talk to you sometime today. In the meantime, please fill out the form in front of you, so *your* case can continue without delay." Once again, the judge appeared to be dismissing Tabitha Herbert.

A jailer tried to lead her back to the row of chairs as the next inmate arrived to the podium— this one lucky enough to have an attorney with her. Before she was out of the video frame, however, Tabitha stopped, pivoted, and got back to the podium just as the other inmate and her lawyer did.

The camera in the holding cell was stationary —no one zoomed in or out to accommodate the new arrival at the podium—so only the lawyer in the middle was fully in the frame.

"I don't have time to be in here if my family is getting gunned down," Tabitha snarled. "I have kids out there who I need to protect. I can't be in here, messing with this foolishness."

"Foolishness?" The judge's surprise was so acute that it was almost comical.

"Yes, foolishness. My kids are out there. Is something not making sense to you people?"

Judge Rohr opened his mouth to respond, but then he did a double take. Something caught his eye, or someone. "Eleanor Pochowski, can you represent Ms. Herbert?" It was a question, but just barely.

There was a beat of silence before the lawyer started shaking her head. "Oh, I simply can't add to my client list at this time, Your Honor—"

"Just for this hearing?"

The woman sighed and then straightened her shoulders. "Certainly, Your Honor, although let the record reflect that I am just now meeting the defendant for the first time and am not familiar with any details of her case." The lawyer spoke with crisp authority. Her outfit was somehow both elegant and simple, and she turned to her original client and gestured toward the back wall. The woman walked out of the camera shot.

Stella looked at Lou and muttered, "Are you getting this?" He didn't answer, but his head was buried between the view finder and body of the camera.

The judge nodded impatiently. "Yes, yes." He looked down at the stack of folders in front of him. "According to my file, the victim was a coworker of the defendant, but—"

"I didn't *work* with Bobby at Hieroglyphics Communications," Tabitha snapped. "He was my ex-husband! It's like no one knows anything here."

"Yes, I'm sorry, of course," the judge was flustered as he spoke again. "Mrs. Pochowski?"

The lawyer had stepped back from the podium. She stared at her client for a moment, her jaw hanging slack, before she shook herself slightly and put an arm around Tabitha. The movement was both calming and controlling, and Tabitha's shoulders rounded in as the lawyer spoke to the judge. "The defendant will plead not guilty." She turned toward Tabitha, covered the microphone on the podium with one hand, and muttered something to her client. Tabitha nodded, and Eleanor spoke to the judge again. "We would also ask for an immediate dismissal of all charges and for full-custody of her children to be returned to Tabitha as early as this afternoon."

It was hard to tell on the small screen, but the judge might have rolled his eyes. "Mrs. Pochowski, this is only an initial hearing. I will enter Ms. Herbert's plea of not guilty. If you could help her fill out the paperwork for a public defender, her case will be ready to move forward."

Eleanor Pochowski and Tabitha Herbert walked off camera.

Stella turned toward her photographer. "*That's why we cover these things,*" she said with a grin, running a hand through her hair. They needed an interview with that spunky lawyer. She looked at her watch. Assuming Pochowski would stay to represent her original client and then leave the jail for her office, they might be able to stake out the side exit and hope for a chance to ask one or two questions.

As they hustled out the door, Stella thought back to the hearing. Why hadn't police told Tabitha about her brother? Police usually notified next of kin when someone was killed—surely they'd have wanted to interview her about a crime that happened at her own house just hours after the first murder. Furthermore, police knew exactly where to find Tabitha. Stella wondered why she had been kept in the dark.

9

Stella was scheduled to lead off the noon newscast with a live shot downtown about the court hearing, but so far, she had been unable to find Eleanor Pochowski. She could do the story without an interview, but it wouldn't be as good.

"Well, what do you want to do, Stella?" Lou asked. His eyes scanned the surrounding parking lots for the tenth time in as many minutes and Stella wondered what he was looking for. "We can go live here, but I'll need to start setting up the live truck soon." They were standing by a side exit to the jail only used by people with the right credentials. Several detectives and jail employees had walked in and out, but not the lawyer Stella was hoping to interview. "Maybe she went out the front door?" Lou offered.

"We'd have seen her," Stella said, shaking her head. "Let's give it another five minutes. If she doesn't come out, we'll just go with what we've—"

The heavy, metal door hinged open with a squeal and Eleanor Pochowski stepped out into the sunshine.

The lawyer had jet-black hair, minimal makeup, and again, Stella noticed that her navy blue suit managed to make her appear both elegant and no-nonsense. Stella bit her lip, hating feeling like she was ambushing the attorney. Then again, this was likely her only chance to get anything on camera from the woman.

"Mrs. Pochowski? I'm Stella Reynolds with NBC News 5. Can I ask you a few questions about Tabitha Herbert?"

Eleanor Pochowski's step faltered as she took in the news crew blocking her path. She recovered quickly, though, and said, "Two minutes, dear. I'm late for a meeting."

Lou raised the camera to his shoulder and Stella flipped a switch at the bottom of the microphone to the "on" position. "You stepped in to help when Tabitha Herbert needed counsel. How common is that?"

Pochowski smiled tightly. "It's not uncommon to stand in for another lawyer for a simple hearing like that. It *is* unusual to then be assigned to her case permanently."

"You... wait, what?" Stella said, looking at the lawyer with wide eyes. "I thought you were just helping Tabitha Herbert with a form today."

"So did I," Pochowski said wryly. "Before I could leave, Judge Rohr assigned me to be her public defender for the duration."

"I've never heard of that happening before."

"It usually doesn't. Judge Rohr is new, though, and he does things differently—and it's certainly no secret that the public defenders' office is over-whelmed. The wait time on cases can be long. Judge Rohr said this case has extenuating circum-stances, with the children needing a parent at home, and I was only too happy to step in."

Stella wasn't sure "happy" was the right word to describe the look on Pochowski's face. "What can you tell me about the case?" Lou stuck his head out from behind the camera to give her a look, and Stella bit her lip. He was right: it was a weak question.

"My client's main focus right now is on her family. She has three children who lost their father Friday, and now their mother is in jail with very little evidence tying her to any crime. Those kids need their mother, and they need to be at home."

"Did she kill Bobby Herbert?" Stella asked, happy to see Lou nod in satisfaction.

"We're pleading not guilty. That's all for now." Pochowski nodded and walked between Stella and the camera toward her car.

"Thank you!" Stella called before turning to Lou and saying, "While you set up the live truck, I'll head back into the corrections center to request an interview with Tabitha. Maybe we can get that by the end of the week."

She felt a light touch on her arm—Eleanor Pochowski was back. "You'd like an interview with my client?"

Stella stifled a groan. Lawyers weren't always the biggest fans of jailhouse interviews, and she didn't realize Pochowski had been listening.

"Oh, well, we haven't really heard from her, yet, and one-on-one interviews come out so much better than sound taken from the video monitor in the jail lobby..."

Pochowski hesitated. She seemed to be sizing Stella up. "I'll set it up. Does three o'clock this afternoon work?"

"Oh, wow. Yes, but usually you need at least twenty-four hours' notice to the jail—"

"Not my clients. I'll make it happen. We'll see you back here at three."

Stella and Lou watched her walk through the parking lot, climb into her car, and drive away.

"That was weird," Stella said. "Why would she move mountains to get me in with her client?"

Lou grinned. "I don't know. Did you see her face when she said she was, 'happy to step in?' She didn't seem too happy about it to me. I think she's going to make the system pay for roping her into this case. It's kind of awesome, isn't it?"

Stella bit her lip. Maybe Lou was right and Pochowski would mix things up. That was a good thing for her story that day, but was it a good thing for Tabitha? She wasn't so sure.

10

"Stop pursing your lips. It makes your whole face tighten."

Parker was glaring at her from across the table in his apartment off High Street. She'd gotten there about ten minutes late after getting stuck behind a slow-moving customer at the mall makeup counter.

"I can't believe I just spent four-hundred-and-twenty-eight dollars on makeup. Do you see this tiny tube?" she held up a lipstick-sized container of makeup. "This was thirty-two dollars. For just this!" She carefully set the tube down on the table and looked over her haul of items, finally adding,

"That's like... what I'd usually spend at the grocery store over the course of six weeks!"

"It's an investment in your career, Stella. Now, what did I tell you about your eyes?"

"You mean about the base layer?"

"No! It's called primer. Use primer, *then* your base color, then your contour color in the crease, and finally the accent color by your brow!"

Stella nodded and looked at an extremely magnified view of her eye in a small, round mirror on the table in front of her. Four steps for eye-shadow application seemed absurd.

"Don't make that face," he said, pursing his lips at her. "Who is the expert here?"

"You are," she said flatly, "and don't purse your lips," she added slyly.

He snorted and continued to direct her on which colors to put where using which brushes for the next twenty minutes. She couldn't deny that, when all was said and done, she looked almost as good as she had when Parker had done her makeup over the weekend. She took out the clip holding her hair away from her face and looked at her reflection critically again.

Highlights. Was Harry right? Did she need to change her hair to be successful at work? Her long, auburn hair hung past her shoulders, and she turned her head to the left and right, trying to picture another color reflected back in the mirror.

It was a relief when her cell phone buzzed on the table.

"Harry wants to know if this jailhouse interview is an exclusive," Beatrice asked without preamble.

"Yes, it is, and I think we were the only ones with sound with her lawyer, too—but don't quote me on that."

"We had to pull Lou—Hope got a line on an interesting drug case downtown—but Devi will meet you in front of the jail at quarter 'til, and you'll stay there to be live at five and six."

Stella put her cell phone back in her bag, along with her new, enormous makeup kit, and stood. "I guess my lunch break is over. Parker, thank you so much for your help; I know you're busy, and it means a lot that you took the time."

"Not as busy as I used to be, anyway," he said with a dramatic sigh.

"What do you mean?"

He made a face and crossed his arms in front of him. "My work at the station is only part time. I also have clients at a salon."

Stella looked around his apartment in surprise. He had enough equipment sitting out that she'd assumed he saw clients right there in his living room. There were salon chairs with the foot crank to raise and lower the seats, plus sink basins, dryers, and boxes of curlers. It looked like he was ready for a perm and a dye job right there at the kitchen table.

"I was supposed to go into business with a friend, and we were going to rent space, you know, and really make it official. We were supposed to open last month." He fell silent.

"What happened?"

"My *partner* took my money and ran."

"That's terrible! How could that happen? Didn't you have some kind of agreement—a contract? Something written down?"

"We did, but apparently it wasn't official enough—just something I scrawled out on a piece of paper."

Stella shook her head. "This person just... took your money?"

"I guess. The space we were gonna rent is up for lease again. I tried to see her, but she's good at hiding in plain sight."

"What does that mean?"

He hung his head for a moment and then shook it gently before locking eyes with Stella. "It's Edie Hawthorne. I contacted a bunch of lawyers and finally found one who will take the case, but it's taking forever."

"Wait, Edie Hawthorne from Channel 7?"

"Yup. We had a great concept for our salon. It was going to be called *Designing the Stars*, since we both worked for TV stations. Great buzz right off the bat. I'd saved up for years, but she would be the face of it all. Since she has her own show, she's got the name recognition—if I may flatter myself, I have the talent. She knew someone who had prime real estate for us, so I gave her some of my savings to secure the lease and used the rest to buy the equipment." He shifted his weight and his arms dropped down to his sides. "And then... nothing."

"Can't you confront her? Demand your money back?"

"I tried. I guess I feel dumb that she was able to take advantage of me so easily. At first, she was just having trouble getting the lease for us to sign, and then her schedule was so busy that she couldn't meet. She stopped returning my calls," his face grew dark, "and now, she's dead to me."

~

AN HOUR LATER, Devi's equipment was set up in the corner of a room in the bowels of the jail. Eleanor Pochowski was pacing the floor in front of them with her cell phone pressed to her ear.

"I know, the whole day has gone to hell. Re-arrange my schedule as best you can and ask the judge to move that case to next week. I just inherited a *murder* case—there's a lot that's out of my control right now." The door to the tiny room opened, and Eleanor hastily slipped her cell phone into her pocket.

Tabitha Herbert was wearing green scrubs with "Franklin County Department of Corrections stamped across the chest. Her hands were cuffed together in front of her, and a guard walked behind her. When all five people were crowded together inside the interview room, the guard unlocked the handcuffs, clipped them to his belt, and said, "Just knock on the door when you're done and I'll come back for her." He backed out of the room and the door closed with a soft click.

Tabitha looked warily at her visitors. The attitude Stella had seen during her initial hearing was nowhere to be seen; instead, she looked tired. "Who are you?" she asked.

Stella opened her mouth to answer, but the lawyer spoke first. "Tabitha, Stella is the reporter who wants to do a story about you. I think it might help with our bond hearing coming up. We need to create some sympathy for you and your kids."

Tabitha looked distastefully at her lawyer. "*Create* some sympathy?"

Her lawyer looked back at her with a steely glare. "Yes, *create*. Right now, police have eyewitness testimony naming you as the trigger woman in your ex-husband's death. You have no sympathy. We need to create some."

Tabitha nodded slowly as the words sunk in. "Okay."

Stella got to work clipping the lavalier microphone to the neckline of Tabitha's shirt. The black cord curled down her shirt until it connected to a black box the size of a pack of cigarettes on the table.

"Ready?" she asked. Tabitha nodded. "All right, what can you tell me about Friday afternoon?"

"No," Eleanor interjected. "My client will only answer questions about her kids today."

"Wha—"

"Listen, *I* haven't even had a chance to properly interview my client, so I'm not going to let her answer any questions about the day of the crime. Only about her kids."

Stella's eyes narrowed. She wasn't there to help Tabitha's case—she was there to report on a news story. Tabitha, however, looked at her lawyer with new respect and clamped her mouth shut. Stella took a deep breath.

"Okay. Tabitha, what are your concerns as you sit here today?"

"I'm worried about my kids and my family. I don't like being in here when they're out there—especially when somebody's out there popping them off—"

"My client is very concerned about the safety of her family," Eleanor interrupted, putting a hand on Tabitha's arm. "We certainly can't speak to motive on any crime, but we *can* say our primary concern is the children's safety and comfort. They need their mother."

"Where are they now?"

"They're with my mom and dad," Tabitha answered, frowning. "They live just down the street from me, so the kids are okay in that sense, but I actually *do* want to talk about Friday. I have an—"

"Tabitha!" Eleanor said, her voice cutting through the interview room like a foghorn. "We cannot discuss the case at all until my office has had a chance to investigate!"

Stella bit back a groan at the interruption. She and Tabitha spoke for another ten minutes with Eleanor interrupting every other minute to keep her client from saying anything she deemed damaging. Stella ended the interview with a final question about Tabitha's brother.

"Tabitha, what was your brother doing at your house Saturday?" She'd asked the question on a lark, assuming Eleanor would stop her, but instead, the lawyer sat back to listen.

Tabitha shook her head. "I'd asked him to pick up some clothes for my kids to make sure they'd be comfortable. Well," she laughed without humor, "as comfortable as possible. You know, we're all close—so close. He'd just moved out of the neighborhood, but up until a few months ago, he lived on the same block as us. He used to babysit for the kids when I had to work late, or early, or... I mean, he was their favorite. My kids just loved everything about him..." She sniffed loudly as she said the words, apparently overcome with emotion as she thought about all the people she missed.

Within just a few days, Tabitha had gone from mother of three to murder suspect and grieving sister, worried about the health and safety of her children. It was a lot to take in, and Tabitha fell silent, refusing to answer any more questions. Eleanor knocked on the door and the same guard from before walked into the room. The only sound was the clanging of metal as he clamped the handcuffs around her wrists and then the sound of the door swinging closed with a bang.

While Devi started breaking down his gear, Stella took a moment to assess Eleanor. Under the glare of the fluorescent lights, she could see that the lawyer's black hair wasn't natural. She leaned forward to get a better look. Blond roots?

Stella sat back in her seat when she realized Eleanor was staring at *her*. "Sorry, I just—my boss has been talking to me about needing highlights," she pointed to her auburn hair, "and I've been balking at the idea. It kind of seems... I don't know, not related to my job performance? He seems to think it will help my career, though, and then I noticed your... well..."

Eleanor threw her head back and laughed. "Oh, Stella, have you got a lot to learn. Yes, absolutely, I dye my hair. Blonds may have more fun, but not in the workplace. I got sick and tired of being treated dumber-than, and I blamed my hair. As soon as I dyed it black, I started to get things done. I haven't looked back."

"It's just hair, though. How could it possibly make a difference?"

"Just hair? It's like the difference between getting a cake from a bakery and one from an Easy Bake Oven. They might both taste good, but everyone would prefer the professional version."

Stella cocked her head, trying to make sense of that analogy, when Eleanor's cell phone rang. She dug it out of her pocket and turned away to take the call.

While Devi changed out the batteries in the microphone, Stella picked up a lock of hair and held it in front of her face. Was she a professional baker, or was she using an Easy Bake Oven? She honestly had no idea.

Devi stood. "Ready?"

They walked out of the interview room together with Eleanor wrapping up her phone call several paces behind them. As they stepped out into the lobby, Eleanor put her hand on Stella's arm. "Do you have a minute?"

"Go ahead, Devi, I'll be right out," Stella said. He shrugged and walked out of the building.

She looked inquisitively at Eleanor as the older woman narrowed her eyes. "I like you. There's something about you that reminds me of me when I was younger." Stella smiled uncertainly. "I don't have any family—lost my daughter to violent crime years ago, and boyfriends have been... unreliable."

Stella stared at her silently, her mind reeling. This woman lost her daughter to violence and was now representing the very people accused of violent crimes? The two things were almost impossible to reconcile. Before she could ask any questions, though, Eleanor went on.

"In fact, being the best I can be at my job is what made me change my look and really dig down and focus on my career to help those less fortunate." She stared unblinkingly over Stella's head and then shook herself slightly. "It's why I wanted to say this: you worry about you. No one else is looking out for you in this world.

"If you need to change your look to succeed, do it, but stay true to you. There's a way to do that, and you need to find it. I decided to fight for those who cannot fight for themselves, and sometimes that means getting assigned to a case I wouldn't normally accept otherwise." She smiled ruefully before adding, "I won't let anything stand in my way, though—certainly not something as silly as hair color."

She squeezed Stella's arm and walked through the security screening into the intake area of the jail, leaving Stella alone in the lobby. As she turned to leave, she saw herself in the security monitor above the door. She'd never given much thought to her hair. Would changing it really make her more successful at work, or was her appearance holding her back, already? It was hard to imagine her hair had that much power.

She shook her head and resolutely walked through the door into the cool, fresh, spring air. She didn't have the answer, but she did know she had the lead story for the news that night: an exclusive conversation with a murder suspect. She would worry about her hair another time.

11

The next day, Stella was heading out to the crime scene, hoping to find someone who knew the most recent victim, Tabitha's brother, Darren.

She was working with Lou again, and this time he was wearing blue jeans, a lime-green button-down, and a black bowler hat.

"Does Hope mind?" he asked, handing her the microphone and putting the camera strap over his shoulder.

"Mind what?" Stella asked, pulling her sunglasses out of her briefcase.

"That you're working on the Lambern murder. Isn't it her story?"

Stella shrugged. "It is, but she's off today, so Harry asked me to see what I could find out."

Lou nodded and they started walking. Stella knocked on doors, hoping to find someone at home who knew the victim, and Lou trailed behind. Instead of getting any information, though, most residents wanted information from her.

"What's going to happen to the kids?" asked one woman who answered the door while nursing a baby.

"FCCS has them now," Stella said, watching two tiny feet kick out from under a blanket, "but I heard the grandparents are trying to get temporary custody."

"Ooh, Lord. Those old folks won't know what hit them, three kids in that house!" She shifted the baby in her arms. "I guess I better call down to Valerie and see if she can organize a babysitting drive. Maybe a food drive, too. Lord knows those poor old people went from no kids to three—they gonna need some help."

"Valerie Osmola?"

"The one and only."

"Which house is hers?"

"She down at the end of the block. See the house with all the windows in the front? It's how she keep such good track of all of us. Shoot, ain't nobody do nothing on this street or the next without Valerie knowing about it."

Stella looked in the direction the woman was pointing and saw what she was talking about. In a neighborhood of homes with faded, peeling wood siding and small, foggy windows, Valerie's house was made of solid, reddish-brown bricks with giant picture windows on either side of the front door. Through the window, Stella could see someone wearing a bright purple and yellow top. The color combination was so bright that her eyes watered.

"Is that her?"

"Probably. She sits there all day, unless she sees something she needs to investigate. That's when she gets up, finds out what's going on, and goes back to her perch. It kind of bugged me when we first moved in, but a couple months after we got here, she saw my Shawna skipping school with some boy from the next street over. I like it, now. It's like having your own security camera, you know?"

"What did she say about the murders?"

"Well, she up and told everyone about Bobby getting shot. It was like a mission of hers to spread the word. I ain't heard nothing about Darren, though. She must be sulking in there, 'cause she missed it. We ain't heard anything from her in days."

Stella walked back down to the sidewalk and called Lou over. "Why don't you get some shots of the neighborhood and Tabitha's house? I'm going to check on something." She didn't think Valerie would want to talk on camera, based on their phone conversation that weekend. If she hadn't let police know what she saw, she surely wouldn't want it broadcast over the airwaves.

Valerie watched her walk up to the front door. She didn't move, so Stella knocked gently. They stared at each other through the glass.

The oddness of the situation made Stella smile apologetically. "I told my photographer not to record anything," she said through the window. "I just want to talk completely off the record."

Valerie finally blew out a sigh. "Fine. Come in. I'm done being on camera, though—it ain't safe."

Stella walked right into the main room of the first level, which was full of light from the two picture windows. Valerie sat on one of the two couches that faced the front windows and stared over her head.

Stella watched her for a few moments before she turned around and saw with surprise a flat-screen TV hanging over the front door, playing one of those judge shows people loved. It was an unusual set up, and before Stella could ask, Valerie said, "I got tired of missing stuff happening on the street when my shows were on, so I moved the TV from there," she pointed to a spot on a side wall under a window covered by blinds, "to right *there*," she pointed over the front door. "That way, if anything happens outside, I can see it. If nothing is happening outside, I watch my shows."

The family room took up the whole front half of the house. All the way to the left, a staircase hugged the side wall of the room, leading, she supposed, to the bedrooms on the second floor. Dead ahead, Stella saw the kitchen through an open doorway.

Valerie nodded to the other couch, and Stella sat down sideways, so she could face the other woman. "What's going on, Valerie? You told me on the phone Saturday night that it wasn't safe and you just said the same thing again. What happened?"

"What happened? Someone else got killed

next door! You think I need something *else* to happen for me to not feel safe?"

Stella bit her lip. Valerie had a good point, but she suspected there was something else at play. "I don't know, Valerie, you tell me."

Valerie shifted in her seat and leaned back against the cushions. She looked out the window with blank eyes, and Stella's gaze followed. Valerie did have a great view: Stella could see the whole street, including everyone's front porch.

Valerie heaved herself off the couch with new energy, but Stella noticed her hands were shaking as she paced the room. "I'll tell you exactly what happened, Ms. Stella Reynolds. I was sittin' where I always sit, and I heard someone pounding on the door at Tabitha's next door. I didn't know who it was, but when you hear that much noise, you get up off your couch and see what the problem is. Do you know what I mean?"

Stella murmured that she did, and Valerie continued, wringing her hands as she spoke. "So, then I see Darren trying to open the front door. I opened my blinds, so I can see what in the heck he's doing." She pointed to the covered window behind her. "I mean, police caution tape was still up over the door! He can't just go busting through there, even if he is Tabitha's brother, right? So, I open the window, and just as I'm about to say, 'Darren, what are you doing,' bam!" She stopped in front of the couch and lowered herself stiffly to the cushion. "He dropped dead. Gunshot came from inside the house. The door opened, the barrel of a gun moved forward, and all of a sudden, Darren jerked back. Blood everywhere! It was... it was..." She slid down in her seat and fell quiet, her chin resting on her chest as she stared quietly out the window in front of her.

"Who was it, Valerie? Do you know who shot Darren?" Stella stared at the window in question. The blinds were lowered and closed now, but she could imagine the devastating images still bouncing around in Valerie's head.

"I didn't see anything, except... just... blood. Blood everywhere. I hit the ground and stayed there 'til the cops arrived."

"Nothing else?" Valerie hesitated. Stella moved from her couch to Valerie's and sat near her. "What else did you see, Valerie?"

"I saw... I saw Tabitha pull the trigger. It was like a nightmare, 'cause it don't make sense why she'd shoot her own brother."

Stella shook her head. It couldn't have been

Tabitha—she was behind bars when her brother was shot. "Valerie, it couldn't have been—"

"I mean, blood just... everywhere..."

Valerie's eyes were glazed over and Stella knew she wasn't seeing the room, anymore. Instead, the other woman was reliving what she'd seen Saturday night.

"Valerie," she tried again, "Tabitha was—"

"You think blood is red, but when it comes from the chest, it's like, dark black. Black as night."

Stella blew out a sigh. She wasn't going to get any more answers out of Valerie; the woman was in shock. She tried another tactic. "Did you call police?"

Valerie's sharp eyes flicked back to life as she turned toward Stella. "Sure, sure, I thought, 'let me give the killer a reason to come after me!' No!" she snapped, "I didn't call police. I damn near peed my pants and just dropped down to the floor and laid as still as I could as long as I could. I didn't even mean to tell you. People getting killed for knowing less than I know, so I ain't knowing anything."

The two women fell quiet, both lost in though. Through the front window, Stella saw Lou looking around. His camera was slung over his shoulder and the tripod was tucked under his arm.

"I've got to go," she said. She turned back before she left to see her still half-lying on the couch, staring out the window. Stella felt as shocked as Valerie looked.

On her way to the live truck, she went over the nosey neighbor's story again. Tabitha was in jail when Darren was killed, which meant Valerie *couldn't* have seen her shoot her brother. If Valerie was wrong about *that*, it also called her information about Bobby's murder into question. It was possible that Tabitha was innocent and the person who killed *two* men was out there.

Out here, Stella thought, looking around the neighborhood.

Worse yet, since Valerie wasn't talking, police didn't even know what they didn't know.

12

As Stella headed down the walk toward Lou, she was accosted by the same ten-year-old girl she had met Friday night.

"You doin' a story on Darren or Bobby?" the child asked. The rumpled pajamas from Friday afternoon were long gone, and instead, the girl was wearing jeans and a tank top. Stella was cold just looking at her. Her gold, high-top sneakers were scuffed at the toe, like she'd stopped herself on the swings by dragging her feet one too many times.

"Darren," Stella said, stopping when she got to Lou. She tried to re-focus on the story at hand. She needed sound with someone who knew Darren—a family member would be best. Tabitha said her parents lived on the block, so Stella's eyes moved from house to house, looking for signs of three kids.

"Who is out here, talking to my child without permission?" a voice screeched, cutting across the stillness of the neighborhood. Stella's head whipped around to find a woman marching her way.

Her mouth was set in a grim line and her arms swung in time with the clacking of her low heels on the sidewalk. Rail-thin, she wore stretchy, black pants that would have been leggings on anyone else. On her skeletal frame, however, the pants hung loosely around her lower half. A red tunic top and gold heels completed the outfit.

Stella grimaced at the accusation, but tried to smile at the woman. "Hi, I'm Stella Reynolds with NBC News 5. We're looking for anyone who might have known Darren—"

"So you're asking a child?" Her nostrils flared at the perceived threat, and she grabbed the girl by the arm, yanking her away from the TV crew.

"No—no, of course not! I wasn't going to interview your daughter. We have—"

"Well, it looked like you were doing just that.

Who is your boss? I'm going to call him and let him know what I think about..."

As the woman continued to rail against the media, Stella's attention was diverted to the house across the street. An elderly blond woman descended the front staircase as if every step hurt. She held a small child in her arms no more than three years old. It was the green pacifier that caught Stella's attention—she remembered it from Friday night, after Bobby had been killed.

She turned to Lou and quietly motioned across the street. That had to be Tabitha's mother and her smallest child. That was the woman she needed to interview for her story that night. When she opened her mouth to say as much to Lou, however, the woman next to her, who was still angrily talking about Stella's lack of moral judgment, stepped around her, so she was between Stella and her photographer.

"I've got another thing to tell you," she said, now one hand on her hip and the other pointed at Stella's face. "Since when is it okay for the media to come into my neighborhood like they own the place? You know, this street floods all the time, but no one ever comes out here to ask why the city doesn't address the aging sewer lines. The minute someone is shot, though, you are all over us like ants at a picnic..."

Stella blew out a sigh as she watched the elderly woman drive away. Her focus shifted to the woman still talking in front of her, and then down to her daughter, who was now wandering away.

"Excuse me, I didn't catch your name," Stella said, hoping to break the woman out of her rhythm.

"I'm Jill DeMario, and you may not interview me."

"Mrs. DeMario, please believe me, I have no plans on interviewing you or your daughter. I am out here on a public sidewalk, where I am legally allowed to be. In fact, my hope is to leave this area within the next five minutes, which I can only do with your help." The woman looked at Stella suspiciously. "I understand that Darren moved to a new neighborhood recently. Do you know where he moved to?"

"Mmhmm," Jill said, staring unblinkingly at her.

Stella raised her eyebrows and waited. Fifteen seconds passed and then thirty more. Stella kept her expression pleasant, and finally, Jill smiled.

"You pretty funny for a white lady, I'll give you

that. I heard that Darren moved over to that new apartment complex off of Kenny Road."

"Thank you," Stella said, turning to go. Before she was halfway to the live truck, though, Jill groaned.

"Where did that girl go this time? She slips away from me like a ghost through the cracks in the door, I swear. Did you see which way she went?"

Stella pointed silently down the sidewalk where she'd seen the girl head. Jill nodded, and Stella heard her mutter as she walked past, "That's right. She went back to our house—that's where she *should* be, back at our house..." While Lou loaded up the equipment, Stella watched Jill walk down the sidewalk and go into a house with blue-tinted, heavily peeling, vinyl siding.

Stella walked around to the back of the truck and watched Lou organize his gear. All of a sudden, from the street side of the van, the ten-year-old girl appeared.

"So, what you need to know?" she asked Stella seriously, as if the last ten minutes hadn't happened.

"Are you trying to get me in trouble today? I think you need to head home."

"It's on my list, but first I want to know what you need."

Stella lifted her eyebrows incredulously. "What's your name?"

"Cara."

"Go home, Cara." She actually would have loved to ask Cara some questions, but she had just told her mother she wouldn't, so Stella stepped back from the van and Lou slammed the doors. They both headed to the front of the live truck and climbed in. Cara stood on the sidewalk, looking up at Stella through the open window.

"I heard Bobby got a new job at some kind of big time company. He made good money. My mama said leaving Tabitha was the best thing he ever did."

"Goodbye, Cara," Stella said, staring out the windshield.

"You know, it wasn't Tabitha who pulled the trigger," the little girl said loudly, over the sound of the engine. "She got problems, but not like that."

Stella watched Cara as they pulled away from the curb.

"What just happened?" Lou asked, scratching his head.

"We learned a lot and have nothing to show for it. That's what just happened."

"So, where are we headed now?"

"I guess we're going to go see where Darren lived."

Lou glanced at her with a confused expression on his face. "What about the other guy?"

"You mean Bobby?"

"Yeah. I'm getting confused."

"Join the club," Stella said grimly. One fact kept looping in her mind: she now knew more than police about the murders. She wondered if that put *her* in any danger.

13

Stella picked up the two-way radio in the live truck and called the assignment desk. Because she and Lou were relatively new to town, she had no idea where the new apartments on Kenny Road were. Luckily, Joy answered the phone on the second ring. She'd lived in Columbus her whole life, and even better, she'd been an assignment editor at the station for twenty-some years. There wasn't a nook or cranny of the town that she hadn't been to or heard of.

"Oh sure, Stella. Those new apartments were built about a year ago. Not quite low-income, but just a step above."

Joy gave Stella directions, and she guided Lou

through a maze of interstates to get to the right part of town.

Twenty minutes later, they pulled up to a campus of two-story row houses that still looked as new as they were. Not only were the buildings in great shape, but the parking lot was gleaming, with perfect, yellow lines marking off spaces every three feet. Each unit had a bright, orange door with a long, narrow window next to it. Opposite that was a larger square window that looked into the kitchen of each unit. The apartments were alternating shades of gray, going from dark to medium to light and then back to dark again. Eight to ten buildings sprawled back from the main road, surrounded by a sea of parking spaces, grass, and the occasional small tree held up by planks of wood.

Stella hadn't been expecting so many units, and she realized with a sinking feeling that they would be hard-pressed to locate Darren's apartment in the hundred or so to choose from.

"We'll have to walk it," Lou said.

She peered out the windshield for a moment before slowly nodding. "Let's split up," she said. "I'll take the ones on the north side and you take the ones on the south. If you get lucky, call me on my cell phone and vice versa."

Lou looked undecided, but Stella set off. "You have my number, right?"

She knocked on four doors before someone finally answered. It was an older woman with her hair in curlers, and she was still wearing a house-coat, even though it was nearing noon.

She peered at Stella through thick lenses and said, "Yes?" After Stella explained who she was, but before she could ask any questions, the woman closed the door with a snap. Stella heard the lock slide into place and then footsteps fading away.

It was the most interaction she had for the next half hour. As she approached the last building, she looked despairingly down the sidewalk. There were ten more doors to try before she could call this story dead.

She raised her hand to knock on the first door when her cell phone rang. It was Lou.

"Jackpot."

"You found Darren's apartment?" she asked hopefully.

"And then some. Meet me at the truck."

Lou refused to explain anything else at the live

truck, only saying, "Follow me. You have to see it for yourself."

They wound their way through the buildings on the south side of the complex, finally slowing as they approached the final building. In the ten-unit apartment building in front of them, *two* doors were shrouded in black crêpe paper. People had scrawled condolence messages across signs hung over the doors, and flowers and candles were piled on both porches.

"What is this?" Stella asked.

Lou shook his head. "Get closer. It gets even weirder."

Stella started walking again, finally coming to a stop when she got to the foot of the porch of the first door. Up close, she could see that the banner on this door read, "*RIP Darren*," with dozens of signatures underneath. A piece of twine nailed to the doorframe was wrapped around a Sharpie, so anyone who came by could sign the paper. Her eyes shifted two doors over and a small gasp escaped her lips. The sign on the second door read, "*RIP Bobby*."

"They were neighbors?" she asked, unsure of the significance, but knowing it was there. "Have you knocked on either door? Is anyone home?"

"I wanted to get you first. We might only get one shot with this—I figured I should be rolling the whole time."

Stella nodded, agreeing with the plan. She rolled up her sleeves, both literally and figuratively, took the stick microphone Lou offered, and walked up to Darren's door. She looked back at Lou long enough for him to give her the thumbs-up to indicate he was recording, and then she knocked on the door.

Bam. Bam. Bam.

The sound echoed in the still air of the apartment complex, nearly empty during work hours. After a few moments, she knocked again.

Bam. Bam. Bam.

Nothing.

She turned around, walked down the porch and over two doors, and tried the next door. She had only knocked once when the door jerked open and she nearly smashed a woman in the face with her fist.

"Oh!" she exclaimed, pulling her hand back.

"What do you want?" the woman asked, looking at Stella suspiciously.

"Did Bobby used to live here?"

The woman, with blond hair pulled back into

a sloppy bun on top of her head, looked at Stella through squinty eyes. "Who wants to know?" She was wearing gray, baggy sweat pants and a black, zip-up hoodie. Her face was puffy, like she'd been crying.

"I'm so sorry to bother you," Stella said before quickly explaining who she was and what she was doing. "I'm so sorry for your loss. Who are you, exactly?"

The woman stared at Stella for another beat before deciding to open up. "I'm Rhonda Leavy, Bobby's girlfriend."

"I hadn't heard yet that he left behind a girl-friend. Again, I'm so sorry for intruding, but would you mind telling us a little bit about Bobby?" Stella held the microphone out and felt Lou step up onto the porch behind her.

Rhonda's eyes filled with tears. She blinked rapidly before starting to speak. "What can I say? I don't suppose there's ever a good time to be mur-dered, but it seemed most unfair for Bobby. He had been doing so well. Just got a promotion at work and had visitation with the kids worked out with Tabitha. To be honest, their relationship fi-nally seemed to be settling down, you know? Really evening out. It just goes to show you never know what people are capable of."

"How long had you two been together?"

"Only about six months. We met at the office... I haven't been back since... since..." She shook her head, unable to continue. "I need to go back. I guess it's time."

"I'm so sorry to have intruded," she said softly. Lou turned to walk down the steps, but Stella asked one last question. "We couldn't help but notice the apartment two doors down. Did you know Tabitha's brother, too?" Rhonda nodded, and Stella added, "I had no idea Darren and Bobby lived so close to each other. Was that awkward with the divorce and all?"

"Not at all." Rhonda crossed her arms and leaned against the doorframe, a sad smile on her lips. "Darren and Bobby have been friends longer than he'd been married to Tabitha. He said the only strained time between them was before the divorce. He and Tabitha fought like cats and dogs, to hear him tell it, but once they decided to separate, everything got better—their relationship with each other, with the kids, and certainly between Bobby and Darren."

"Police said Darren's murder might have been

retaliation for Bobby's. Do you know anyone who'd want to do that?" It was a tricky question to ask, considering Stella was talking to one of the people who might want to retaliate against Tabitha. Rhonda was so caught up in her grief, however, that she didn't take offense.

"I can't think of anyone—not a single person—who'd want to hurt him. It just doesn't make sense."

As Stella walked back to the live truck, she had to agree: something wasn't adding up.

14

The next day when Stella got into work, she found a Post-it note from her boss attached to her computer screen. *Come see me.*

She was filling in for Vera that night for the first time, anchoring the evening news at six. Despite the fact that it was supposed to be her day off and she was supposed to be in Tennessee visiting Lucky, she felt good. She set her bags down before going to find her news director.

"Come on in, Stella," Harry said, leaning back in his chair so he could see around the file cabinet by the door.

Stella held up the yellow Post-it. "What's up?"

He tapped the keyboard on his laptop, stared at the screen for a moment, and then nodded. He turned the computer around on his desk, and Stella was confronted with a very unflattering screenshot of herself taken from a recent live shot. Her eyelids were half-closed, her mouth half-open —it wasn't pretty.

She made a face. "Why do you have a still shot of that?"

"Whoever posted the audio clip of you from the other night is updating pictures of you on a daily basis. I don't think we need to do anything about it, yet; I just wanted to you to know we're monitoring the situation. Right now, it's only got..." he swiveled the computer around so he could see the screen, "twelve-hundred views. No big deal—we can ignore it. If it takes off, though, we'll need to address it on air. That's all."

She walked slowly back to her desk. She didn't like the way Harry had said, "if it takes off." It almost sounded like he was rooting for it to do just that, and the thought made her uncomfortable. As she was logging into her computer, her desk phone rang.

"NBC News 5, can I help you?" she said.

A muted, nasally voice asked, "Will you accept

a collect call from the Franklin County Correctional Facility?"

Stella leaned over to dig a notebook out of her bag. "Uhh..." She found a pen in her top drawer and bit the cap off. "Yes," she said, when her tools were gathered. After a few clicks and clanks on the line, there was a moment of silence, and then Tabitha Herbert started talking.

"I need some help."

"Help?"

"Listen, I'm worried about my kids. I need someone to make sure they're okay."

"Kids?" Stella was so surprised to be on the phone with Tabitha that she couldn't get past wondering why the inmate had called *her*, instead of her lawyer.

"Yes, can you not hear me well? These phone lines are terrible." There was a shifting sound and she said, "Someone is threatening my kids! I think it's Bobby's ex. She's gone mad with grief, or something, and wants to get back at me. My kids are in danger!"

"Wait—hold on, Tabitha. I just met Rhonda yesterday. She honestly seemed very calm to me about everything."

"Calm? I just got a crazy letter from her. She is

not calm, okay? She's going to hurt my kids to get back at me, I just know it!"

"Have you told police? Did you show the letter to anyone at the jail?"

"I can't get anyone here to do anything fast— and I can't wait, Stella. I need your help!"

Stella realized she was standing; Tabitha's terror and stress were transferring over the phone line. She ran a hand through her hair and said, "I'm not sure what you want me to do. Should I call your lawyer? The police?"

"I want you to do what you'd do if they were your kids!" Stella wanted to say, *Still not clear,* but instead she murmured a calming sound and Tabitha continued. "If you find out someone is threatening to hurt your kids, you move mountains, for God's sake! You make sure they're safe!"

"I understand you're feeling helpless, but let's not overreact. Can you read the letter to me, please, so I can have all the information I need to move forward?"

Tabitha took a shaky breath and said, "I just opened it today. She's crazy—I'm telling you, she's a nut. She wrote: *You selfish, selfish woman. You took what I love most dearly. In my heart, I know the same will happen to you. You reap what you sow, and if I were you, I'd never sleep another night without worrying about those you love dearest meeting the same terrible fate as my poor, loving boyfriend. Rot in hell."*

"Wow." Stella said, breaking the silence that followed. "And she signed it?"

"Well, no."

"Oh. Uh... how do you know it's from Rhonda?"

"I just—"

"Your call will disconnect in thirty seconds."

"What was that?"

"Damn jail phones. We're out of time. I'm counting on you, Stella! I need you! My kids need—"

Click.

She jumped at the harsh dial tone. She'd been pressing the phone against her ear and wasn't expecting the loud noise. Stella slowly lowered the receiver and sat down. The Rhonda she'd met the day before had seemed so collected. Grieving, but pragmatic—not the kind of person who'd send a threatening letter to the jail. What was she supposed to do? She was a reporter—not child protective services or police.

Police!

She picked the phone back up and punched in some numbers.

"Coyne."

"Sergeant, it's Stella." She quickly ran through everything Tabitha had told her. When she was done, Sergeant Coyne sighed deeply. "Is there anything you can do?" she asked.

"It's not that easy, Stella," he said. "There was no direct threat, only her gut feeling about who wrote the letter. I guess I can send a crew out to do a welfare check on the kids, but that's about it."

It seemed better than nothing, but it wasn't exactly moving mountains. After they hung up, Stella paced behind her desk. She felt like she needed to do more. Because she was anchoring, she wasn't expected to do anything but read through scripts before the news. She figured it wouldn't take too long, so she should have time to sneak out and do some reconnaissance for Tabitha.

She scanned the newsroom and found Devi checking email at an open desk. "Hey, Devi, are you busy?"

He gestured to his email account. "Not really. Why?"

"Just wanted to check something out."

He stood, grabbed the keys off the desk next to him, and said, "Let's roll." Once they were inside a news car, he started up the engine and then looked at her and said, "Where to, boss?"

"Hieroglyphics Communications." At his confused look, she elaborated, "It's downtown, off Fourth Street."

"What's the story?"

"I'm not entirely sure," she said, looking out the window, lost in thought. Rhonda might have fired off a passionate letter right after the crime. She had seemed calm the day before, but maybe she'd been putting on a show for Stella and the camera. She wanted to see Rhonda at work and hoped she'd be able to tell if the woman was simply grieving or if it was something worse.

"Right now, it's just a fishing expedition."

THE BUILDING WAS in a deserted section of downtown Columbus. Empty, neglected buildings surrounded the communications company, making the long, gray, modern structure with a mix of concrete, dark wood, and shiny, glass windows look dark and imposing, despite the late afternoon sunshine.

"Hieroglyphics, huh?" Devi said.

Stella cocked her head and looked at the sign. "It does seem an odd name for a company. Hiero-glyphics are completely confusing, yet you assume the company wants you to believe they're good at communicating."

Devi shook his head. "There must be some strategy we're missing."

"I'll head in and ask some questions, but I don't want anyone getting nervous. I'll call you if I can get an interview." Devi nodded and cranked the radio up as Stella climbed out of the car. She heard the automatic door locks clunk over as she walked toward the office building.

Inside, she was greeted by a woman who looked to be in her early forties; she had blond hair and wore a black dress with chunky, orangish-red accessories.

"Rhonda's not in today," she said, answering Stella's question with a lowered voice. "She had a death in the family and needed some time."

"Oh," Stella said, disappointed. "Yes, we heard about Bobby. Did you know him?"

"Of course—we all did."

"I'm so sorry for your loss," Stella said. She took a bracing breath before continuing. "I'm actually working on a story about his murder today. I don't suppose there's anyone here who'd be willing to talk on camera—someone who knew Bobby well?" Stella wasn't exactly assigned to do anything about Bobby that day, but since she was there, she didn't see the harm in trying to get an interview.

"Well, I'd have to check with Paul for that. He's the owner here." The admin disappeared around the corner and Stella took a moment to look around the lobby. There were many silvery-metallic accents on the furniture, and even though exposed ductwork hung down from the ceiling, some warm wood tones kept the office from feeling impersonal.

After a few minutes, the blond receptionist was back with an attractive, middle-aged man by her side. He had a shock of white hair, his skin had the healthy glow of someone who spent a lot of time outside, and his physique matched. He walked toward Stella with his arm extended. "Paul Blackwell. So nice to meet you, Stella. We're all still in shock over the whole thing. Bobby was a great employee—in fact, I had just given him a huge promotion. We can't believe he's gone."

"Mr. Blackwell, would you be willing to go on camera to talk to me about what kind of employee Bobby was?"

"I'm afraid not, Stella, but I'd be happy to tell you off-camera how much we liked him." He motioned to a set of chairs in one corner. Before she sat down, two other employees walked through the lobby: blond women both wearing black and both quite attractive. "He'd only been with the company some six months, but I could tell he was a rising star."

Stella nodded. "We've only heard great things about him. I'm so sorry for your loss."

"What's the latest on the investigation?"

"Police aren't telling us much—then again, I don't think there's much to tell. I'm sure you've heard they have Bobby's ex-wife in custody."

He shook his head, his expression drawn, but he looked up and smiled happily as another employee crossed through the lobby. Not that she was keeping count, but it was another blond. "Molly, great work last night," he said with a wolfish smile. Stella looked up in surprise at the woman and saw her blush before she hurried out of the lobby. She looked back at Paul and saw he was staring at the empty door where his employee had disappeared, the crass smile still on his face.

She cleared her throat. "So, not much of an update for you, I'm afraid," she said. He startled out of his trance and arranged his face back into one of proper sadness.

"Well, it really was a shame."

She was getting a funny vibe from this whole office; it was filled with women employees who appeared to be carbon copies of one another. She didn't necessarily like his tone when he addressed them, either. She was preparing to stand to leave when yet another blond approached the pair.

"Paul, I'm sorry to interrupt, but I have the papers you requested." She held a stack to Paul and then handed him a pen. "They just need your signature, and then I'll be able to send them on to the client."

Paul leered at this new employee as he took the file. "Felicia, I told you to bring these to my office later today."

"I had a meeting crop up, so I wanted to get them to you now," she said, taking a couple of steps back. Her face looked slightly familiar, and Stella stared for a moment, trying to place this woman. As another employee walked behind Felicia, though, Stella realized it was simply too many blondes in a row—they were all starting to look alike.

She stood from her chair. "Well, I've taken up enough of your time, Paul. Thank you so much for sharing your thoughts on Bobby with me." Paul gave her the creeps and she didn't want to stay any longer than she already had. He stood, too, and reached for her hand. They shook, but he held on a little too long and pressed into her palm a little too familiarly. She struggled to keep her face expressionless as she turned and left the office.

In the parking lot, she tried to open the door to the news car, but it was locked. Devi scrambled to open the door, and when she climbed in, he said, "No dice?"

"No interview, but I did learn a few things."

"Like what?"

"Like Bobby's boss is kind of a jerk."

"What does that have to do with the murder?"

"I'm not sure. At this point, everything seems important."

15

Stella's cell phone rang at one o'clock in the morning. She had gotten home around midnight after anchoring the news with Mark and had climbed into bed to read. She must have drifted off to sleep, and although she couldn't have been asleep for long, she felt like a bear interrupted from winter hibernation. The combined buzz of the battery pack against the nightstand and the jingle of her ring tone finally roused her, and she blearily fumbled for the source of the noise.

"Hello?" she croaked.

"Can you get here in ten minutes?" a man asked.

Stella rubbed her eyes and squinted at the screen. She didn't recognize the phone number. "I think you have the wrong number."

"Stella, girl, I know I have the right number, mmkay?"

Parker's signature sound finally connected the dots in her brain. "What's—wait, what?"

"Can you be here in ten minutes? I'm almost out of time."

"Can I be where in ten minutes?" she asked with a groan. Why was Parker calling her in the middle of the night with a confusing question?

"I'm in the middle of an operation. After you and I talked, I couldn't get out of my head that I was just letting Edie Hawthorne railroad me. So, I came up with a plan, but I need you to help me right now. Can you get here in ten minutes?"

"No."

Silence met her single syllable answer, and then Parker's voice took on a pleading tone. "I'm just down the street. Please, help me. Be here in twenty minutes—and wear a hat."

Stella flopped back against her pillow and threw an arm over her eyes. She had a feeling she was going to regret this. "Fine. Tell me where to go."

~

APPROXIMATELY THIRTY MINUTES LATER, Stella pulled up to the curb behind a popular restaurant and bar just a few streets away from her apartment. During daylight hours, she would have walked, but at 1:34 in the morning, she'd decided to drive.

It was nearing closing time at Bernard's Bar and Tavern, but raucous laughter and music still floated out the back door. Stella spotted Parker leaning against the back of the building. He was between street lamps in the alleyway, but the glowing ember at the end of his cigarette helped Stella spot him.

"Since when do you smoke?" she asked, looking at his cigarette with surprise.

"Stella," he said, waving her comment away, "I'm ready to enter phase one of my revenge plan."

"Revenge plan? This doesn't sound like something I should be involved in."

"I just need you to act as lookout while I get close to Edie's car."

"Parker, what are you talking about?"

"Operation Crab Cake is about to begin." In one hand, Parker jiggled a small, white, take-out bag that she hadn't noticed before. "It's pretty simple, actually," he said, lowering his voice. "I have one of Club 21's finest crab cakes wrapped in foil inside this bag."

"Okay," she said, dragging out the last syllable.

"I'm gonna slip the crab cake into the pocket behind the passenger seat in Edie's car." He looked at Stella triumphantly.

"Why?"

"Can you imagine how infuriating it's going to be for her? This crab cake is going to slowly rot, and she'll have no idea why the inside of her car smells like a Dumpster outside an oyster bar. It's genius."

"How does this help you get you your money back?"

"Oh, it doesn't. It just gives me intense satisfaction, and that, my dear, is priceless."

Stella's nose wrinkled in distaste. "No. I can't be a part of this."

"You don't have to be."

"Why did you call me here, then?"

"I just need you to monitor a distraction." Stella opened her mouth to ask what he meant, but before she could, he leaned into the bar through the open door and reached his hand around the wall. Seconds later, the blaring scream of a fire alarm pierced through the noise. In one moment, everyone was pounding shots and playing darts, and in the next, there was chaos.

"What are you doing?" Stella shouted over the deafening noise.

Parker grinned. "She's in the front room. Make sure she doesn't come around back until I'm gone."

"How will I know when—" but Stella was talking to herself. Parker had turned and sprinted down the alley. Stella looked uncertainly into the bar. Even though she knew there wasn't a fire, it still went against her every instinct to walk into a building with a smoke alarm sounding off its warning.

She blew out a breath and grumbled, "I should have stayed in bed."

After stepping through the door, she joined the queue of customers heading to the front exit. Slipping between people, she scanned the crowd, looking for the tall, statuesque figure of the Channel 7 fashion reporter. As she made it through the front exit and back out into the fresh air, she finally spotted her.

Edie was standing like a swan among ducks. Her shiny, black hair gleamed under a street lamp, and at least four men vied for her attention. As Stella watched, she noted that Edie somehow gave each of them enough to keep hanging around: a word to the muscle T-shirt guy here, a gentle touch on accountant guy's arm there, a wink to the undertaker, and a tinkling laugh at something the alt-rocker said.

Edie was good. Stella could understand how Parker was taken in, and even she was slightly awestruck. Wading through the crowd of evacuating bar patrons looked easier than breaking into the man-fort surrounding Edie, but Stella was in luck. Edie caught sight of her and a look of rapture overtook her face.

"Stella Reynolds? Is that really you? I never see you out! Don't tell my bosses, but I watch you every weekend!"

Stella grinned and said, "Don't tell my bosses, but I watch you, too!"

The women smiled at each other, and Stella had to remind herself that Edie's friendly demeanor was deceptive.

Edie waved off her admirers and asked Stella how she was settling into town. Before she could answer, though, the woman interrupted, "I'm sorry... what exactly are you wearing right now?"

She fingered Stella's flannel pajama pants and barely contained a gasp of horror when she took in the Chuck Taylors on her feet.

"Oh, um... I was already in bed for the night when a friend convinced me to come out..."

"Ahhh, right. Well, you look comfortable, that's for sure," Edie said with a smile. Stella tried to ignore the fact that the word "comfortable" had come out sounding like a curse word.

Edie looked like she'd never worn sneakers in her life. Her four-inch platform heels were the least-provocative part of her outfit: her dark hair was sleek and loose around her face, and a red corset-style top stopped an inch above her black, leather pants, showing off a small, glittering ring at her belly button. Edie cleared her throat and Stella looked up from the jewelry, her cheeks red.

"So, uh... how long have you worked at Channel 7?"

"A year, now."

"You're such a natural—you do a really great job."

Edie smiled like she'd heard that a million times before and started gabbing about her job, which was what Stella had hoped would happen

—flattery and curiosity will almost always encourage someone to get chatty.

As Stella nodded and smiled her way through hearing Edie's resume, she surreptitiously looked for Parker in the crowd. The area in front of the bar was clearing out; most people had taken the fire drill as a sign to head home for the night.

There was no Parker in sight.

She wondered how long she'd have to keep Edie engaged, but she looked at the fashion reporter with fondness. She seemed so kind; it was difficult to remember she'd cheated someone out of thousands of dollars. Stella finally tuned back into what Edie was saying.

"When I saw that so many people don't know how to dress themselves," Edie was saying while running her fingers absent-mindedly down the arm of Stella's rugby shirt, "that's when I knew I was meant to teach people how to do it on TV," she finished. "What about you, Stella? When did you know?"

Stella looked at her sleeve, where Edie's fingers had just been, and felt herself stand a little straighter. She smiled at the woman. "Oh, I guess for me, it was when a college professor of mine was murdered and prosecutors charged my best friend for the crime. Of course, I knew she was innocent, but no one else did, so I had to help find the real killer." Edie's face scrunched up in confusion. "Oh, and I like dressing up, too, and realized I could do that every day on TV," Stella added sweetly.

Edie returned Stella's smile uncertainly. Stella's grin widened when she saw Parker wave to her from inside the bar. The ringing of her cell phone gave her the perfect excuse to walk away. "Well it's getting late, but it was so nice to run into you, Edie." She turned and walked back into the bar, which was quiet again.

Some employees were carrying racks of glasses from the dishwasher to the shelves, and the bouncer glanced up at Stella and said, "We close in five minutes—you missed last call. Time to go home."

"My car is parked out back. I'm just gonna cut through, if that's okay?"

The bouncer nodded, and soon Stella was back outside in the alley. Parker was sitting in the front seat of her car.

"How did you get in my car? I definitely locked the doors."

Parker shrugged. "What can I say? I got skills, mmkay?"

"So, how did everything go?"

"Operation Crab Cake was a success. I'd say one or two days of bright sunshine on a nicely paved parking lot will do the trick."

Stella shuddered at the thought. "You didn't put anything in my car, did you?"

Parker looked shocked at the thought. "You are a friend, Stella. Only my enemies should fear me."

"I'm headed home. Can I drop you somewhere?" Parker gave her directions, and in a few minutes, she pulled up in front of his apartment. She rolled down the window after he got out to say goodbye; he stopped halfway across the sidewalk, and they both turned toward angry voices.

A man and woman were headed their way, still halfway down the block, but both were stumbling —maybe drunk. The longer Stella watched, the more she realized they weren't having an argument, but simply a loud, drunken conversation. Parker must have come to the same conclusion, because he shrugged and gave Stella a wave before bounding up the steps to his apartment.

Stella started rolling up her window as the couple walked by.

"Stella?"

She stopped the window halfway up and squinted into the darkness. "Yes?"

"Stella, it's me, Rhonda," the woman slurred.

The man with her muttered some curse words that amounted roughly to, "I ain't got time for this," and kept going down the block.

Rhonda, a bit off balance, braced herself against the roof of Stella's car and smiled down at her. "What are you doing here?"

Under the streetlamp, it was clear that Rhonda's bleach-blond hair was overdue for a dye job. Dark roots showed for the first quarter-inch from her scalp before the white-yellow hair took over. The whole thing was pulled back into a tight, slicked-back ponytail. She looked sad and over-tired, like she hadn't slept in days.

"Just dropping off a friend and heading home. How are you, Rhonda? I stopped by your office the other day—they said you hadn't been back since Bobby's death. How are you managing?"

Rhonda's eyes filled with tears at her boyfriend's name. "I'm not gonna lie, it's been real tough. I don't see how it'll get any better any time soon."

"Well, you know what they say: write your

thoughts down on paper, like a letter—but, you know, never send the letter. Rhonda, do you know what I mean?"

Even through her drunken haze, a flicker of understanding passed through her eyes. "Never send it? That sounds like real good advice, Stella."

"Be careful tonight, Rhonda."

The woman stepped away from the car, looking lost and alone on the sidewalk. Before Stella could get too far away, she called out, "Wait!"

Stella stepped on the brake and looked at her expectantly.

"I've been thinking ever since we met... I wanted to tell you something. I honestly don't think it means anything, because I definitely think Tabitha is the one who pulled the trigger, but I can't get it out of my mind. Doesn't seem big enough to tell police, but I feel like I should tell someone."

"What is it?"

"It's something that happened at work. Right after Bobby got the promotion, someone started leaving him angry notes. Apparently, they thought they should have gotten the job, instead of him."

"Who?" Stella asked, looking at Rhonda suspiciously. Were these just words from a confused, grieving woman, or were they worth something?

"That's just it: we never could figure it out. A couple of anonymous notes were left in his drawer and an angry voicemail on his cell phone."

"Well, who else was up for the promotion?"

"I guess everyone. It was a new position Paul had created to lead the team. We used to all be on the same level—well, I guess we still are, now."

"You have no idea who was so angry?"

"See, why I didn't tell police?" She shuffled down the sidewalk a few steps and then turned back one last time. "Goodbye, Stella."

She watched her walk away through her rearview mirror, her mind working overtime. It wasn't a lot to go on, but it might have been a reason for someone to kill Bobby. Love, power, and money were the big motives for murder. Tabitha didn't love Bobby anymore, and by Rhonda's account, the two had been getting along better than ever. That left money and power as good motives for the murder, and with Rhonda's information, everyone who worked with Bobby could be suspects, including Rhonda.

Maybe police needed to take another look at Hieroglyphics Communications.

16

Stella's weekend was compressed enough that it certainly didn't make sense to drive to Knoxville, and that's exactly why she was already an hour into the trip. Surely Lucky would appreciate her effort to see him, even though she only had one day off.

Her weeknight anchoring debut had been fun; she and Mark paired well together, and Harry had made a point of calling after the late news on Thursday to tell her she had done a great job.

She'd awakened as early as she could Friday morning and had started driving, and she couldn't wait to see the look on Lucky's face when she rolled up to his house in Knoxville. The six-hour drive meant she would get there right around lunchtime. Lucky had to leave Saturday morning for his press tour, and Stella would head out when he did and just make it back in time for her shift Saturday afternoon.

She cued up some of her favorite playlists on her phone and made frequent stops for coffee. One interstate blended into another, and Ohio soon turned to Kentucky and then Tennessee. Before she knew it, she was pulling into Lucky's driveway.

He lived in a stately, stucco home on the outskirts of the western edge of Knoxville, and the house blended into the hill on which it was built. A wrap-around porch welcomed visitors in the front, and down the steep hill was a walk-out basement at the rear of the home. White window frames set off the dark gray stucco, and a fire engine-red front door drew your eye to the very center of the home.

She waved to the gardener, a friendly man named Ben, who even then, at noon on a Friday, was hand-weeding the beds by the front door, a wide-brimmed sun hat blocking the rays from his tanned and weathered face. She used a code to open the garage door and then used her key to open the inner door before stepping into a spacious mud room. She followed the hallway into a gorgeous, professionally-outfitted kitchen; stainless steel appliances gleamed, and when she flicked a switch, light bounced off the shiny, granite countertops.

"Lucky?" she called out, certain, even before the sound of her voice stopped echoing in the cavernous room, that no one was home. Was he out running errands?

She plucked her phone out of her bag to call him just as it rang in her hand. Lucky's voice was so garbled that she couldn't make out what he said.

"What? I can't hear you!" she spoke loudly, as if that would improve their poor cell connection.

"I said: I'm in the air, right this minute, flying as close to Ohio as I'll be on this trip. Just wanted to say I love you and I'm sorry I was cross before I left. I hate leaving on bad terms."

"In the air? I thought you didn't leave for D.C. until tomorrow morning?" Stella said, sinking onto a barstool at the island.

"They booked me another radio interview for seven o'clock tomorrow morning, so I left a day early. Where are you?"

"Oh," Stella said, feeling at once angry, sad, and silly. Why hadn't she called him yesterday when she'd made her plan? The whole idea of surprising him at his house now felt idiotic. "I'm uh..."

"Not at work again?" Lucky asked, his voice taking on a mother hen tone. "They need to give you time off. There has to be some kind of OSHA violation there, working so many days in a row. It's not like you get overtime pay!" Lucky sounded cross, even from ten-thousand feet up.

"No, no, I'm not at work. I'm... well, I'm just putting my feet up. It *was* a long week," she added, putting her feet up on the next bar stool to make what she said true.

"Oh, Bear, I miss you. We'll get this long-distance thing figured out. I know we will," Lucky said with his usual boyish charm. Stella didn't answer. "Bear?"

"You're right. It's only been a few months—I'm sure we'll figure it out," she said, stifling a groan.

"Don't forget you owe me a trip to Knoxville. I can't always come to Ohio."

"Oh," Stella said, finally heaving herself off the seat and heading for Lucky's well-stocked refrigerator, "don't I know it. Knoxville for sure, next time."

She grabbed a can of soda and held it against her forehead. She could feel the blood pumping at her temples and hoped this wasn't the beginning of a migraine.

They said goodbye, and she carefully set her phone back in her bag, walked out of the house through the mudroom into the garage, and then raised her head to the ceiling and screamed at the top of her lungs.

"Miss Stella?" She broke off mid-curse and opened her eyes. The gardener was looking at her with concern. "Is everything okay?"

She clamped her lips, swallowed her emotions, and then forced out a smile. "Yes, Ben, sorry. I hope I didn't startle you. I didn't realize Lucky would be out of town."

"Can I get you anything?"

She laughed without humor. "No. I guess I'm just going to head home."

"To Ohio?"

"Yup." She reigned in her frustration long enough to send Ben an embarrassed smile and then laughed again as she climbed back behind the wheel.

She realized she must have sounded like a mad woman, screaming in the garage, and she sat in her car for several minutes, her emotions at war. She rested her head against the steering wheel, her chest tightening as tears threatened. Breathing deeply through her mouth until she got her emotions in check, Stella straightened her shoulders, picked up her phone, and tapped a name on her contact list.

"Where are you?" she asked.

"On a hike."

"Who is this, and what have you done to my friend?" Stella asked suspiciously.

Janet crowed with laughter. "Don't I wonder the same thing, these days? Jason is an avid hiker. Who knew?"

"So now you're an avid hiker?" Stella asked her former roommate in wonder. Picturing Janet on a hike with her boyfriend was like picturing a lion that didn't eat meat. Stella and Janet had met in Montana years earlier where they formed an unlikely friendship. They'd been roommates up until Stella had taken the job in Ohio.

"No," Janet clarified, "I am a grudging hiker who knows that the best way to get sex out of my boyfriend is to earn it through good deeds."

Stella chuckled. "What is your good deed?"

"Hiking this damn mountain for no other reason than to say we've done it." Janet's breath was heavy as she navigated the trail. "What's up?"

"Oh, nothing. I thought maybe we could hang out later. I'm in Knoxville with, uh, nothing to do."

"Hmm," Janet said, and she must have stopped moving, because after a few more deep breaths, she spoke normally again. "Sounds like the best offer I've had today. If you're free now, that gives me a great excuse to start heading *down* this mountain, instead of continuing *up*."

Stella laughed a real laugh for the first time since she'd arrived at Lucky's house, and she made plans to meet Janet at her place in an hour.

When she pulled up to the duplex, she didn't get out of the car. Instead, she sat, staring at the home. When she'd lived in Knoxville, she and Janet had shared an apartment in a slightly dodgy section of town. Their apartment had been spacious, but plain with chipped Formica countertops and special security bolts on the outside doors. As Stella looked at Janet's new home, though, she couldn't help but be dazzled by how *nice* it seemed. New, beige, wood siding cut sharp, perfect lines along the front of the house with two doors tucked discreetly away from each other, so you wouldn't have to stare at your neighbor if you looked out your own front window.

Small, red and white flowers burst out of the planter boxes just under the sparkling windows on the main level. Stella snorted out a laugh when she noticed, upon the second glance, that the matching flowers on the second floor might have been plastic—they weren't blowing in the breeze like the flowers on the first floor.

Janet leaned out the doorway of the unit on the right and yelled, "You coming in, or what?"

Stella looked at her friend fondly and climbed out of her car. Janet was shorter and curvier than Stella with medium length, light brown hair and brown eyes. When they'd first met years ago, Stella had thought Janet was much older than her. Appearances could be deceiving, though, and just then, with her face flushed from the hike and free of makeup, Janet looked, well, radiant.

"Are you actually getting younger every year?" Stella asked, holding her friend at arm's length before they hugged.

Janet cackled out a laugh and walked into her home. "No, but apparently quitting smoking is good for your health."

"Imagine," Stella said dryly. "Next thing you know, they'll say hiking and regular exercise are good for you, too."

Janet shot her a dry look before shoving a drink into her hands. Ice cubes clinked happily against the glass, and Stella took a long pull of the drink before sitting next to her friend.

"I really needed that."

"I know. I'm a professional bartender, remember? I know when people *want* a drink and when they *need* a drink. From your voice on the phone, I knew you *needed* a drink."

"What time is it?" Stella asked guiltily, looking at her watch.

"It's never too early for a Bloody Mary," Janet pooh-poohed. "So, what's wrong?"

Stella took another sip and then plucked the celery stalk from her glass and took a bite. "Eh, I'm boring lately. I want to know about this house! It's gorgeous," she said, looking around.

They had walked directly into the sitting room; Stella was on a dark, leather couch with a cool-blue and cream rug underfoot. Janet sat on one of two matching armless chairs, upholstered in a modern pattern of grays and blues that complimented the rug. Looking past Janet, Stella saw the kitchen was under construction.

"Where's Jason?" she asked, wondering where her boyfriend was.

"He decided to finish the hike and then run back home," Janet answered nonchalantly.

"Run home? Where were you hiking?"

"Sharpe Ridge—not far," she answered. "Jason's been stuck inside forever renovating the kitchen, and just needed a break. He can't wait to see you, though—said he'll join us for dinner tonight."

Stella nodded. She would be glad to catch up with Jason. He'd stuck with Janet through some pretty big ups and downs and seemed like a great guy. "I knew Jason was aces with electronics, but he's a carpenter, too?" she asked, eyeing the ongoing construction project.

"We're making some investments," Janet said, suddenly interested in her own drink.

"Like this house?" Stella asked.

"Right: the duplex, the bar, things like that."

"You own the whole duplex?" Stella asked, setting her drink on a coaster on the dark cherry coffee table between them and leaning forward.

"Wait, you bought the bar? That's—that... how?" she finally spluttered.

"It was time to settle down, you know?" Janet said, stirring her drink with her celery stalk. "I manage the finances and run the bar and Jason does all the hard stuff."

"I wouldn't say running a bar is easy," Stella interjected, defending her friend.

"No, it's not, but he does the wood working, fixes things that are broken—you know, the stuff I could never do."

"Wow," Stella said, sitting back and looking at her friend with new respect. "That's really something, Janet. I'm so happy for you!"

A small smile appeared before her friend forced a frown back. "So, spill it. What's going on with you? Why are you suddenly in Knoxville with nothing to do?"

Stella sighed and looked down her nose at her drink for a moment. She spent the next thirty minutes telling Janet everything from the situation with the online clip to the murder cases she'd been working on to her recent rocky road with Lucky. When she'd finished, Janet blew out a loud sigh, took their empty glasses to a bar in the corner, and silently made new drinks for them both.

She handed Stella a new glass and then sat back down.

"Vodka with lime?" Stella asked.

"A serious talk needs a serious drink."

Stella nodded, steeling herself for her friend's words. Janet didn't spend time on frivolous niceties; she got right down to business, and all of a sudden, Stella wasn't sure she was ready to hear her friend's bald assessment of her life. It was too late, though.

"First of all, Reynolds, this audio clip? You just can't worry what anybody thinks about you. I know, I know," she said, cutting Stella off before she could launch into her explanation. "I know your whole messed up business is all about what people think about you—what kind of ratings you brought in for each newscast, polling viewers on your likability scores. It's ridiculous." She sipped at her drink with a hand out to keep Stella quiet. "What I'm telling you is: you'll never get anywhere in life or at work if you're only concerned with others' opinions."

"I'm not—"

"Now, just hear me out. Lucky is another matter. No one ever said long distance would be easy, but I think if you two can make it six months, you can make it for good. You just need a system—a plan for regular visits with a few surprises thrown in."

"Well, that's what I was trying to do today—"

"When I say *surprises*," Janet said, leaning forward with a cagey expression, "I don't mean driving half the day without first knowing the other will be there. Jason works with all of this technology." She looked slyly at Stella from under her eyelashes. "Do you know what you can do with a small camera and a hot lingerie set?"

Stella held her hands up. "Ugh, Janet. Say no more."

"I mean, you can get right in there—"

Stella covered her ears. "Janet! Stop. I know what you mean!"

Her friend's cackle cut through her covered ears and Stella chuckled, too. Janet's face took on a contemplative look. "As for the murders, I'd keep an eye on the boss man."

"Paul Blackwell?"

"Yes. He sounds slippery, and I worry that, when police do catch the real killer, this Paul guy will get away with his crimes."

"Well, we don't know—"

"Not for sure, I know, but it sounds like he's

been abusing his power at the company. Someone needs to stand up for those women at his office, Stella—they still have to work there. I think that someone is you!"

After their talk, Janet excused herself to take a shower, and Stella settled back into the couch, paging through a magazine from the coffee table. She stared blindly at the pictures, thinking about Paul and his many blonds. Were there crimes going on at Hieroglyphics Communications, or was Paul Blackwell just a really bad boss?

She was glad she'd come to Knoxville, if for no other reason than for Janet to remind her there was more going on in Columbus than murder.

17

"Stella, what do you have?"

She looked around the conference table on Monday morning. She'd survived her night in Knoxville and a surprisingly easy weekend shift—easy, because Spenser and Amanda had the weekend off to celebrate their wedding anniversary. She'd never been so thrilled for someone else's wedded bliss. Now she was sitting in the morning meeting, where every reporter and producer was expected to pitch a story for the day ahead.

Beatrice cleared her throat, waiting on an answer, and Stella said, "Tabitha Herbert will be in court today on a bond hearing. Her lawyer is trying to lower her five-hundred-thousand dollar bond so she can take care of her kids until the trial."

Beatrice nodded. "Sounds good. Take Lou, and plan to be live at noon."

"I don't care what anyone says," Lou said fifteen minutes later, taking in the huge swaths of glass that made up the front of the courthouse, "that cannot be energy efficient."

The building was relatively new—the giant glass, metal, and concrete structure loomed over a block of High Street downtown.

"I don't know about that, but it's very symbolic, isn't it? You know, the transparency of justice, and here they have built an actual transparent building."

Lou shrugged and gathered his gear. One of the security guards recognized them when they walked into the building and waved them through the screening process. The criminal division was on the first floor, so they wound through the hallway and quietly entered the courtroom. Court was already in session for the day, so they crept along the back wall, heading for an open space in the front row of the gallery.

Lou painstakingly lowered the legs on the tripod, trying to make as little noise as possible, while Stella took a seat next to him and got her notebook out. There were a number of inmates sitting in the jury box, waiting for their turn in front of the judge. Stella scanned their faces, looking for Tabitha, and finally spotting her at the far end of the second row. She then turned to look for Tabitha's lawyer in the gallery, but she didn't see Eleanor anywhere.

It was a full docket, and after twenty minutes, Stella felt herself zoning out. It seemed as if every defendant except Tabitha was called up to the podium for their case. Two in a row were called up simply to reschedule, because their lawyers didn't show up. Another hour passed before Tabitha's name was finally called.

"Case number OH-567731, State of Ohio versus Tabitha Herbert. The defendant is represented by Eleanor Pochowski," the bailiff recited the words monotonously. Tabitha stood from her spot in the jury box and walked to the podium.

Stella saw, guiltily, that Tabitha didn't look bored at all. Her way of life for the next six to eight months was on the line, after all. If the bond hearing went well, she'd be on her way home; if it didn't, she'd have to continue her stay at the

Franklin County Correctional Facility. Stella craned her neck, again looking for Eleanor Pochowski.

After a moment of confused mutterings and shuffling of papers, Tabitha muttered, "Well, this is just great."

The prosecutor stood and addressed the judge. "Your Honor, may I suggest we reschedule this bond hearing until the defendant's lawyer is able to join us?"

"Mom, no," a slight voice squeaked out from the gallery. Stella looked sharply to the right and recognized Tabitha's mother sitting in the front row with Tabitha's three children. It was the oldest who had spoken—he looked to be around ten. One tear streaked quickly down his cheek and his hand trembled as he held it out toward his mother.

"Quiet in the courtroom," the judge said, banging his gavel, but even he couldn't take his eyes off the sad scene unfolding in front of him. His usually sharp tongue directed at anyone breaking the rules of the court softened slightly as he looked upon the children. "Ma'am, you might need to take the kids out of the courtroom." He looked over the top of his glasses at Tabitha's mother and added, "This is no place for children."

"Excuse me, Your Honor?" Tabitha tore her eyes away from her kids and faced the front of the courtroom again. "Why should I pay the price for my lawyer not being here? Can we continue with the bond hearing? Is there someone else who can represent me?"

"I'm sorry, Ms. Herbert, but we'll need to reset this bond hearing for..." he looked down at his calendar, "one week from today. My office will let your attorney know about the new date."

"All rise," the bailiff said as the judge stood and walked through the door behind the bench into his private chambers.

Tabitha stood, gaping at the empty seat where the judge had been just moments earlier. A bailiff walked over to escort her back into the jury box, and her anger bubbled over onto him. "What just happened? I'm supposed to have a bond hearing today!"

"You heard what happened," he said, leading her away. "Your lawyer was a no-show. Don't worry. You'll be back."

A jailer led all twenty inmates through a side door. The rest of the courtroom started to empty, and soon, only Stella, Lou, and Tabitha's family remained.

Stella took a deep breath, really hating her job sometimes. Over the sound of the oldest child's sniffles and the youngest child lightly singing a song to himself, she said, "Excuse me, Mrs. Lambern? I wonder if I could ask you a few questions."

Tabitha's mother looked up at her in surprise and then slowly nodded.

Stella took the microphone out of her bag and waited for Lou to take the camera off the tripod. When he was ready, she said, "How are you getting along?"

The woman laughed sharply, without humor. "Well, it's been a terrible few weeks. I'm losing one daughter to the criminal justice system, and then I had to bury a son, all while I'm trying to keep three kids alive. It's just... it's been a terrible few weeks," she repeated.

Stella grimaced and nodded sympathetically. "Police haven't made much progress on your son's murder. Is there anything you want to say to anyone watching who might have information?" Stella was thinking specifically of Valerie, an eyewitness to the crime who hadn't yet stepped forward.

"I guess I just want to say we need your help," the woman shifted her gaze from Stella to Tabitha's kids sitting next to her. She shook her head sadly before continuing, "These kids need their mom, and I need some closure. We just need some—" She broke off and looked at the camera as if it was a person. "Wait, can I tell people that we really do need their help? My husband and I are on a fixed income and now we have three growing kids in the house."

Stella nodded thoughtfully. "Absolutely. We can make that part of the story today, if you want."

The older woman nodded and squared her shoulders. "We need help," she said, staring straight at the camera. "We need your prayers, but we also need your generosity."

After a few more questions, the interview was over. Stella thanked the woman for her time, and she and Lou headed into the lobby.

A storm had popped up while they were inside the courtroom, and rain pelted the many windows they now faced, pouring down from the gray, cloudy sky. Stella's phone buzzed with a new text from the assignment desk warning her about the severe weather. The note read: *Call in ASAP. Court story is dead. Harry is moving you to weather.*

W3 had gone into full-effect while Stella and Lou were in the courtroom. He covered up his camera with the rain gear he'd stashed in his backpack and then took off, running through the parking lot for the live truck. Stella detoured to the bathroom on the first floor.

Just as she was finishing up in the stall, the main door opened and someone walked in, talking on their cell phone.

"The case is moving forward, but I'm doing everything I can to stall it."

Stella's ears perked up. The woman's tone was rushed and stressed—peculiar enough that she decided to stay hidden in the stall. She peered through the crack between the door hinges, but all she could make out were flashes of a gold top, black pants, and dark hair. Stella couldn't see the woman's face at all.

"Well, of course the judge will just reschedule it, but it's clearly a conflict of interest. I can't imagine anyone would ever find out, but if they did..."

Stella froze—there was something familiar about the woman's voice. She shifted again, trying to get a glimpse of the speaker without announcing her own presence. She squinted through the cracks again, this time making out a tattoo on the woman's upper left back. It was in shades of black and gray—something with wings.

"No, like I said, I think it's the only way. We'll talk later."

Stella's mind raced as the woman turned on the bathroom faucet. Someone was talking about a conflict of interest in a case that they weren't planning on disclosing—the very definition of news.

No longer worried about being seen, Stella took a breath and pushed against the stall door. It didn't budge; the lock was sticky. She pushed again, finally heaving the door open, but it was too late. By the time she got out of the stall, she was alone in the bathroom.

Stella hustled out into the hallway, grabbing a squirt of hand sanitizer from a dispenser on the wall as she went. Through the crowd of people heading in and out of the building, however, she couldn't find anyone who matched the woman from the bathroom.

She looked at her watch, knowing Lou was waiting for her, and then jumped when someone tapped her on the shoulder.

"Stella?" She turned in surprise and found Edie Hawthorne standing behind her. She had a slight smile on her face as she looked Stella over. "Look at you! No flannel pajamas today, eh?" She nodded approvingly at Stella's black business suit. "Nice accessories, too."

"Where did you come from?" Stella asked, taking in Edie's gold top and black pants. Had she been the woman in the bathroom? What kind of conflict of interest could she have been talking about?

The gold looked more sparkly than she remembered, but she'd only seen the back of the shirt. Edie had a raincoat over her arm, and she started to shrug into it while Stella watched. Realizing this was her only chance to see if Edie had a tattoo on her back, she leaped forward to help Edie put the coat on. A small struggle broke out between the women with Edie turning sharply to one side, finally shoving her arms into the coat, and fiercely tying the belt together in one swift motion.

"Thank you, Stella, but I've got it."

Flustered, Stella straightened her own jacket and forced a smile on her face. "It's really coming down out there, huh?" She looked suspiciously at the other woman, realizing it was possible that Edie had been talking to someone about the case between her and Parker. Was she getting unfair help from a judge to keep his case against her from moving forward? "Are you here visiting a, uh... friend?" Stella asked, trying to keep her voice light.

Edie's face reddened. "Oh..." she looked down at her nails and then cleared her throat. "Yeah, something like that."

"Oh. Well, good luck," Stella said faintly. They parted ways, and she tried to make sense of their encounter as she headed out of the courthouse toward the live truck.

Her cellphone rang, interrupting her thoughts. "Hello?" she answered, climbing into the news van. She spotted her galoshes sitting between the two front seats and smiled. She now put them in the news car every time she went anywhere, so she wouldn't be caught unprepared again.

"W3 is on. We'll need you live as soon as you're ready! Harry was thinking you could go to that low spot along the Olentangy," Joy said breathlessly into the phone, referring to the news director's goal of wall-to-wall live weather coverage. "They interrupted the *Ellen* Show. Viewers aren't too happy, to tell you the truth."

"Live by the river?" she said, looking at Lou. "We'll start heading that way."

Lou rolled his eyes—the river might have been the station's go-to place for a weather live shot, because it flooded practically before the first drops even fell from the sky, but Lou seemed to think it was a boring one. Nevertheless, the engine roared to life and he pulled out of the parking lot.

Stella looked up at the black sky and tried to redirect her brain to the task at hand. Edie, Tabitha, and the murders would have to wait.

18

———

Lou stepped on the gas and the van skidded a bit as they rounded the curve of the cloverleaf on-ramp. Another fifty feet and he pumped the breaks.

"Crap," he muttered. With the driving rain and black skies, it was impossible to see how far the backup on the interstate might last. "We'll never make it," he growled, switching lanes for the third time in an attempt to find one that was actually moving.

Stella chewed on her lip and stared thoughtfully at the road ahead. At this rate, it would take them an hour or longer to get to the low-lying spot along the Olentangy River where they could usually get good visuals of flooding, and they needed to get their live shot up and ready to go much sooner than that.

"Take this exit," she said, pointing to the side of the road. Her cell phone rang—the station was ready for her live phone interview on the storm. "Get off here at King and take Fifth all the way to—"

"The murder neighborhood?" Lou interrupted with a questioning look.

"A neighbor told me it always floods when it rains. Let's see if she was exaggerating," Stella said grimly before answering her cell phone.

"Stella, we're ready for your phoner," Beatrice said crisply.

"How much time should I fill?"

"I've got you down for a minute-thirty, but if you go long, it's okay—Vera and Mark could use the break." Stella looked at the clock and realized they'd likely already been live in wall-to-wall weather coverage for half an hour while Stella and Lou had been in the courtroom. "Standby, Stella. I'll connect you now."

She gripped the handle above her door to steady herself as they went around a corner, and she heard the anchors finishing a segment with the main meteorologist through her cellphone.

Mark: Bob James, we'll come back to you in just a few moments with more on the storm that's sprouting tornado warnings to the south and east of our coverage area. We turn now to Stella Reynolds, on the phone for us. Stella, where are you and what are you seeing?

Stella: Mark, we just got off 315 north-bound, where traffic was at a standstill, and are now winding our way east through the city, looking for any flooding that might be causing problems. We have some serious rainfall coming down almost faster than our windshield wipers can handle. The skies are very dark to our south and east, wind gusts are strong, in fact—

Stella paused; her ears perked up at a pinging sound through the windshield. They were stopped at a red light and Stella lowered her window to be sure.

I want you to take a listen to this.

She held the phone up to the windshield for a few seconds and then brought it back to her mouth.

Yes, that is pea-sized hail you're hearing, pounding against our windshield as we approach Cleveland Avenue. It's not big enough to do any damage, yet, but we'll certainly keep an eye on the storm and bring you the latest update soon. For now, reporting live, I'm Stella Reynolds. Back to you.

She stayed on the line until Beatrice said, "You're clear, Stella, thanks. Bob says you're in the only pocket of hail in the area. Stick with it for now and see where it takes you."

Stella groaned after she disconnected the call and relayed the information. That was the problem with W3: you never knew when it would end.

She and Lou talked only when necessary. The noise of the hail against the metal roof of the van would have made conversation difficult, but the added strain of driving in the rapidly deteriorating conditions had them both silent as the photographer navigated the slick streets.

Much of the traffic was gone, but it was still slow getting across town. Lou finally turned the van onto Journey Street and said, "Thank God, it's flooded." Stella stared at him silently, and he said, "Oh, you know what I mean. Not thank God it's flooded, but thank God we can get the live shot up."

Stella grinned. "I knew what you meant. It's just... anyway, let's go."

They both zipped up their jackets, tightened the drawstrings on their hoods, and then opened their doors in sync.

"Ow," Stella said, as the first tiny pellets of hail stung the exposed skin on the backs of her hands.

Mounds of hail formed on the high spots of ground around them and the low spots were flooded from the earlier downpour. It was a surreal visual, and Stella understood her photographer's excitement when they'd pulled up—it would make for a great live shot. While Lou worked on raising the mast from the middle of the live truck,

Stella got her IFB plugged into the box that would connect her to the anchors and producer back at the studio.

"Dialed in!" Lou shouted over the noisy storm. Stella kept her head down, so the stinging hail wouldn't get her face, and she grabbed the tripod from the back of the van while Lou ran cable to the front of the van.

"Gah, it's so wet," he said, wiping his hands on his pants and trying to connect the cable to the camera for a second time. Stella found an umbrella in the passenger side door of the van and opened it over him, so he could work without getting pinged by the hail. "Okay, great. Thanks, Stella."

Lou took his cell phone out of an inner pocket of his jacket and called the station. "We're ready—okay, yup, I'll tell her," he said, and then he turned to Stella. "They're with Bob right now, but as soon as he's done, the anchors will toss it to you."

Stella nodded, pulling her hood further up over her head. The hail was relentless, and her hands and face burned.

She could barely hear Beatrice through her earpiece. "Standby, Stella. Coming to you next."

The audio switched over to live programming, and she heard Mark and Vera wrapping up another segment with Bob.

> **Vera:** Bob, we'll check back with you in just a moment, but first we want to go to Stella Reynolds, live in—okay, Stella, I'm hearing that you're east of the city. Stella, what are you seeing out there?

A sudden gust of wind blew the umbrella out of her hand, and she sucked in a shocked breath as it flew behind her with the speed of the storm. By the time she turned around, it was already a block away.

> **Stella:** Oh!

When she turned back to the camera, tiny hail pellets hit her square in the face. She took a steadying breath and tried to adjust her hood with her free hand.

Well, the hail is...

It was no good; she was looking directly into the wind, which was blowing hail painfully into her face. She tried adjusting her hood again, keeping her other hand steady as it held the microphone. Both hands stung and her eyes watered, but she did her best to describe the damage to buildings and cars that was happening right in front of her eyes. After ninety seconds, Beatrice came into her earpiece.

"Wrap and toss directly to Bob, Stella," she said in an oddly strangled voice. Was she laughing? Stella obviously couldn't ask, so she did what she'd been told to do.

> So again, we advise staying inside, if you can, in a safe place away from windows, just in case the hail gets even worse. Let's go straight to Bob James, now, with the latest on weather conditions across the viewing area. Bob?

"Clear."

Stella and Lou raced back into the safety of the live truck and locked eyes. They were both smiling from the adrenaline rush of making the live shot.

She was ready to high-five her partner when she noticed that his eyes weren't just full of excitement, but also full of mischief.

"What?" she asked over the pounding hail and call of the wind from outside.

"You are a trip, Stella," he said, barely containing his grin.

"Did I look funny out there?" She tried to keep her tone light, but the words stung almost as much as the hail. After all, she'd just braved a hail storm on live TV—couldn't Lou cut her some slack?

"Oh," he looked at her with surprise and then forced a neutral expression onto his face, "I thought you made a joke on purpose. You know, when you said it was a 'hail of a storm,' I almost burst out laughing."

"I did?" Stella's brow wrinkled. She hadn't meant to say that; it must have come out while she was shielding her face from the barrage of pellets. "Did anyone laugh?"

"I couldn't hear..." he trailed off, his brow furrowed. He then said, "What is this?"

Stella followed his gaze out the windshield. A caravan was turning onto their street, headed directly for them. The first in line was a white pickup truck with a full camper bed attached to the back. It had "Storm Spotters" painted on one side and a satellite dish attached to the top of the cab. There were two cars behind it, and all three vehicles stopped and people climbed out like ants at a picnic. Many were identically dressed in matching jumpsuits, but a camera crew came out of the last car; when she craned her neck, she saw that it looked like an out-of-state news car. After reaching over and turning the wipers on high, she leaned forward and squinted.

"No!" she gasped, sitting back abruptly. "Is that..."

"That is one motley-looking crew," Lou said, filling the silence as they watched the men in jumpsuits scurry around, setting up equipment against the driving hail. "What are they doing out there, anyway?"

Stella ran a nervous hand through her hair and straightened her shirt when she noticed half the news crew was headed their way. She resisted the urge to check her reflection in the mirror—it wouldn't be good after standing in the hail for ten minutes, and there wasn't time to fix anything, anyway.

The man walked to her window, his gait sure

and steady, despite the weather. As he got closer, he pushed his hood back slightly and smiled. Her heart fluttered unexpectedly and she toggled the switch to lower the glass.

"Hey, stranger," he said with a smile.

"John, what are you doing here?"

19

John Stevenson might as well have been starring in an action movie. A streak of lightning flashed behind him and he glowed slightly as he leaned in through the window. Drops of rain and glittery hail dripped off his hood onto the windowsill, and he brushed his lips against her cheek in greeting. His dark brown hair was damp from the storm, and his blue eyes sparkled with warmth, despite the chill in the air.

"I can't believe it's you!" he said, smiling down at her.

She grinned back, and they stared happily at each other. The silence stretched, punctuated by hail pinging off the dash of the van and the street.

Finally, Lou cleared his throat. "Hey, man. Can you lower the mast? We don't want to be killed by lightning at a time like this."

Stella jumped at the noise, but John reached to the side, opened the door directly behind Stella, and with a quick glance at the control panel mounted just inside the door, pressed down on the lever to lower the giant, steel antenna. His eyes hardly left Stella's.

Finally, when Lou cleared his throat again, she pulled her eyes away from John's and said, "Lou, this is John Stevenson. He's one of the main anchors in Knoxville, Tennessee. We used to work together—"

"Everywhere?" John interjected.

Stella laughed. "Feels that way, doesn't it?" They locked eyes again for a moment, and she felt the familiar pull behind her belly button whenever John was near. She forced herself to break the contact. "So, why are you here?"

"We're shooting a sweeps piece that'll run in May on these tornado chasers from Knoxville," he said, motioning to the crews behind him. "They drive for days following storm systems. It's…"

"Interesting?" Lou offered, scratching his head as a guy from the crew held his weather radio in the air.

"Exhausting, I was going to say," John chuckled. "We've been following this storm since about five this morning, and they don't show any signs of slowing down."

"When other people take shelter, the storm chasers take action," Stella intoned in her best promotional-sounding voice-over.

"That's it exactly," John said with another chuckle. "So, how are things?"

"Good. Things are good. How's Katie?"

"She's fine. I mean, I hear she's fine." He looked away at the mention of his ex-girlfriend, before asking, "And Lucky?"

"He's, uh, good. You know, long-distance can be challenging, but—"

Another flash of lightning and crash of thunder—closer this time—made all three jump.

"Dang that was close," Lou said. "I'll call it in and tell them we're out until the lightning calms down." He tapped the numbers into his phone and turned away.

John reached into the van, put his hand on

Stella's, and gave it a gentle squeeze. "You look great."

She laughed. Bedraggled and nearly drowned were the words that came to *her* mind, but when she looked up at John to tell him that, she stopped, her breath caught in her throat. John looked... dreamy. Mist from the storm surrounded him, making his blue eyes stand out even more than usual. He sparkled where the storm had touched him.

She finally said, simply, "So do you."

The sound of engines firing up broke the spell. "Looks like your ride is leaving," she said to John. "It was so nice to see you," she added with feeling. John was so uncomplicated, and of course, he understood her job and her business so well. They would never fight about a story or a work schedule.

He leaned toward her and brushed his lips against her cheek again. She closed her eyes for a moment and wondered what would have happened if she'd never left Knoxville.

"Bye, Stella," he said. Was it her imagination, or was there a wistful tone to his voice?

She watched him walk away. "John!" she called, jumping out of the truck into the hail. He turned back. "Be careful!" she shouted over the pounding noise. He raised a hand and waved before climbing into his news car. Stella watched him drive away.

"You know what really sucks?" Lou said. He set his phone into the cup holder between them, letting Stella watch the convoy drive away before speaking again. "When old flames look so good you can't remember why they're old flames." He gave her a knowing look, and Stella didn't even try to disagree.

AN HOUR LATER, they were back in the live truck with two more live shots under their belts. The lightning had passed, the hail was over, and even the rain was lessening to a regular storm versus the previous deluge. As they sat silently, save for the drips of water running off their slickers and dropping on the all-weather mats in the van, the two-way radio on the dash came to life.

"Harry is ending W3. Shoot enough for a wrap-up package for the ninety."

It was just after three and they had plenty of time to shoot their story before the evening news deadlines. She fished for a granola bar from the bottom of her bag while Lou took an apple out of his lunchbox. "Nothing like a five minute lunch break," he said.

Stella chuckled through her first bite. Three minutes later, she said, "Okay. Back to work."

Lou grinned. "Why does it feel unreasonable for us to ask for a lunch break? Shouldn't it be unreasonable for them to ask us *not* to take one?"

"What is reason to a news director?" Stella asked, climbing out of the van. Her foot splashed into a river running down the street that covered her entire foot. The puddles they'd seen when they had first gotten to the neighborhood had expanded to ponds in the front yards on either side, and storm sewers, so overwhelmed with the rain, had stopped draining long ago.

"You came!" someone called over the driving rain. Stella's head swung toward the voice. Jill DeMario, the woman who'd spent the better part of twenty minutes yelling at Stella the last time they'd met, was headed her way with her daughter, Cara, huddled under an umbrella. She had a friendly—or maybe victorious—smile on her face. "I told you about this here drainage problem, but I never thought you'd come to see it for yourself.

What do you think?" she asked, coming to a stop on the sidewalk. "Bad as I told you, ain't it?" Before Stella could answer, she added, "I can't tell you how many times I called the city to complain. It's like nobody cares about us out here in this part of the city. Nobody!"

"Well, I care—I'm here. We'll show everyone what this street is like in a rainstorm."

"It ain't just the street!" Jill said indignantly. "Come see my basement! It floods every time it rains. Okay, not every time, but if it rains more than ten minutes, I can count on it flooding. The first time, it ruined all kind of stuff. Now we just know we can't keep anything down there."

"Have you, I don't know, called a plumber out? Maybe it's not the city's—a" Stella gulped. The look on Jill's face was textbook outrage.

"Not the city's fault? Like the water building up out here on the street has nothing whatsoever to do with my basement flooding?" She glared accusingly at Stella, who held her hands up in defeat.

"Okay, okay, sorry. Let's go—show me." She turned to make sure Lou was ready, and he hefted the camera onto his shoulder and nodded. Stella clipped the wireless microphone onto Jill and said,

"Lead the way. We're recording, so just tell us what's going on in your house."

Cara went first, her mother followed, and Stella walked behind Lou, so she would stay out of the shot. They sloshed their way to the house, finally hitting dry land on the fourth step of Jill's front porch. Cara opened the door and stepped aside, allowing her mother to take the lead.

"Follow me." Jill marched down the main hallway, past the family room, and into the kitchen. "Pardon the mess," she said as she opened the door and headed down the basement steps. The counters were neat and tidy, but spots in the middle were faded, showing signs of constant use. In the ten seconds it took Stella to walk through the room, Cara opened a cabinet door and pulled out a snack from the packed shelves within.

"As you can see," Jill said, "well actually, you can't—we lost power ten minutes after it started raining. It always shorts out, I think because of the water."

Lou flipped a switch and the light on the top of his camera illuminated the basement. Stella peered around him and saw nothing but water.

"It's hard to tell from here, Jill, how many stairs are underwater."

"The bottom three. You can see on this fourth step where the water came up to last time." She looked earnestly at Stella, "Like I said, we don't keep anything down here, anymore, so I'm not out property, but it's hard to dry the space out. I worry the mold is gonna make this place bad to live in and impossible to sell. That's not good for me, and it's not good for my daughter."

Stella asked a few more questions and then went back up to the kitchen to make room for Jill to show Lou around the flooded area.

Cara sidled up to Stella. "I been wanting to talk to you. You seem like you might be able to help my friend's mom."

"Who's your friend's mom?"

"Tabitha. You know she didn't shoot Bobby."

"I don't know anything," Stella said gently. "I only know police are still investigating the case."

"Well, *I* know she didn't kill Bobby, because I saw her doing something else at the exact same time Bobby was shot."

Stella turned toward the little girl. "What do you mean?"

Cara motioned out the back window with her chin. "Shawna and I were playing cards when it happened. She had her back to the window and I was sitting right there." She pointed to the seat closest to the basement door that looked out over the backyard. "Shawna was dealing us a new hand, so she didn't see it."

"Didn't see what?" Stella asked.

"Didn't see her mom sneak across the backyard to the next street over to meet with her dealer."

Stella's eyes widened at the information. "You saw Tabitha buying drugs? Did anyone else see it? Can anyone else confirm that?"

"You think I'm gonna tell Shawna something like that about her own mother? She doesn't need to know that." She gave Stella that same disappointed look she'd given her the day of the first murder, when Stella had asked if the girl had spoken to police.

"That's interesting, Cara, but I'm not sure what I can do with that. The word of a ten-year-old is not likely to hold much weight against adult eyewitnesses police have already spoken to. Plus, why wouldn't Tabitha have given police her alibi, if that was the case?"

"It doesn't have to be just my word," Cara said, staring meaningfully out the window. Stella's gaze followed hers. "Flooding looks just as bad over

there as it does over here," she added enig-
matically.

Stella stared out the window, but didn't really
know what she was looking for. Cara sat down at
the table, looking at her cell phone, and Stella
continued staring out the window through the
backyard to the street beyond. "All I can see is the
bus stop."

"Exactly."

Stella's eyes widened. The bus stop! Devi had
told her weeks ago that police had installed a security camera after a riot at the bus stop around the
corner years ago. She turned to look at Cara with
new eyes. This girl wasn't just your average ten-
year-old; she was more like an investigative reporter in training, although she figured Cara
wouldn't want to hear that.

"Thank you," she said to the top of Cara's head,
as the girl was back to ignoring Stella while she
texted. She called past the child, "Lou! We need to
get moving!"

It was three-thirty; if everything went right—
green lights, no traffic, and helpful employees at
the transit authority—they'd have time to get the
video and still make it back for their first live shot
at five o'clock.

20

"All I'm saying is I don't know why we had to leave in the first place!" Lou said, pulling cable from the huge spool in the back of the van. "What a waste of time," he muttered.

It was four-fifty, ten minutes until their live shot, and the producer back at the station was already calling for mic checks.

"Give me a minute!" Lou said in a clipped tone into his cell phone before tossing it into the van. "They think checking on me every two minutes is going to speed the process up?" he asked as he leveled the tripod and slammed the camera into place.

Stella watched him connect cords, and then she hastily pulled out her notebook. Everything had *not* gone their way at the transit authority's security center. The receptionist hadn't been there and no one was authorized to speak to the media, anyway. A high-level office clerk did know there was a process—though she nor anyone else knew what it was—that media outlets had to go through to request video from security cameras.

All told, they'd wasted an hour while Stella tried contacting anyone and everyone at the city for permission to look at the security footage from the bus stop camera. They ended up with nothing, except a frustrated photographer and no time to get ready for their five o'clock live shot back on Journey Street.

Stella's IFB crackled to life. "Where have you been?" Beatrice asked crossly. Stella knew she was juggling a dozen things back in the control room at the station.

"Following a lead that didn't pan out. Lou will send our package over as soon as he's tuned in."

"It'll be tight."

Stella didn't answer; she'd caught sight of Jill DeMario standing on her porch. "Still flooded down there?" she called.

Jill nodded. "Worse than last time—it's not going down."

Stella chewed on her lip and then waved frantically at the camera to get Beatrice's attention back at the station.

"What's up, Stella?" Beatrice asked through the earpiece.

"Can we scrap the package? I can do a live walk and talk. I've got the woman from my story—she can walk us through her house, show us her flooding, and talk to us about the problem?"

There was a pause while Beatrice considered Stella's offer. "Yes, let's do it. You've got five minutes to prep. You're live off the top."

Lou ran around the van to pull more cable. "You'll have to guide me."

Stella ran to Jill to explain the plan. Sooner than anyone was ready, the live shot was underway.

Stella: Residents along Journey Street tell me every time it rains, the storm sewers back up, not only turning the streets and gutters into rivers, but also wreaking havoc inside their homes.

Stella turned and beckoned to Jill.

Joining me live now is one resident who's fed up with all these water woes. Jill De-Mario says her basement has flooded no less than five times already this spring. Jill, when did the flooding first become an issue?

Jill: We moved in about five years ago, and the very first rain after, our basement flooded.

Stella: You're not talking about a little bit of water in the corner, either.

Jill: No, ma'am; I'm talking about two to three feet of water. I saw a bin of baby clothes float by the first time it happened—literally floated right on past the steps, like it was a durn paddle boat on the river.

Stella: Let's take a look at the situation, Jill.

She led the way into Jill's house and then held the door open as Jill and Lou followed her in. Lou flicked on the camera's light as soon as they stepped into the dark house—still no power—and Stella prompted Jill forward.

Stella: Jill, let's see how your basement looks two hours after the rain stopped falling. Careful on the steps there...

Lou wobbled as he stumbled over a pair of slippers and Stella grabbed his elbow to steady him as they continued forward into the house. Once again, Stella quickly peeked over his shoulder at what lay beyond the basement door.

Stella: I understand that, after the first flood, you realized you'd have to keep the basement totally empty, Jill?

Jill: That's right, I did. The problem now is that, every time it floods, it trips our fuse box, so I gotta get the power company in here to fix things. Not only does it cost me the time to get this place drained and dried out, but it's also a two-hundred dollar bill from the electrician to fix the power in my house. It ain't right. It just ain't right.

Stella saw that Lou was stuck. From his spot halfway down the steps, it would be extremely dangerous to try to pivot and walk back up the stairs blind, his face buried behind the viewfinder with long cords trailing, waiting to trip him. They hadn't had time to work out the logistics, so Stella had to figure it out live.

Stella: I'm going to have Lou, our photographer tonight, carefully stay there on the steps. We've got phone calls into the city and hope to have their response to this flooding fiasco when we see you again at six o'clock. How long will residents have to deal with faulty storm sewers and flooding? The answer in less than an hour. Reporting live, I'm Stella Reynolds. Back to you.

Twenty minutes later, Stella rolled her neck around and stretched out her back by the live truck. She was finally catching her breath for the first time since the storm had broken out.

She shook her head, amazed at how many times she'd been in this neighborhood over the last few weeks. As she faced the houses on the south side of the street, she saw from left to right

Valerie's house was on the corner, Tabitha's home was where the murders had happened, and next to that was Jill and Cara's now-flooded house.

In the waning sunlight, she noticed for the first time the side window to Valerie's house—the side that faced Tabitha's home—was a mottled, bubbled glass. Was it glazed? She took a few steps closer to get a better look; it wasn't quite as opaque as a glass-block window, but it wasn't far off. She found it hard to believe you could see clearly out that window. You might have been able to make out general shapes and colors, but you certainly couldn't definitively ID a shooter.

Did police know that their star eyewitness in the Bobby Herbert homicide had been looking through a funhouse window when the murder happened? She picked up her phone to call Sergeant Coyne to ask that very question, when it rang in her hand, instead. She didn't recognize the number.

"This is Donald Monroe from COTA. I have a message here to call you," came the gruff voice on the other end of the line.

Stella punched the air in celebration. She needed to see the security video from the bus stop, and someone from the Columbus Ohio Transit

Authority was finally on the line. She quickly explained what she was interested in, worried that any questions would lead to a much longer phone conversation than she wanted. Luck was finally on her side.

"Listen, Stella, I'm trying to get out of the office tonight for my granddaughter's birthday party, so Alissa Collier in the security office is expecting you," he said hurriedly. "I told her to help with anything you need. Anything else?"

"Thanks, that's it," she said with a smile. It was time to see if Cara's story would hold up.

21

Instead of heading home after her six o'clock live shot, Stella drove straight to the COTA security office.

The building not only housed the security center for the transit authority, but also had a bus maintenance shop and employee lounge. It was bustling with activity, even at seven o'clock at night.

"What exactly are you looking for?" Alissa Collier asked with a pen poised over her notebook and a confused look on her face.

"I'd like video from today from the bus stop off Passage Avenue, but I'm also interested in video from the same location from three weeks ago. I want to... uh, compare water levels from two different storms," Stella said, hoping her request wouldn't raise any suspicions, since it had also rained on the day of Bobby's murder.

"The system is set up to keep video for thirty days. After that, if it hasn't been requested by anyone, it gets recorded over. Sometimes the cameras are disabled, though—sometimes they're vandalized, especially out at those satellite locations—so I can't make any promises. We just won't know until we check. Do you want to come back and look with me?"

"Sure," Stella said, her fingers crossed.

Alissa led her back into a dimly-lit utilitarian space. The brown carpeting had a path worn down the middle, which they followed to a bank of security camera monitors and a tall stack of computer towers. "Everything is recorded digitally." She sat down in front of one computer monitor and punched in some keys. "I'll call up the camera on Passage Avenue," she said, and Stella heard the click-clack of keys as she started the search. "Let's see what we've got."

It took a few minutes for Alissa to locate the right camera, and when she finally got it set up on a playback monitor, the speakers overhead came to life.

"Alissa Collier to the maintenance office, please."

She blew out a sigh. "People keep vandalizing the buses and I have to sign the report," she said apologetically.

"Do you mind if I keep going without you?" Stella asked. "It's getting late," she added, looking at her watch.

"Sure, Stella, no problem. If you find the clip you need, just write down the time stamp. When I get back, I can email it to you, okay?"

Stella nodded and watched Alissa leave the office. She then smiled in the empty room. That couldn't have gone any better; she was alone to look through any footage she wanted.

She sat in Alissa's seat and saw the view from the security camera on Passage Avenue. It must have been situated on top of the pole of a streetlight, because the angle was a wide, bird's eye view of the bus stop and surrounding area. The bus stop consisted of a lonely bench cemented into the sidewalk, but the shot from the security camera also included the sidewalk and grass of the neighboring yard.

212 | LIBBY KIRSCH

Stella fussed around with the computer keyboard, finally figuring out how to rewind the footage. She went all the way back to just before the time of Bobby's murder and played the video back in real time.

She watched it once and then rewound the video a second time.

Stella was so shocked that she didn't say anything for a few minutes. She watched what appeared to be Tabitha walk up to the bus stop and sit and talk with a person for several minutes before making some kind of exchange. Based on Cara's narrative, it was likely drugs for money.

Even better for Tabitha, both the woman and man in the video jerked visibly and ducked down at the same time, almost as if they'd heard a gunshot. Looking at the timestamp at the bottom of the video, that was likely exactly what had happened.

True, the video wasn't crystal-clear, but it certainly corroborated Cara's story that Tabitha hadn't been home at the time of the shooting and couldn't have pulled the trigger.

When Alissa walked back into the room, Stella couldn't contain her excitement.

"I found it! Can I get a copy of this right here?"

she asked, forgetting all pretenses about the flooding story.

"You're the second person interested in this clip in the last two weeks," Alissa said, eyeing the screen innocently.

"I am?" Stella asked, the news pulling her up short. "Was the other person older, with black hair? Kind of... elegant?"

"Yes, that's exactly how I'd describe her. Elegant, just like you," Alissa said.

Stella looked down at her water-stained suit and multiple frazzled wisps of hair escaping the braid she'd twisted her hair into earlier that day and thought Alissa was being awfully kind.

"Did you send her a copy, too?"

"No, she just saw it and said she might be back for it later."

"Hmm," Stella said, staring moodily at the screen. She wanted to put this video out there as soon as possible, but not at the risk of ruining Tabitha's case. She'd have to call the woman's lawyer first thing in the morning.

"Are you doing a story on drug dealers working at the bus stop? 'Cause we've got a lot of that video, honey," Alissa said, scratching her nose before she hit the appropriate keys on the keyboard to send a

214 | LIBBY KIRSCH

video copy to Stella's inbox. "Honestly, we've got a lot better video of that going down than this."

Stella's ears perked up at this information. Although she wasn't here for that, it certainly sounded like a great story for another day. "Is it a problem for the transit authority?"

"Of course it's a problem for us! Here we have thousands of covered benches all over the city, and dealers and their customers use them to stand out of the elements. Drug dealers *love* the transit authority."

"What can anyone do? It's not like you guys can patrol each and every bus stop."

Alissa shook her head, frustrated. "There's really nothing we can do, that's true. We talk with police and they increase patrols for a while at a trouble stop, but things go right back to normal a couple weeks later. Dealers know it and users know it, too." After a few more minutes, Stella asked, "How many different video clips do you have?"

"I can think of around twenty right off the bat that made people in this office stop and take a second look." Stella looked hastily at her watch again. It was late and she had a lot to do, yet, this evening. Alissa noticed and said, "I'll put some clips together and email them to you. Does that sound okay?"

"You won't get in trouble?" she asked doubtfully.

"The director told me to help you however I could," Alissa said with a sly smile.

"I'm guessing you use the bus?"

"Every day to get to work. I'm so tired of having to share the space with criminals. Something should be done!"

Stella nodded. "All right, you've got my attention."

It was almost eight o'clock when she got back into her car. Stella was drained, but she knew she had to make one last call.

"I need help talking to an inmate last-minute."

"Not even a, 'hello, how are you today?' Just right down to business?" Coyne said.

"Hello," Stella said, grinning into the darkness, "how are you today, Sergeant Coyne?"

"I can't get you into jail at the last minute," he said, ignoring her belated greeting. "That's run by the Sheriff's Office. Not only do I hold no weight over there, but they also have policies and procedures as long as the day is."

"You have *no* contacts over there?" Stella asked incredulously. "You don't know *anyone* at the jail?"

Coyne blew out a sigh. "Let me make some calls, but I'm telling you, they're not just going to do it because I asked. It takes man-hours and re-sources to set up interviews at the jail."

After they disconnected, Stella parked by her apartment and sat in the quiet car, drumming her fingertips against the steering wheel. She was tempted to go straight to Coyne's office, play him the video, and set Tabitha free, but she wanted to talk to Tabitha first. She needed to find out why she and Eleanor hadn't told investigators the truth, yet—the truth that Tabitha was innocent and she didn't kill her ex-husband.

Stella opened her car door and walked through the dark parking lot to her apartment. If Tabitha didn't kill Bobby, who did?

22

"How was the press tour?" Stella asked as she wrapped the curly cord of the wall phone around her finger and leaned against the counter. Lucky had tracked her down in the makeup room, likely by sweet-talking the station operator at the front desk.

"Fine. It was fine," Lucky said. His slight twang and raspy voice sent chills down her spine, despite the heat coming from the bulb lights surrounding the mirrors.

"The night race is only a couple of weeks away," she said, thinking back to her year in Bristol, Tennessee, and going to the NASCAR track there. The race was held under huge stadium lights, which only added to the drama of the event. "Is your team ready?"

"We're ready. You should come to the race. I want you to come," he said suddenly. His voice was friendly, but Stella sensed an underlying edge—a simmering challenge—to his invitation.

"Come to the race in Bristol?" she repeated, stalling.

It was becoming a sore spot between them, and Stella didn't want to rehash it just then. She had exactly ten days of vacation each year, and because Lucky had never had a "real" job before, he didn't appreciate Stella's restraint when she couldn't fly away for a long weekend every time he suggested it.

"Fly in first thing Saturday and you can be back home Sunday night. You won't miss a single day of work," he said, once again trying and failing to sound casual.

"Umm..." Lucky never remembered that she worked weekends. The trip would take two vacation days. She tried to imagine what a ticket would cost only two weeks out.

"My treat," Lucky said, guessing correctly.

"No," she laughed, "I can buy my own ticket. It's a great idea, Lucky," she added. "Of course I'll be there." Parker walked into the room, ready to get to work on Vera for the early shows. "I actually need to get back to the studio," she said, smiling at Parker. "I'll call you on my dinner break, okay?"

She disconnected the call and turned to her friend accusingly. "I've been trying to get in touch with you since yesterday."

"Why's that?" he asked, pursing his lips and eyeing Stella's outfit. "Was it to ask if you should wear that today? I would have said an emphatic NO."

Stella looked down at her light gray suit and bit back a retort. "No."

"The suit is fine, it's that shirt you have on underneath, I mean—"

"Parker, I saw Edie at the courthouse yesterday." He finally took his eyes off Stella's outfit, and she filled him in on her suspicions.

He frowned. "I don't like the sound of that."

"I don't know for sure, but it's possible that she has a contact at the courthouse."

"How can we find out?"

"I don't know," she admitted. "I don't know what the plan is on that front."

He forced a smile onto his face. "I'll tell you the plan," he said, glancing at the clock on the wall. "I have fifteen minutes until Vera gets here. Let's tame that mane of gorgeous, auburn hair and maybe no one will notice your terrible shirt."

Stella snorted. "Thanks, I guess."

AFTER THE SHOW, Stella sat at her desk, holding her cell phone in her hand. She knew she owed Lucky a call, but she tapped in a different set of numbers, instead. On the third ring, Paul Blackwell answered.

"Go," he barked, sounding impatient already. After Stella explained why she was calling, Bobby's old boss warmed considerably. "Oh, Stella. I had a hunch I'd hear from you again."

She made a face at his sugary voice. "Really?"

"I felt a... connection. I thought you might have felt it, too."

She rubbed the spot between her eyes and tried to keep her voice friendly. "It turns out Bobby didn't have a lot of family, and I was hoping you'd reconsider going on camera to talk about him to really let us know what kind of guy he was, you know?"

"Hmm," he murmured, as if Stella's pretense

for calling was so thin that he could see right through it. "Let's do that. Meet me at the office. I'm free right now, as a matter of fact."

"Let me see if I can get a photographer—"

"Oh—it won't be just the two of us?"

"Well, I'm a *TV* reporter, you know? I kind of need to capture our interview on TV."

"Harrumph. Well, I guess that makes sense." They set up the details and Stella told Harry what she was planning.

"Will you turn the package tonight?"

"Yes. It'll be ready for the eleven o'clock news."

Twenty minutes later, she was in a news van with Devi.

"So, what's the plan?" he asked.

"I guess some kind of memorial piece on one of the recent homicide victims."

"You guess, or it is?" Devi navigated the streets of downtown Columbus with ease.

"I guess," she said, wrinkling her brow. "There's something off about the homicides; I just want to dig around Bobby Herbert's old office. Fair warning--there's something weird about his boss."

They drove in silence, Devi concentrating on the route, and Stella coming up with a list of questions for Bobby's boss.

When they pulled up to the office, Stella was surprised to see a full parking lot. She looked at the clock on the dash and noted that it was well after seven at night.

"Full house, huh?" Devi said.

Stella didn't say anything as she grabbed her bag and got out of the van. Inside the office, the same beautiful, blonde woman greeted them at the reception desk. "Mr. Blackwell asked that you set up for the interview over there," she said, pointing to the same grouping of chairs in which Stella had sat with Paul once before. "He'll be out in just a few minutes."

A few minutes turned into twenty, and there was still no sign of the boss. Stella looked at her watch and then walked over to the receptionist. "Any idea on timing? This whole thing will only take ten minutes, but if he doesn't come out soon, we'll be out of time."

"It should be any minute," the receptionist said with an apologetic shrug.

"Can you call and ask?" Stella asked insistently.

The receptionist looked uncomfortable, but was saved the trouble of coming up with an answer when the door behind her opened and Paul Blackwell walked out of his office.

"Stella!" he said, coming around the desk and embracing Stella's hand with both of his and trying to pull her in for a hug. She took a step backward, instead.

"Sorry," she said, reaching into her bag. "Let me just put this on silent while we talk." As she turned to lead him to the chairs in the corner, she saw one of the many blond employees slink out of his office, avoiding eye contact with anyone.

Stella locked eyes with Devi, whose expression let her know he'd also witnessed the strange situation. She tried to ignore his look of intrigue and carry on with her interview.

"If you can just take a seat right here, Devi will get you hooked up with the microphone." Stella shot him an apologetic look. She just couldn't deal with getting that close to Paul Blackwell; his very presence set off alarm bells on the inside. "It's so busy—everyone working late tonight, eh?"

"Well, you understand deadlines, I'm sure. We all have to work together to get the job done, especially now with Bobby gone," he said loudly enough that Stella got the impression he wasn't only speaking to her.

The microphone was on and Devi nodded.

"Paul, just a few questions about Bobby. First of all, what can you tell me about what kind of person he was?"

Paul leaned back in his chair and tucked his button-down shirt in so it looked neat. He then leaned forward and adjusted his suit jacket, buttoning the top two buttons, and finally he smoothed down his hair with one hand. "Okay, I'm ready."

Stella nodded encouragingly, but Paul seemed to be waiting for her first question. She blew out a silent breath and repeated it.

"What can I say? He seemed like a great guy. He'd only been with our company a few months, but I could tell he was a go-getter—someone you wanted in your corner. In fact, I had just given him a major promotion to lead my marketing team here."

"Did he get along with everyone?" Stella was thinking back to Rhonda's words from the other night. She knew there was someone here who wasn't happy about Bobby's promotion. The question was: did Paul know about it, too? She watched him closely, but he didn't appear to be hiding anything.

"We're just one big team, here, and we all root for each other. Bobby's success was, in a way, a win for the whole team."

"Jesus," Devi muttered, barely loud enough for Stella to hear. She had to agree, Paul was laying it on pretty thick.

"Who will be taking over for Bobby, now that he's gone?"

"We've got a crack team," Paul said, lowering his voice. "I'm still determining who'll take over as project manager. It seems vulgar to move on so quickly, but of course, I do have a business to run." He glanced back at his office before focusing on Stella again. "I'm still deciding who the best fit for the job is."

Devi cleared his throat, and Stella looked down at her notebook so Paul wouldn't see the look of revulsion on her face. Was this guy for real? *Trying out his employees* appeared to mean more than checking their marketing qualifications.

She asked a few more questions—enough for her story—and soon she was standing by the front door, shaking Paul's hand once again.

"It was great to see you again, Stella. I knew I would." He slowly pumped her hand up and down, and with some difficulty, she managed to extract her hand from his grip in a way she hoped was not overly obvious that she was trying to get away.

"The story will air tonight at eleven. Once again, we are so sorry for your loss." Stella turned and held the door for Devi, but was prevented from following him out when Paul grabbed her arm.

"You'd be great at marketing, Stella. I bet we'd pay you more than that TV station, too." He flicked a card into her hand. "Call me, Stella—anytime."

She smiled weakly and walked quickly out the door, happy to get away from him. He gave off a creep-vibe that was hard to ignore.

When she got to the van, Devi was talking into the microphone of the two-way radio. "Do you want her to call in?"

"No," came the tinny response, "just let her know the change."

He hung the small, black microphone back on its hook and said, "That was Joy. She said Dave just went home sick with food poisoning. Anyway, they want us to stay out here for a live shot, instead of going back to the studio for the eleven."

"Can they send us a bodyguard?" she asked,

looking uncertainly at the dark parking lot. There was something about Paul that made her not want to be alone in the dark anywhere near him.

"I've got your back if you've got mine," Devi said grimly. "That guy was awful. I pity any woman who works for him."

Stella nodded, realizing Rhonda was in that group. Had Paul been inappropriate with Rhonda? Was she upset that Bobby had gotten the promotion over her? Furthermore, where did Darren, the other homicide victim, come into play in all of this? The more she dug, the less she seemed to understand.

23

"Stand by, Stella," Devi said from behind the camera. She was standing in a halo of light with one spotlight pointed directly at her face and another behind her. "We're thirty seconds away from the show open."

Stella looked down at her notebook one last time and then pressed her earpiece into her ear a little more snugly as a pop of music started the newscast. She heard her own voice as her prerecorded tease played during the cold open of the newscast, followed by snippets of two other stories that would play later in the half-hour show.

"You're off the top, Stella. We're coming to you

in twenty seconds." That was the eleven o'clock producer, Chloe.

Mark: Good evening, everyone. I'm Mark Markus, and Vera has the night off. We begin tonight with a plea for justice from the very people who never thought they'd have to ask for it.

Stella Reynolds is live near downtown Columbus with that top story tonight. Stella?

Stella: Good evening, Mark. When Bobby Herbert was gunned down in cold blood, he had just been offered a promotion here at this marketing firm behind me. Now the owner of Hieroglyphics Communications says he hopes whoever pulled the trigger pays the ultimate price.

Take Package
Paul Blackwell: We are still in shock. Bobby was on his way up and the whole office knew it.

Stella Voiceover: Bobby Herbert had only been working here for six months, but his boss says he was a star employee headed for greatness.

Paul Blackwell: I could tell he was a go-getter—somebody you wanted in your corner.

Stella Voiceover: Unfortunately, though, someone else wanted him dead. Bobby Herbert was killed while trying to pick up his kids for visitation just weeks ago. Now, Bobby's ex-wife is in custody, charged with murder.

Paul Blackwell: Throw the book at her. She doesn't deserve any kindness.

Stella Voiceover: Now, Paul finds himself without a star employee, trying to pick up the pieces.

Paul Blackwell: I haven't filled his spot, yet. I don't know when I will.

As the package continued, a hubbub inside the office made Stella lose focus. She heard screaming, shattering glass, and more yelling over the loud generator that powered the live truck.

She and Devi locked eyes and both turned to watch someone storm out of the office, jump into a car, and peel out of the parking lot.

Stella didn't get a good look at whoever had just left—only a glimpse of blonde hair as the person drove away. She took a step toward the building when Devi said, "Standby, Stella. Back to you in ten seconds."

"But I want to—"

"In five, four..."

The sound of engines starting distracted her. As she looked over, she saw an exodus from the office building. Stella stamped her foot in frustration. Something happened inside that building, but she was trapped until she could wrap up the live shot.

"Go!"

Stella tore her eyes away when she realized she was live on TV. "Back here, live, everyone still trying to pick up the pieces from this terrible murder, including Bobby Herbert's parents, who are struggling for many reasons in the weeks since his death. Reporting live, I'm Stella Reynolds. Back to you."

By the time she got the all-clear and unhooked herself from wires and microphones, the office in front of her looked deserted. While Devi tore down the gear, Stella approached the building with caution. One car remained in the parking lot, so she knew someone was inside.

She looked through the glass door and saw the receptionist sweeping up something. When she tapped lightly on the door, the woman jumped, visibly shaken. Stella waved, and the woman reluctantly walked over. She unlocked the door and opened it just a fraction.

"Paul's gone. You'll have to come back tomorrow."

"What happened? Is everyone okay?"

"Everything's fine, I guess. I don't really know. Paul wanted us to stay and watch the story, and then Felicia lost her mind. She threw a lamp across the office that shattered against my desk. Paul stormed off after her. Everyone else was so glad they could finally leave, and here I am, stuck cleaning up the mess again."

"Why was Felicia so upset?"

The receptionist shook her head and didn't answer.

Stella took a business card out of her bag and slid it through the small opening the door. "Call me if you think of anything. Even small things sometimes make a big difference."

As she walked back to the live truck, she wondered if Felicia had been upset to learn that Paul didn't know who would get the promotion, now that Bobby was dead. If she was going with the theory that Tabitha was innocent, she had to add Felicia to the pool of possible suspects.

24

Stella got back to the station, ready to head home take a shower to get rid of that grimy feeling Paul Blackwell gave her and collapse into bed. She gathered her bags and zipped up her coat. Her keys were in her hand when the phone at her desk rang; she took a step toward the door as it rang again. Stella looked back over her shoulder and took another defiant step away from her desk—her workday was over. When the phone rang for third time, however, she dropped her bags and answered.

"Will you accept a collect call from the Franklin County Correctional Facility from Tabitha Herbert?"

Stella jammed the phone between her ear and shoulder and ripped open her top drawer, looking for a notebook and pen. "Of course."

"Hello?" Tabitha said after a series of clicks connected them.

"Tabitha, I'm so glad Sergeant Coyne got a message through to you!"

"Who?"

"Sergeant Coyne. Did he tell you to call me?"

"I don't know who that is. I'm calling you be-cause—wait, why did *you* want to talk to *me*?"

Stella shook her head to clear the confusion from the last twenty seconds. "Tabitha, I know you didn't shoot Bobby. I know you were buying drugs one block over when he was shot."

Silence met this proclamation. Stella let it ride. Finally Tabitha said, "How do you know that?"

"First, tell me why you didn't tell police the day of the crime."

There was a pause and all Stella heard was rustling. She could imagine Tabitha wrapping the phone cord around her finger, or fidgeting with her hair, stalling. Finally, she said, "Well, at first I was scared that I'd be in trouble for the drugs. I mean, I know police could have arrested me for child endangerment, felony drug possession—

heck, they probably could have added on something else. It never occurred to me that I'd be
charged with Bobby's murder. By the time I was
ready to tell the truth, there wasn't anyone around
to listen."

"What do you mean? What about your
lawyer?"

"She's a ghost—I never see her. She's missed or
rescheduled half of my hearings in the last week
and a half. She never returns my calls—"

"I can't believe it! Eleanor is so highly-regard-
ed," Stella interrupted.

"I knew it," Tabitha said, blowing out a disgruntled breath. "I knew you wouldn't believe me.
I can't believe I wasted my one call this week on
you."

Stella felt her back stiffen. She had just spent
the evening being half-groped by a disgusting
man, all in an effort to investigate a crime police
thought was already solved. She opened her
mouth to say as much to Tabitha when she
stopped. It was easy for Stella to judge—she was a
free woman. Tabitha likely thought about her case
for twenty-four hours a day, sitting alone in a cell
away from her children.

"Tell me what's going on," she said, her voice calm.

"Thank you," Tabitha said, and Stella could feel her relax slightly on the other end of the line. "Pochowski isn't doing the job. I told Eleanor I have an alibi, and she says she checked it out, but can't find any evidence. She says it'll just come down to my word—the word of a druggie. Now, I know this isn't going to win me any mother of the year awards, but it's the truth: I left Johnny in charge of the youngest two just for five minutes. He'll back me up, I just know he will. I met my supplier by the bus stop, and I was there when I heard the shot. I wasn't even in the house, no matter what Valerie thinks she saw."

"He doesn't have to back you up, Tabitha."

"What? Why?"

"The bus stop on Passage Avenue has been under video surveillance ever since a riot nearly broke out there five years ago. I have video evidence that you weren't home when Bobby was shot. I wanted to talk to you to find out what you want me to do with it. I figure we can play it for police, prosecutors, the judge—everyone. You could be home with your kids by the weekend!"

They sat in silence for several seconds while

Tabitha processed all that Stella had said. "My mom said you were really nice when the kids were in court that day. It means a lot." There was another pause, and then Tabitha said, "How long did it take you to get the video?"

"Well, I mean, I found out about it yesterday afternoon from Cara."

Tabitha barked out a laugh. "That girl doesn't miss a trick."

"I had to finish up at work, but once I got in touch with someone from COTA, it took, I don't know, maybe an hour or an hour-and-a-half?"

"So why didn't Eleanor find it?"

"She did! Well, I think she did. Someone at the security office said someone who looked like Eleanor was there and that she saw the video. I left her a message so I could ask her about it."

"Well, the last time she actually came to see me, she told me she couldn't find the video. That woman is trying to railroad me. She's missing my court appearances, not answering my questions, and then she said she couldn't confirm my alibi— the same alibi you confirmed in an hour."

"You need to go straight to police."

"Police won't talk to me unless Eleanor is there, and Eleanor isn't! She isn't here; she's missing appointments and not showing up in court! Something's not right!" Stella didn't say anything. "Just let me figure some things out before you show that video to anyone, okay?"

"Take care, Tabitha." After she hung up, Stella was practically vibrating, she had so much energy. Whereas ten minutes earlier, she couldn't wait to collapse into bed, now she realized she'd never be able to sleep that night.

If what Tabitha said was true and Eleanor was ignoring Tabitha's case, even going so far as to railroad the investigation, it seemed like the best way forward was to play the video for everyone and show the world that Tabitha was innocent. Tabitha wanted her to wait, though.

Stella gathered her bags and picked up her keys off the desktop once again, making a quick decision about how to move forward. She was going to go straight to Eleanor. It was possible the lawyer wasn't intentionally trying to keep Tabitha in jail, and instead, just didn't have all the information Stella did. There was a lot of work to do before she would know the truth, and she couldn't believe she had to wait eight hours before she could start digging again.

25

The warm, gorgeous scent hit her as soon as she opened the door to get the paper Wednesday morning. A dozen roses were sitting at the bottom of the steps, just inside the landing of her apartment. The owner of the stationary shop next door must have let the delivery person in.

Stella scooped up the vase and carried it to her apartment, finally taking the card out of the holder when she'd set her bags on the counter in the kitchen.

I love you, but it's not enough if you can't make time for us.

Enclosed with the card was an airplane ticket.

She couldn't imagine how Lucky had pulled it off from two states away. She looked at the card, written in a florist's unfamiliar scrawl.

Love.

It's not like he hadn't said it before, but it still gave her pause to see it written. Her feelings toward Lucky were so complicated. Dating him had some very real challenges—he was so famous that whomever he dated was famous by proxy, and then only famous for dating him. Even if she was an accomplished rocket scientist and dating Lucky Haskins, she'd only be known as Lucky's girlfriend. It was a difficult thing to work around, especially when Stella wanted to make it on her own. She wasn't going to get to network by being Lucky Haskins's girlfriend.

She tapped the screen of her phone a few times and listened to it ring. It was early, still—not yet eight—and the call went straight to voicemail. Stella thanked him for the flowers, but didn't mention the ticket.

Seconds after she disconnected the call, her phone rang. "I knew you were awake," she said with a smile. Even though she was trying to figure out how to make things work between them, she somehow knew they would. "The flowers really are beautiful."

"Flowers!" Parker crowed. "There must be trouble in paradise if you're getting flowers on a Wednesday morning!" he added with a cackle.

"I thought—" she pulled the phone away from her face and saw with a grimace that it was, indeed, Parker's name on the screen and not Lucky's. "Never you mind about the flowers. Why are you calling so early?"

"It turns out my plan needs a little outside help. Before you can say no," he spoke over Stella, "it doesn't involve any property damage this time."

"What you have in mind?"

"I just saw a commercial—a promo—on Channel 7. Edie is going to be doing makeovers outside the Horseshoe before the spring game on Saturday."

Stella nodded; she had seen the same commercial earlier that day. Edie's station was billing it as a magnificent makeover, which meant they were apparently hoping to harness the massive ratings they got on home football game days. The makeover show would air just before the pregame show on the ABC affiliate. It was prime television real estate, and the fact that Edie was hosting the show meant her station had big plans for her.

"You work on Saturday, don't you?"

"I'm anchoring the news that night. Why?" she asked suspiciously. She wanted to help Parker, but not at the risk of her career, or embarrassing someone else on live TV, no matter what they'd done.

"I just need it to look like I'm working on a story near Edie."

Stella rubbed her forehead. "I can't believe I'm telling you this, but I'm scheduled to be there that morning. I'm covering a kid with the Make-A-Wish Foundation. A little girl with cancer wanted to go to the spring practice game and the team is giving her the royal treatment: breakfast with the coach and hanging out with the team in the locker room pregame. So yeah, I'll be by the Horseshoe Saturday morning."

"Perfect, just perfect."

"I want to know exactly what you're doing this time," Stella said.

"I'm not sure, yet, but I'll need the camera and a microphone."

"Listen, we can't photobomb—"

"I promise, nothing vulgar or beneath us,

mmkay? Just good, old-fashioned detective work we can capture on film."

She disconnected with a grin. She didn't know what he had planned, but she was glad he was going to do *something*. Edie needed to be held accountable and at least give Parker his money back.

She looked at the flowers again. She could probably get time off for Lucky's next race—it would just mean not being able to take vacation days for Thanksgiving or Christmas. Who was she kidding? She was the new kid in the newsroom; she probably wouldn't be able to take those holidays off, anyway.

Before she headed to her room to get ready for work, Stella called the newsroom. Joy picked up on the second ring.

"I'm going to start downtown this morning," she said, "so I might be late."

"What are you doing?" Joy asked curiously.

"I'm going to try to talk to Eleanor Pochowski about her client, Tabitha Herbert. I heard she's ghosting Tabitha, and I want to get to the bottom of the charges."

"Rumors, or is the information credible?"

"It's from someone pretty close to the case," Stella answered, dodging the question.

"Okay. I'll send Devi downtown, in case you get anything. Is this interview already set up, or is it an ambush?"

"Ambush."

"Well, good luck, then," Joy said before hanging up.

Three cups of coffee and one hour later, Stella waved to Devi from across a parking lot downtown.

"Morning," he grunted after she'd walked over and leaned down to talk through the open driver-side window.

"I don't think she'll go on camera, but if I luck out, I'll call you on your cell."

"Can't hardly wait," he said, lighting a cigarette.

Stella walked away before his first exhale and headed into the office building on Spring Street. They were at the southern edge of the Arena district, and the area surrounding the professional hockey team's home rink was full of restaurants, shops, apartments, and even a farmer's market.

According to the directory board in the plain, beige and white lobby, Eleanor's office was on the second floor.

She pushed the door open and came face to face with a wispy woman with baby-fine, dark brown hair frizzled around her face. She was sitting at a reception desk, and there were doors to three spaces around her. The open door led to a small conference room, and the two closed doors, Stella suspected, were offices.

"You're early!" the woman said, standing and coming around the desk to take Stella's coat.

"I... I am?"

"Oh," the other woman laughed, "don't worry, I won't make you wait outside. Eleanor should be here any minute. Why don't you wait in her office? Can I get you a cup of coffee?"

"N-no, I'm fine, thanks."

The woman propelled her into an office and deposited her on a chair across from a desk before bustling back out of the room to answer the ringing phone.

The office was professionally decorated with wood plank flooring and deep-gray walls that were kept from making the space too dark by the white, leather furniture and glass desktop. Matching leather-bound books lined the floating shelves to one side of the room and several diplomas hung in matted frames on another.

After a few minutes, when it was clear the receptionist wasn't coming back and Eleanor wasn't in, yet, Stella got up to look around the room. She started with the floating bookshelves. Some were the legal books she'd spied when first entering the room, but there was one shelf full of everyday books. She saw titles like, *"How to Win," "A Civil Action,"* and *"Anatomy of a Trial."*

She wandered around the room, finally stopping behind Eleanor's desk. There were two pictures of a little girl at different stages of childhood. With a pang, Stella remembered Eleanor saying she had lost her daughter to violent crime years before. The little blond had pigtails in one picture and a sleeker bob in the next. Her sweet smile in the second picture showed silvery, metal braces.

Stella sighed and moved back to the chair the receptionist had originally put her in when something else silvery caught her eye. A black, wire trashcan by the desk was empty, save for a silver locket at the bottom.

Stella paused, listening hard, but only heard the receptionist talking on the phone. She then doubled over and grabbed the locket from the trashcan. The large oval had a decorative engraving of a bird with its wings open mid-flight.

She opened the locket and found two pictures inside: a young woman and a handsome man.

Stella's eyes flitted back and forth between the picture in the locket and the picture on Eleanor's desk. The little girl's sweet smile in the picture on the desk had morphed into a Cheshire Cat grin, but there was no doubt about it that this was the same girl. She had the same small gap between her front teeth, apparently not fixed by the braces. Instead of detracting from her beauty, however, it seemed to make her beauty just a little more unique.

Stella sighed. To lose a daughter in the prime of her young adult life—she couldn't imagine the heartache. Her eyes moved to the other picture. The handsome man's dark hair was graying at the sides, and he wore wire-rimmed glasses and a somber expression. While the picture of the girl appeared to be professionally taken—maybe her final yearbook picture—this second photo looked like it had been cut from a larger picture.

Stella started at the sound of the outer door to the main office opening and closing. She glanced around guiltily and then took out her phone and snapped a picture of the open locket before quickly tossing it back into the trash can. She made it back to her seat moments before the receptionist stormed in.

"I'm so sorry, but I think there's been a mistake," the woman said, flustered. She looked nervously from Stella to the door and back again. "I thought you were Mrs. Pochowski's ten o'clock appointment, but she's only just now arrived!" She bit her lip and wrung her hands, the picture of distress.

Stella smiled apologetically. "Yes, I'm sorry, I was confused earlier, too, and you were moving so fast that I didn't have a chance to explain. I don't have an appointment, but I was hoping to get a few minutes of Eleanor's time. I'm Stella Reynolds from NBC News 5."

"Oh, no, no, no! I'm afraid her schedule is booked solid today. She won't be able to squeeze you in."

Stella stood. "Here's my card. Please have her call me as soon as she can. It's important—about new evidence in the Herbert murder case."

When she stepped out of the office building into the cool sunshine, she waved at Devi parked across the busy, four-lane street. He raised his hands to ask whether she got the interview and she shook her head, so he nodded and drove away. She put her head down against a sudden cold gust and headed to her car.

Eleanor was avoiding Tabitha and maybe Stella. It seemed like getting everything out in the open was the best way to move forward for all parties. She needed to play that bus stop video on the news and see what shook loose. She owed it to Tabitha and her kids.

26

Stella sat in her car outside a coffee shop downtown, sipping an extra-large latte. She should have been driving back to the newsroom, but she was feeling low after striking out at Eleanor's office.

She replayed the video from the bus stop on her phone and a sense of urgency made her stomach clench. She set her drink down in defeat.

Simply put, she was running out of time. The video would be deleted from the COTA server soon as a matter of regular operations, and Stella needed to make sure it was copied in an official capacity, so it could be used in a court of law to prove Tabitha's innocence.

The copy Stella had would make for good TV, but not necessarily good evidence in the courtroom. She glared through the sunlight streaming in the windshield and realized she had no choice —she'd need to disobey Tabitha's wishes and get the video out there. If she played it on the news, prosecutors would be forced to investigate. Eleanor might be off the hook for how she was representing her client, but at least Tabitha would be off the hook, too. She nodded resolutely and fired up her engine, determined to pitch the story to her boss for the news that night.

The ring of her cell phone forced her to put the car back in park.

"You owe me," Sergeant Coyne said. "Big time."

"What?" Stella asked, somewhat incredulously.

"You're in. My second cousin is married to the shift commander. Just so you know, I'll never hear the end of this."

"You're the best! That's why I called—"

"Save me the BS," he interrupted, "and let me know what's going on as soon as you can. My guys say their star witness isn't answering her phone and they're worried their case is falling apart."

Stella was momentarily sidetracked. "Valerie Osmola isn't talking?"

"Mmhmm. The mayor's breathing down our necks to find a suspect in the other homicide, too. You let me know what you're so busy doing before you let the public know, all right?"

"Deal. I'll call you as soon as I have something concrete," Stella promised before hanging up.

She pulled out into traffic. There were two jails in the city of Columbus and Tabitha was being housed in the one closer to downtown. Within minutes, she parked her car again and tightened the ties on her coat against the chill as she walked several city blocks toward the jail.

It took a few minutes to get into the secure facility, and after walking through the metal detector and having her bag searched, she checked in at the visitor's window. After a few minutes, a tall, lanky, balding man came out from behind the secure door.

"Stella? Ed Dyer. Brandon tells me I'm to treat you well. He says you're 'one of the good ones.'"

Stella smiled. "Did he really?"

"Yup. You can have ten minutes with Tabitha. I've got her set up in an interview room over here." He pushed open the secure door through which he'd just come and escorted Stella through a maze of security monitors and dispatcher desks, finally coming to a stop outside a regular-looking office. "It's usually reserved for lawyers and their clients, but I'm making an exception for you."

"Thank you," Stella said, slightly taken aback that she was being given such special treatment. He knocked on the door softly and then inserted a key and pushed it open.

Tabitha was sitting at a table in an orange prison jumpsuit. There were no handcuffs or ankle cuffs, but there was a resigned air about her that made Stella realize it didn't matter. The door closed softly and she took a seat, alone in the room with Tabitha.

"I don't know how private this conversation is," Stella said, looking warily into the corners of the room for a hidden camera or microphone.

"What did you find out?" Tabitha asked, brushing aside Stella's concerns. Her blond hair hung greasy and limp beside her face, which was pale, making the dark circles under her eyes stand out.

"Really... nothing. Eleanor's not returning my calls and she wasn't in when I went to talk to her. That's why I'm here. I think we need to move forward with the surveillance video. We'll worry about Eleanor later. Let's get you out of jail now."

"No. At least, not yet," Tabitha said, rubbing her forehead with both hands.

"Why not? Don't you want to go home?"

She leveled a withering glare at Stella. "Yes, I want to go home, but first I want to know what kind of corruption I'm dealing with. Look, when Eleanor volunteered to represent me, I thought I finally caught a break in this whole case, but now—"

"Wait," Stella interrupted, "Eleanor *volunteered* to represent you? She told me she was assigned to your case by the judge at your arraignment."

Tabitha shook her head. "No, the judge asked her to help me with a form, and as we were filling it out, something came over her. I watched it happen. She was very no-nonsense—all business—but as we got to the bottom of the form, something changed. She looked at the judge and said she'd like to be assigned to my case. The judge was happy. Heck, I was happy. She really seemed to know what she was doing, and you never know what you might get through the public defender's office."

"But—"

"Something's going on. Don't you see that? I want her to pay for what she's doing to me."

"We're running out of time. Don't *you* see that?" Stella said, jumping up to pace the small room. "The video files at the transit authority are only kept for thirty days. That gives us some time, but I wouldn't want to push it. We need to get prosecutors to officially request this video *now,* while we know it's there."

"I think Eleanor is out to get me. I want to know why before we go to police."

"No!" Stella shouted. She then clamped her lips together and sat down. "I'm sorry, Tabitha, but we need to go to police so *they* can figure it all out."

The woman shook her head. "They have failed me in every way in this case. If I get out of jail, they forget all about me. They won't investigate Eleanor, because they still have a murder to solve. They won't give me or her another thought." Tabitha stood, finally injected with some of the energy that Stella had seen the day they first met. "I don't want her part in this getting swept under the rug."

"Tabitha, listen—"

"No, you listen. You need to ask questions about Eleanor. I want to know what I'm up against —what my kids are up against."

Stella nodded slowly. She may not have understood Tabitha's reasoning, but she certainly understood her motivation. Keeping her kids safe was her priority.

"I've known it since the beginning, but now you know. Someone else killed my ex-husband and my brother. I need to know who and why."

"Bobby's girlfriend said he was having trouble with someone at work. Do you think—" There was a soft knock on the door to the small interview the room, and the door swung slowly open as Ed Dyer walked in.

"Time's up, ladies. We've got a shift change coming up and I need to get Tabitha back to her cell."

By the time Stella got back to her car, the beginning of an idea was forming. She needed to play this video alibi for Eleanor. How she reacted to it could be very telling, and *that* would get Tabitha one step closer to being home with her kids for good.

27

"All right, let's do this," Stella said as she stood to find her jacket. "Edie's going to be on the south side of the stadium and that's good news for us."

"Why is that?"

"Because that is where we're meeting our Make-A-Wish child. Since you'll be with me, you have a legitimate reason to be near Edie."

Stella buttoned up her suit jacket, and then lifted the long strap of her messenger bag over her head to wear it across her chest. Her days off had passed in a blur of working out, grocery shopping, cleaning, and setting up the details for her story today.

"Want any more coffee?" she asked, heading to the kitchen.

"Nah," came Parker's voice from across the room.

Stella filled her to-go cup, screwed on the lid, and headed to the door. She took a sip and turned to find Parker still sitting on the couch, his bag untouched on kitchen table and his coat still hanging on the hook by the door

"Are you okay? We need to leave soon to meet Devi at the stadium." She looked at her watch and said, "Traffic's going to be nuts with the game. It's a three-thirty start, though, so if we get a move on, we might..." She turned back from the door for a second time to find Parker still sitting on the couch. "Parker?"

He was slumped back against the cushion, his hands clasped over his head, but his feet tapped out an urgent beat on the floor. He was the picture of confusion; even his body wasn't sure if he was exhausted or energized.

"What?" she asked, unable to make out Parker's mumbled words. His lips moved, but he didn't answer Stella, and she finally realized he must have been going over his plan.

He was a nervous wreck. Perhaps the full

weight of what was about to happen was finally settling in. This would be his best chance yet to confront Edie in a meaningful way, potentially setting the wheels in motion to get his investment back.

She stood uncertainly by the door for a moment and then set her bag and coffee cup down on the table before walking over to Parker. "I'll help you through this," she said, sitting next to him. "Let's go make some TV magic." The silly line quoted from Spenser somehow broke through Parker's growing sense of panic. He lowered his hands and smiled at Stella.

"You're right. Let's do this." He stood slowly, nodding to himself, and then turned back to pull Stella up, too.

They caravanned to the TV station, and then hopped into a news car to drive to the stadium together. With game day traffic, they needed the official call letters painted across their vehicle to be able to maneuver through road blocks and traffic snarls with ease.

Devi would meet them by the stadium—he was coming from another shoot and would be heading out somewhere else after Stella's story. Although their first newscast of the day wasn't until six that night, crews would be out all day shooting video for the news stories that would fill it.

"Are you going to take 315?" Parker asked suspiciously.

"Yes."

"You'll never get through that way."

"I'm going to cut over on King and then try to sneak through the medical campus."

"They'll have it blocked off. "

"I think they'll let us through, though, since we're in the news car."

"Tsk," Parker said, shaking his head.

"Well," Stella said irritably, "which way would you go?"

"It's gotta be Olentangy River Road to the north of the stadium and then cut over on Lane Avenue."

"Go past the stadium? Lane Avenue? You're nuts!"

Their bickering was interrupted when the two-way radio came to life. "Stella, are you headed this way?" Devi asked, his tinny voice interspersed with static.

"Yup, I'm about to hop on the interstate."

"Don't! It's backed up south of the city. I'd stay

on Olentangy and cut through on Fifth Avenue. There are lots of lights, but I think it'll be quicker."

"Thanks," Stella answered and hung the microphone. She looked at Parker and saw her own irritated expression mirrored back. The sight made her laugh. "I guess neither of us were right."

He pursed his lips and then allowed a small smile. "Don't sass me, Stella, mmkay?"

They fell quiet as she made her way through traffic. Every few blocks, the interstate came back into view, and Stella was glad Devi had called in the navigational tip. Traffic was at a standstill as thousands of fans made their way to the stadium for the game.

"This is crazy," Parker said. "It's not even a game. It's a glorified practice!"

She and Parker crawled through campus, hitting every other light and making slow progress. The energy in town was contagious. It was warmer in the high fifties, but the sun was shining brightly, and Stella had her window down. Occasionally, a passing fan shouted, "O-H!" Each time, without even thinking, Stella shouted back "I-O!"

Parker smiled. "Good to be back in the home state, huh?"

"You act too cool, but I see you're wearing scarlet and gray socks. Explain yourself."

He grinned. "My jersey's in the wash." Stella barked out a laugh.

Parker grew more contemplative as they got closer to the stadium. Devi was parked in the main lot across from the stadium and she pulled in next to him and looked at her companion. "You can come with us or wait here until we're done."

"I'm with you. You can't leave me at a sporting event and expect me to survive!"

Stella rolled her eyes. "As long as you support the team, you're one of the good guys." She started to walk away when an aggressive voice made her turn back. A large, burly man wearing a scarlet jersey and gray cargo pants with his face painted red had stopped several feet away from Parker.

"Where's your scarlet and gray?" he asked accusingly.

Parker looked at Stella as if to say, "told you so."

The man didn't like being ignored. "I said," he took a step closer to Parker, "where's your scarlet and gray?" Upon closer inspection, Stella saw a can of beer inside a drink cozy in the man's hand, plus suspicious lumps in his cargo pants pockets that made her think he was hiding at least a half-dozen more cans in his pants.

She hurried to Parker and hooked her arm through his. "Let's go. The photographer is ready for us."

"He ain't got game day colors on," the man said to Stella, as if to explain his behavior. Stella, herself, was wearing a gray business suit with a scarlet top underneath—she was no rookie.

The man drained the beer in his hand and pitched it in a perfect arc to a trashcan several feet away. It landed with a clang, and before the trash inside had settled, he was reaching into a pocket to extract another.

Stella leaned down and pulled Parker's pant leg up, revealing his socks. "No, he's good. See?"

The super fan nodded, his face quickly morphing to a smile. "O–H!"

Stella looked expectantly at Parker. He finally chanted back, "I–O."

They hurried off toward Devi and disappeared into the crowd.

~

"Man," Parker said an hour later as they came out

of the stadium, "kind of puts everything in perspective, doesn't it?"

The morning sun had been replaced by cool clouds while they'd been inside shooting their story. Stella took a deep breath and tried to clear her mind. She'd been blinking rapidly for the last forty minutes, determined to keep her emotions in check. The nine-year-old girl they had just spent an hour with was amazing.

"I mean, she just plows ahead every day, even though she doesn't know..."

"So brave," Stella added, blinking again. "Did you see her give the coach a high-five? I'm pretty sure Devi got it on camera—it will be the perfect way to end the story."

"Nice face paint," Parker said with a barely-concealed smile. She blotted her tears with a tissue and it came away red.

"Well, I couldn't very well say no to her—not after hearing her talk about her illness!" Stella said, catching a glimpse of herself in a nearby windshield.

She wiped her eye again—it was stinging painfully. The girl had wanted to paint everyone's face for the game, and now Stella's entire face was scarlet on one side and gray on the other.

She smiled at Parker. "You couldn't say no, either."

"I know," he said, hitching the camera up higher on his shoulder.

Devi had to stop in the bathroom, so Parker was carrying the camera and Stella had the tripod under one arm as they walked back to the news car. Parker's face was gray and scarlet, the mirror image of Stella's.

Her eye twitched again, and she blotted it once more with the tissue.

"Are you okay?" Parker asked.

"Yup," she said, tucking the tissue into her bag and supporting the tripod with her free hand. It was only twenty pounds, but it was awkward to carry, so Stella stopped and set it on the sidewalk next to her so she could regroup. A terrible stench made her eyes water for another reason.

"That's awful," Parker said, fanning the air with his free hand. "Let's get a move on, mmkay? I can't handle the air over here."

Stella quickly wrestled the tripod off the ground and they started moving only to be hampered a few feet away by a huge crowd heading in the opposite direction, toward the stadium. Loud laughter and a squeal made Stella stop, but before she could move out of the way, a woman in the group tripped and the red plastic cup she had been clutching crumpled. Beer sloshed out of the cup, directly onto Stella.

"What the—" Stella stuttered, trying in vain to wipe the cold liquid away.

"Jeez, lady, if you want a beer, just ask for it."

"What are you talking—" Stella looked in confusion at the group, her eyes finally settling on a small woman staring irritably back at her.

The sound of the cup rolling to a stop on the ground caught everyone's attention, and a man at the edge of the group snorted. "Jamie, *you* just tripped and spilled beer all over that lady—she didn't take the beer from you."

The large group of fans guffawed, all eyes on the large, wet splotch over Stella's chest. The cold liquid was seeping through the fabric against Stella's skin, and she couldn't decide what was worse: the smell, or the cold, wet feeling.

Either way, she ripped the suit jacket off and shivered involuntarily—her sleeveless shell wasn't enough against the elements.

"That's not gonna work," the man standing next to Jamie said, crossing his arms while he assessed Stella'a outfit. He untied a windbreaker from his waist and handed it to Stella. "Here, take this," he said with a grin.

"Oh, thank you, but I couldn't—" Another involuntary shudder ran through her.

"Phil, give that idiot your jacket. His outfit needs to match his face."

A second matching windbreaker came shooting from the crowd and hit Parker square in the face.

"That's so... uh, nice, guys. Thank you, but—"

"I insist," the first man said before moving his group off toward the stadium again.

Stella looked at her suit jacket ruefully, hoping the beer would come out at the dry cleaners. She turned to find Parker grinning at her.

"You gonna put that jacket on?" he asked, his expression making it clear that he wouldn't touch a stranger's jacket with a ten-foot pole.

Her expression turned haughty. "Yes, I am. What a polite thing to do. I'm sure someone so kind is okay, in my book." She slid her arms into the fleece-lined windbreaker and hoped her words were true.

"It looks like you've been swallowed by a hippopotamus," Parker said. He was now gripping his coat with his thumb and forefinger, as if it might attack. The crowds were thicker now as the game was closer to kickoff, and more groups of celebratory fans swarmed past.

"Where's your scarlet and gray, man?" A particularly burly fan chanted repeatedly as he approached. Stella grabbed the camera from Parker and he quickly shrugged into the red coat.

"Now we both look like hippopotamuses," Stella said with a satisfied grin before rubbing her eyes again. They hadn't stopped stinging, yet.

"Are you okay? I think you're having some kind of reaction to the face paint."

"What? No, I'm fine."

"Stella, your eyes are swollen."

"No, they're just—" She stopped speaking when her fingers pressed against the swollen skin around her right eye. Her vision was blurry, and she squinted to see Parker before shaking her head. She didn't have time for an allergic reaction.

She put a new baseball cap on his head and then squashed one down on her own. The coach had given her the hats during their shoot, and she thought they completed their new look nicely, minus the swelling. She handed Parker the camera, switched the small microphone pack from one

270 | LIBBY KIRSCH

cold hand to the other, and then used her free hand to pick up the tripod once again.

"I have makeup removing wipes in the car; I'm sure, once I get this off my skin, I'll be just fine. Let's keep moving, okay?"

An irritated voice came from her left. "You guys, where have you been? You were supposed to get here twenty minutes ago." Edie Hawthorn buzzed past them and said, "Let's go, let's go!" She added in a mutter, "You just can't hire good help, anymore."

Stella's eyes flew to Parker's. Did Edie honestly not recognize them? It seemed impossible, but she turned and beckoned to them, at once annoyed and condescending. "I want to go over the plan for the live show. Get over here now!"

28

S tella could just make out the set for Edie's live shot under construction some fifty feet away. An area was roped off by crowd barriers where a pair of technicians connected wires to the sound board and set up a lighting kit. Both engineers working on the set wore jackets similar to the ones Stella and Parker had on. Their coats were obviously official ABC station jackets with call letters stitched onto front, but it was close enough that she understood how Edie had made the mistake.

Stella stumbled after the fashionista, intent on setting her straight. Before she could, though, Edie turned back. "Honey, maybe in the future we'll do an in-house makeover. Even in bad weather, you should find a coat that fits properly—one that might do amazing things for your figure, whatever it is under there."

It was almost as if Edie found her so repulsive that she couldn't make eye contact with Stella. Instead, she spoke to Stella's arm. It was absurd and, frankly, so offensive that, instead of setting Edie straight, she looked at Parker with watery eyes. He had planned to confront Edie in front of her coworkers, hoping to shame her into giving him his money back, but this might have been better. The ball was firmly in his court now, as far as Stella was concerned. A slight smile crossed his face.

"Give me the microphone," Edie said, grabbing the wireless clip-on microphone Stella was holding. "I'll just put it on my coat and it should be able to pick up the audio from me and the people I interview, don't you think?" Again, she didn't make eye contact with either hippopotamus in front of her.

As the other woman clipped the microphone onto her jacket, Stella stared fixedly at Edie, certain she would realize her mistake.

"Let's go over the plan," Edie said, inspecting her reflection in the camera lens that Parker now had pointed directly at her. With the bill of his hat pulled low and the camera blocking the right side of his face, it could have been anyone behind the camera. "We'll have Ugly One and Ugly Two standing here on the dais, and I'll go over what we're planning to do for each person's makeover," Edie continued. "My assistant will then whisk them away, and that's when we'll have our sponsor segments—we've got a lotion company, a local makeup store, and a sunscreen company on set with us, talking about their products."

Edie shuddered, "The makeup is God awful—you should see the online reviews. One woman says she got such a bad case of hives after using their foundation that she had to go to the hospital. Can you imagine? Total crap. Anyway," she shook her head with a smile, "sales told me they paid a pretty penny to be on my show, so whatever pays the bills, am I right? After the commercial break, we'll check in on our uglies, and then we're back to me for an fashion advice segment. It won't be until just after the final break in the half hour that we'll show the transformation to swans—or, at least, less-ugly uglies," she laughed meanly.

"Sounds great," Parker said, his face still hidden by the camera and hat combination. "The camera can really bring out a person's true colors, I guess."

It was only then that Stella realized the red light on top of the camera was on. Parker had been recording Edie's entire awful summary of her broadcast.

Stella bit her lip. If that tape got out... well, it wouldn't be good for Edie's blossoming career.

"I think that's a wrap, mmkay?" Parker said.

At the humming sound, Edie looked up sharply at the pair. "We haven't even started, yet."

Parker dropped the camera to one side and took his ball cap off with his free hand. "Hi. I think we've got enough."

"No, I haven't even gone over the..." she finally looked up at Parker and her face paled, even under the five layers of makeup she wore. "I-I don't know..." she fell quiet, staring at the ground. "That wasn't fair, Parker." She still hadn't looked at Stella.

"What's not fair," Parker said, still rolling, "is you taking my money."

"Well, th-that's just totally beside the point!" Edie stuttered.

"I'm sure your sponsors would love to know

what you really think of their products," Parker said grimly, tapping the camera. "What did you call it? 'Total crap?'"

She shook her head in disbelief. "Why would you do that? Over a little money?"

"A *little* money?" Parker repeated, outraged. "That's half of my life savings! Why did you take it?"

Her face fell, defeated. "I—I'm so sorry, Parker. I had debt collectors calling at all hours. I just needed to take care of a credit card that had gotten out of control. These clothes," she pointed to her outfit, "they don't come cheap, you know?"

Parker shook his head. "So the money's gone?"

"It was, but I—I should have your money back by the end of the weekend."

"Why didn't you just tell me?"

"I was embarrassed. Bill collectors. Ugh." She looked up, her lower lip trembling. "I really am sorry, Parker."

Stella wasn't buying Edie's show of remorse, though, especially after seeing her at the court-house. She didn't want Edie to sell Parker some sob story, only to have his case thrown out later.

"I know about your friends downtown," Stella

said. "Don't think you can get away with asking them for unfair help if Parker sues you!"

"What are you taking about?" Edie spat. "I don't know *anyone* downtown."

"What were you doing at the courthouse last week, then, when I saw you outside the bathroom?"

"What are you—Stella? Is that you?" She looked in horror at Stella from the ground up. "Those shoes... is that a windbreaker?" she asked, her face scrunched in distaste. "What happened to your *face?*"

"Just answer the question, Edie. Why were you at the courthouse?"

"Oh." Her cheeks colored again, heat turning her already-rouged face even redder. "I had to get a copy of the title of my car," she said defensively. "What's it to you?"

"Your car title?" Parker asked.

"Yes. I'm selling it—immediately." She looked past them into the nearby parking lot. Stella's gaze followed, and she saw a group of people walking by a white, four-door car suddenly make faces and then pivot to keep a wide berth around the vehicle.

"What's... uh, is something wrong with your car?" Stella managed to choke out.

"None of your—" Edie bit off her retort with a groan. "It's just time for an upgrade, okay?"

"Stella!" someone called from some distance.

She searched the perimeter of the area, finally spotting Devi near the news van. "I need my camera!"

"Coming!" she yelled back.

Parker cleared his throat. "If I don't get my money back by the end of the weekend, I'll post this clip online," he said, reminding Edie what was at stake.

Edie tore the lavalier microphone off her jacket and hinged her arm back, as if she was going to throw it at Parker. Stella cringed, wondering how much trouble she would get into for ruining a five-hundred-dollar microphone. Before Edie could do it, though, a photographer from her station appeared and grabbed her arm.

"Edie!" he exclaimed. "Treat the equipment with respect, or I swear I will never work with you again." He extracted the microphone and handed it to Stella apologetically. Edie spun on the spot and stormed away. The other photographer said in a low voice, "I'm the last photographer at the station who will work with her. She such a pain in the—" he shook his head and started up again.

"Most of you on-air people are okay, but some…" He shrugged and walked back to the set.

Stella and Parker headed to the news car in silence. Stella was almost afraid to look at Parker, as if seeing the joy on his face might render the entire thing as part of her imagination. Finally, she couldn't hold it in any longer. "You did it!" she squealed.

He shushed her. "Here, I swiped this makeup remover for you. Get that face paint off before you go blind."

"But—"

"Let's hold off on celebrating until I actually get the money back."

She bit her lip; he had a good point. As she gingerly wiped her face with the cloth, her eyes still watering in protest, a gagging sound made her turn. A little girl headed to the game with her dad dry-heaved as she passed Edie's car. A strong, rotten smell wafted their way, and she saw that all four windows were rolled down completely.

Parker let out a huge laugh and then gagged as he sucked in another breath. "Good God," he exclaimed, "so many victories today!" He reached in through the back window and extracted the deteriorating takeout bag. The crab cake sloshed and dripped as he gingerly carried it to a nearby trashcan. At her look, he said, "I want to make sure she gets a good price for this car."

She shook her head. What an unbelievable day.

Just as they got to Devi, who was waiting impatiently for them at the live truck, Stella's cell phone rang. It was her boss.

"Stella, we've got a situation here at the station. Views on your video have exploded today."

"My video? What are you talking about?"

"The audio clip from the newscast a couple weekends ago. It's up to one-hundred-thousand views. You better come in; we'll probably need to release a statement and maybe even address it on-air."

Just like that, Stella's elation turned to a rock in the pit of her stomach. The day kept getting stranger.

She was quiet on the drive back to the station, ignoring Parker's busy chatter. Only one thing could break through her concern about the audio clip: Edie couldn't be trusted on many things, but Stella believed her when she said she was downtown getting her car title. If it wasn't Edie she'd overheard talking about a conflict of interest in a case, then who was it?

She felt like she was missing something—something important—but she couldn't concentrate on the bathroom mystery until she'd met with Harry about the new crisis.

29

As Stella walked into the newsroom, she was expecting anger and accusation. Instead, everything appeared to be business as usual.

"Have a seat, Stella," Harry said without taking his eyes off his computer screen. Stella lowered herself into a chair and waited. She still had to ask about taking next weekend off for Lucky's race, but now didn't seem to be the right time to ask. Harry tapped out something on his keyboard before looking at her. "So, more than one-hundred-thousand people have heard you talk smack about a coworker. What are we going to do?"

She leaned in to look at the screen. The number indicating the huge amount of views made her mouth go dry, and she looked up from the screen at her boss. Harry wasn't angry, but he obviously expected Stella to make things right.

She wasn't having it, though. She leaned back against her seat and crossed her arms. "I've already apologized to Spenser. I'm not sure what else we can do, except find out who posted this video and go after them!"

Why hadn't Harry already done that? Surely they had lawyers who could send a cease-and-desist letter to whomever had posted the unauthorized audio clip.

"Isn't the audio copyrighted or trademarked?" she asked. "Can't you send a letter to the host website and let them know they need to take it down?"

"That's something we're considering for the long-term, but what are we going to do now?"

Stella forced herself to stay calm. She wasn't about to apologize to Spenser on-air, if that's what Harry was suggesting. That self-important jerk had been trying to mess with Hope on live TV and Stella wasn't one bit sorry for helping out her coworker.

Harry and Stella locked eyes. She was the first to blink. "Do you think I need to... apologize... to viewers?"

Harry nodded once. "Great idea, Stella. Let's do it at six, right off the top of the newscast. We'll play the clip, explain how many views it has, and then you can make the apology. We can put this whole thing behind us."

"That's a pipe dream," Stella muttered as she stood to leave. Spenser and Amanda would never forget this, especially if her discussion with Spenser went out over the *station's* airwaves for a second time—it would be like reopening a wound. She turned back to look at her boss. "How did this thing get so much traction? Last time I checked, it only had a few thousand views."

Harry was back on his computer screen, his fingers flying over the keyboard. He didn't look up, but said, "Hard to say how these things go viral, Stella. We'll probably never know."

She walked slowly back to her desk and glanced up at the producers pod where Amanda and Spenser had their heads together, working at desks next to each other. Now, instead of writing up her Make-A-Wish story, she would be writing an apology. She sat down at her desk and stared at her computer screen, trying to find the right words.

~

"STANDBY, STELLA," Amanda said through her earpiece. Harry was in the booth with her, so for today, at least, she knew she would get the cues she was supposed to get throughout the newscast. "Cold open starts in thirty seconds and then we go to your apology story right off the top."

Stella bent her face toward the scripts in front of her, but she couldn't help but notice Spenser standing on his box at the side set. Harry had decided she would start the newscast by herself at the desk, and after she made her apology, she would toss to Hope for the first live shot. She would then join Spenser for the next read at the wall.

She didn't feel nervous, exactly, but she certainly wasn't used to making such a personal statement on air. It was usually all business—all about the story—and maybe some banal chatter about the weather or a sporting event. This would be quite different.

A pop of music played in the studio, accompanied by the graphics that started off each newscast. Stella sat up straight in her seat, ready.

Stella: Good evening, everyone. I'm Stella Reynolds. Before we get to the news tonight, we wanted to alert you to a situation that's been unfolding online over the last several days. Some weeks ago, I was giving myself a private pep-talk after a particularly stressful situation in the studio. Somehow, my words, which were spoken off camera during a commercial break, were recorded and put online. In case you missed it, here's a short clip.

As the audio played in its entirety, Stella had to work hard to keep her body relaxed, especially with Spenser getting tenser by the second. She watched his face change from tan to dark red in less than a minute. Once the clip ended, the light on top of Stella's camera glowed red again.

Of course, I have already apologized to my colleagues, but I would like to take a moment to apologize to you, our viewers. Not only were my words inappropriate, but they were also unprofessional, and I hope you'll understand that, sometimes, in an effort to get you the news first and fast, tensions can spill over. With that said, I'll toss things over to Hope, live at the county fair with our top story tonight.

Stella smiled warmly at the camera as she tossed the newscast over to the reporter. Harry came into her ear, "Great job, Stella. Very smooth."

Harry had co-produced the show that night with Amanda, and in an unusual move, the rundown called for Stella to join Spenser at the side set in the middle of the first block of news. The green screen was usually used by the weather and traffic anchors, but, instead of maps, the graphics guys had designed a virtual set for that evening. On TV, it looked like Stella and Spenser were standing in front of a big screen TV with a brightly lit studio behind them, but from the studio, it was just a plain wall painted lime green. Stella and Spenser stood next to each other, and to compensate for the height difference, Spenser stood on a box next to Stella.

Once they were both in their places with scripts in hand, the computer-controlled, auto-mated camera swiveled around from the weather center. This part of the show had been added at the last minute as something Harry had been working on up until Stella left the newsroom to touch up her makeup.

Stella quickly read over the script—she didn't want her first time reading the lines to be on live TV—and did a double take at the words on the page in front of her. Spenser, in the meantime, was looking at himself in the playback monitor, ad-justing the handkerchief square in his breast pocket. She wondered if he knew what was com-ing. Amanda gave them a five-second cue, and soon it was their turn to talk again.

Spenser: Tonight, a story of redemption—a story of a little man getting ready for a big change.

Stella hesitated for a fraction of a second, not sure if this was some kind of joke. The teleprompter had her lines, however, presumably written by her news director, so she soldiered on.

Stella: Sometimes, small things need to get off their high horses, and that's exactly what happened today in western Ohio.

Stella continued reading the story about a six-year-old boy who trained an abandoned circus pony to work on his farm after his own horse died unexpectedly, but the video that was supposed to play over the script didn't roll. Instead, the automated camera started acting oddly; the close-up two-shot of Stella and Spenser started to slowly zoom out as the camera trucked backward, showing a wider shot as it went.

By the end of her script, you could see the edge of the weather wall and even part of the lights hanging from the ceiling. That also meant that all of Stella—and Spenser standing on his box—was in the frame. Spenser didn't know what to do. He started to step off the box, thought better of it, and nearly lost his balance before widening his stance and staring straight at the camera.

Stella had no choice but to continue with the story, finally ending with:

Stella: What a lovely story—and now, of

course, the little pony knows his place in the town.

Spenser was supposed to read the tease for the next block that took them into a commercial break, but he stood, speechless, on the box. Stella quickly tossed them to break, and before she could unhook herself from the wires to get back to the anchor desk, the side door to the studio opened and Harry stuck his head in.

"Does everyone know their place here on this newscast, now?"

Stella stared at her boss. Spenser, whose face was now more purple than red, stared at the floor.

"No one is irreplaceable here. Do I make myself clear? Ohio is an at-will employment state. If you don't measure up—if you play with posting clips online anonymously that embarrass the station—you're gone. Does that make sense?" Stella and Spenser nodded mutely.

She wasn't sure what had just happened. It felt like her boss was giving her co-anchor an ultimatum, accusing Spenser of posting the audio clip online. It seemed like a victory, but she didn't feel victorious.

After another moment of stunned silence,

Spenser stormed out of the studio. Stella hustled back to the anchor desk, plugged in her earpiece, and looked into the camera in front of her, waiting for direction from Amanda. It was Harry's voice, however, that came into her ear some thirty seconds later.

"Stella, you'll be solo anchoring the rest of the newscast. I'm taking over for Amanda." Stella stared, unblinking, into the camera until Harry spoke again. "Back to you in ten." She shuffled forward through the scripts on the desk, realizing she'd now be reading the entire newscast, which meant almost half of the stories would be cold-reads. She quickly scanned the next script and plastered a smile on her face.

Stella: Welcome back, everyone.

The rest of the newscast was the smoothest Stella had experienced in weeks. With Harry, a former news producer, manning the controls, she didn't worry about any surprises. They had no technical problems—no cameras whirling suspiciously around—for the remainder of the newscast.

The underlying tension that had been in the

studio for weeks was suddenly gone. She even felt a sense of lightness when she wasn't on camera, during sports and weather.

After the newscast ended, Harry walked into the studio. "Nice job tonight, Stella."

"Well," she said ruefully, "I don't think my apology made things any better between me and Spenser." Despite the fact that Spenser had stormed out, the rest of the newscast had been so pleasant that it made Stella realize how unpleasant the weekend shows had been. She wasn't looking forward to going back to the way things had been.

"Spenser and Amanda will be taking their talents to another TV station," Harry said dryly.

Stella bit her lip. "I didn't want anyone—"

"It's been a long time coming for Amanda. I shouldn't tell you this, but her personnel file is a foot wide. The video she posted of you finally gave us legal cause to fire her." At Stella's shocked look, he said, "Oh, yes. Our lawyers were able to track down the anonymous online poster. Not only was it posted from Amanda's personal email account, but it was done from Spenser's desk here in the building. My guess is they did it together."

Stella frowned, wondering when Harry had

found that out and why the video hadn't been taken down immediately. Before she could ask any of those pressing questions, though, he spoke again.

"I tell you that, Stella, so you know Amanda is responsible for her own actions. Spenser's behavior, quite frankly, was a surprise—I thought he was a bigger person than that." Stella looked up sharply at his words, and he held up his hand. "I shouldn't have phrased it like that, but it's what I meant. Listen, Stella," he said, taking a step forward and resting his elbows on the anchor desk. "In this business, you either make the changes necessary to survive—fix your makeup, improve your writing, contribute to the other shows—or you're out. It's that simple. You survived—not everyone does."

Stella nodded slowly. "So, what's going to happen now?"

"We'll bring in a dayside producer, obviously, until we can fill the slot permanently. I think, for now, we'll have you solo anchor, until and unless I see a need to bring in a co-anchor." He held her gaze for another few seconds before nodding, and then he turned and walked out of the studio.

Stella couldn't deny that she felt a sense of relief mixed sharply with guilt, and a little frustration. Two people were out of a job, not necessarily because of her, but she couldn't deny that she'd played a part in what happened. But more pressingly—with Spenser gone, she wouldn't be able to take the following weekend off for Lucky's race. There was no one who could fill in on her shift on such short notice.

She taped the news teases that would play during prime time shows that evening and then went back to her desk. She would normally head home for dinner, but there was extra work to be done, now that they were down a producer and an anchor. She was actually glad for the busy work— it gave her an excuse to put off calling Lucky with the news about his race.

As she worked on the rundown and updated scripts, she thought back to the video evidence she had that proved Tabitha was innocent. She didn't want to sit on that story any longer—she couldn't wait. She picked up her desk phone and punched in some numbers.

"Eleanor Pochowski, this is Stella Reynolds. I'd hoped you would have called me back, but the matter simply can't wait any longer. I'm running a story tomorrow and you're going to want to see it first. Call me—it's urgent. I think there's a lot we need to discuss about your client's case before I go on air with some new evidence that proves her innocence."

She hung up, happy with her voicemail. If it didn't get Eleanor's attention, nothing would.

30

"This all seems a bit much," Eleanor said, eyeing the news camera and lights.

She had called Stella back Saturday night before the late news, and Stella had insisted they meet first thing Sunday morning. She had briefed Devi on what was going to happen, and he ignored the lawyer, but Stella saw his smirk as he turned to adjust a filter. He knew things were about to get interesting.

Her cell phone rang as the station called her and she fumbled to switch the phone to vibrate mode so she could do the interview uninterrupted. She set the device on top of her bag and then turned the wireless microphone on. She clipped it to the lapel of Eleanor's dark maroon suit jacket and then watched the woman clip the battery pack to the waist of her pants.

"Can you count to five, please, so Devi can check levels?"

Eleanor was getting more and more uncomfortable by the minute, and Stella worried she might just cancel the whole interview. The lawyer, however, gamely counted off the numbers until Devi nodded and clambered behind the camera to zoom in to focus the shot before backing the lens out again.

"I'm ready," he said.

"Great. Eleanor, thanks for taking time to talk today."

"You know I can't discuss many details about the case, though, right? Ask anything you want, but just know that it's more than likely I won't be able to answer it."

Stella nodded. She had a feeling Eleanor wouldn't be able to answer the few questions she had prepared, but only time would tell.

"Before we get started, I'd like to play you a short video clip and get your reaction," Stella said, pointing to a tablet lying innocuously on the desktop between them. "Let's watch."

She ignored Eleanor's surprised expression and tapped the screen to bring it to life. The footage from the security camera at the neighborhood bus stop came up in full, grainy color. The lawyer grew still and silent as they watched Tabitha and her dealer at the bus stop. There was no audio, but after both people on camera flinched and hit the ground, they watched as the dealer ran away from the shooting and Tabitha ran toward it.

"I'm not sure if you noticed, but the time stamp in the lower right corner indicates that, what looks like a drug deal between your client and an unknown person, happened at the exact time her ex-husband was shot a block away at her house. I understand from the transit authority that you've also seen this video." Stella watched Eleanor closely for her reaction, but the lawyer's face was still, giving nothing away. "Have you brought this evidence of her innocence to police or prosecutors?" Stella pressed.

Eleanor blinked under the lights. "Uhh... there are many things I can't discuss about the case—"

"If this video is accurate, though, it seems like Bobby's killer is still unknown. Do you have any idea who police are looking for?"

"Well, no. Right now, we can't say for certain. It's not like I have..." she cleared her throat and started again. "Police still consider Tabitha their best suspect." Eleanor squinted up at the lights again, beads of sweat forming at her brow. She took a deep breath, then, as if she couldn't stop herself, her eyes were drawn back down to the tablet, frozen on the final shot of the empty bus stop.

"Surely this video changes everything," Stella said, laying it on thick. "Why haven't we heard about a search for a new suspect?" Eleanor glanced at her office door and Stella worried she was formulating her escape plan. She needed some answers first. "I understand that Tabitha told you about her alibi nearly two weeks ago. Did you tell police or prosecutors about this video?" she asked again.

"I don't think... it's not for me to say..."

"Have they seen the video, Eleanor?" Stella was unyielding. "What exactly was their reaction?"

Silence descended on the office, broken only by the buzz of Stella's phone vibrating again. She glanced down and saw with disgust that the station calling her *again*. They knew she was in the middle of something important! The phone went quiet and she let the silence stretch for five seconds and then ten.

Suddenly, Eleanor's chair scraped back against the wood floors. She remained seated, but it was as if she needed more physical room around her to breathe. "Where did this come from? I—I mean where did *you* get it?" she asked, her nostrils flaring. She was breathing hard and her face had gone from pale to splotchy red. "I had no idea anyone... it's..." She took a deep breath as she tried to get her emotions in check. She lowered her voice. "I—I'm so glad it's out there. Maybe this will finally move prosecutors to give us a new hearing."

"A new hearing?" Stella asked doubtfully. "What are you saying? You've showed this video to prosecutors and they said it didn't matter?"

"Yes! Yes, that's it exactly," Eleanor said, standing and pacing quickly in front of the desk. "They were unmoved. Now, maybe with the light of the press, they'll give Tabitha a fair shake." She looked wildly around the office. "Excuse me," she headed to the door. "I need to visit the bathroom."

Eleanor was out of the office before Stella could say anything to her amazing proclamation.

"Did you get it?"

Devi grunted, "Everything."

After a few minutes of silence, Stella couldn't stand the suspense. "Well, let me see it while we're waiting."

Devi rewound the video and turned up the speaker on the camera. They both watched on the small, fold-out screen as Eleanor became increasingly upset throughout the interview. Tiny speakers on the camera played back the audio. When it ended, Stella felt a sense of elation—it couldn't have gone any better. She turned to say as much to Devi when the sound of a faraway ring tone wafted out of the camera.

"What is..."

Eleanor's voice then answered the call.

Stella looked at Devi, confused for a moment, until he said, "She's still wearing the wireless. The bathroom must be pretty close."

Her eyes opened wide. "Can you record this?"

Devi shrugged and pressed a button. "Sure."

Eleanor's voice came through the camera. "Well? Did you get my text?" her voice echoed. After a short pause, in which Stella imagined whoever was on the other end of the call said something, Eleanor snapped back, "I'm not going to blow everything. I'm just telling you I was blindsided by the tape—I don't know how they found out about it." There was another pause, and then the lawyer said, "Everything's fine. I was just surprised. I'll control the message."

They heard a door close and Stella moved back to her chair. Eleanor came striding into the office seconds later and sat down without hesitation. She'd obviously regrouped in the bathroom and was once again the picture of calm authority.

"I'm about out of time, Stella, but thank you for helping us shine a light on this situation. The press is so important in cases like this."

Stella's eyes narrowed. "Eleanor, what is next for Tabitha? Will you be asking a judge to dismiss all charges against her?"

The woman sighed dramatically. "We are working within the constraints of the system right now, Stella, and we just hope we can get through. We certainly hope the video is admissible in court, but even if it is, it's gone too far for us to demand that Tabitha be released. Unfortunately, the video evidence shows my client in the middle of a drug transaction, which is not exactly what a lawyer hopes for when it comes to an airtight alibi. Now it's up to a judge to determine where the case goes from here."

Stella's brow wrinkled. "So, you're saying that,

despite mounting evidence of Tabitha's innocence, you're *not* going to ask for a new hearing?"

"It's not a matter of me asking, Stella!" Eleanor exclaimed, her visage of calm wiped clean. "We're too far into the process! We'll continue to talk to witnesses and do our best to get the case ready for trial." She stood and straightened her jacket with a huff. "I'm afraid we are out of time." She walked past the camera and the lights and called to her receptionist, "Madeline, please see them out when they're ready."

"That was weird," Devi said under his breath as he started breaking down the gear.

Stella looked shrewdly at the tablet as she tried to catalogue all the lies she had caught the lawyer in about this case. Eleanor had not been assigned to the case, as she'd told Stella on that first day, but had volunteered to represent Tabitha. Stella was also certain that prosecutors had never seen the bus stop video. Furthermore, she and Devi had overheard her talking to someone about the case about how she wasn't going to "blow everything."

What else was Eleanor lying about?

While she waited for Devi to collect the gear, she inspected the framed diplomas on Eleanor's wall: an undergraduate degree from Kent State and law school at OSU. The third frame wasn't a diploma, instead it was some sort of letter. Stella walked closer and saw a pencil drawing of a familiar bird with the loopy writing of a child next to it. The note read, *Love you, Mama. Fly, fly, fly away to better things. Joanne.*

Eleanor walked back into the office, desperate to hustle them out, but stopped short when she saw Stella reading the letter.

"This is so lovely," Stella said, looking sadly at the picture.

"Thank you. My daughter... before the... before."

Stella nodded and then walked slowly out of the office ahead of Devi.

Now she realized where she'd seen the bird before. It had been on the locket in Eleanor's trashcan, but also tattooed on a woman's shoulder.

Eleanor had been the one on the cell phone in the courthouse bathroom, talking about a shocking conflict of interest.

What was she hiding?

31

As Devi put the camera into its bag and heaved the strap over his shoulder, Stella's cell phone buzzed yet again. It was the newsroom calling for the third time in less than twenty minutes.

"What in the world is going on?" Stella exclaimed.

Beatrice, who'd been called into work on her day off to fill in for Amanda, wasn't happy with the terse greeting. "I thought you'd want to know that a 10-28 just came over the scanner. The victim is Rhonda Leavy."

"What?" Stella asked, dropping her bag to the

floor with a thump. 10-28 was dispatch code for body found. "Rhonda Leavy is dead? Are you sure?"

"Hope just got to the scene with Lou. It's an apartment on Kenny Road. She hasn't confirmed all of the details, yet, but she said there's no ambulance—just the morgue."

"Does Hope know Rhonda was Bobby Herbert's girlfriend? We just interviewed her a couple of weeks ago!" She started walking toward the door and then realized her bag was still on the floor by the receptionist's desk. "Let's go, Devi!"

"Wait—Stella, I need you back at the station. You have to get ready for the newscast!" Beatrice said, making Stella curse.

"Gah, you're right. I just can't believe it! Rhonda Leavy, dead." She shook her head as she pushed through the outer door from the reception area to the hallway.

At one point, Stella had thought *Rhonda* might have been the one responsible for killing Darren as retaliation for Bobby's murder. Now she was dead, though. She held the door open for Devi, loaded down with the camera and light kit. When she looked up to nod at Eleanor's receptionist in thanks, she saw Eleanor standing in the open doorway of a second interior office. The lawyer's face was pale and her mouth hung open. The door swung shut before she could make sense of her expression, but Eleanor looked as shocked and upset as Stella felt.

She bit her lip. It was the right call for Beatrice to make to bring her back to the station, but she didn't like it. She had been to the victim's house, and it felt strange not to go there now. Her mind was racing, and when they climbed into the live truck a few minutes later, she put a hand on Devi's arm, stopping him from starting up the engine. Another more sobering thought entered her mind.

"I think we need to head to Tabitha's mother's house." She squinted at the dash. "We'll still make it back to the station in plenty of time."

"Why?" Devi asked. "What are we going to do there?"

"I guess I just want to... I don't know, check on the kids?" she said feebly. It sounded silly, even to her ears. They weren't police officers, after all, but a lot of bad things were happening to Tabitha's circle of family and friends. First, her ex-husband and brother were shot to death. Now that her ex-husband's girlfriend was dead, Stella worried about anyone else connected to Tabitha.

Devi gamely cranked over the engine. "Sure. I'm on the clock—doesn't matter to me where we go." They drove north, staying on surface streets as they made their way to Journey Street. Traffic was quiet, and Stella suspected that, at eleven on Sunday morning, people were either at church or still holed up in their homes.

"Do you want to get out?" he asked as they turned onto Tabitha's street.

"No, let's just make sure everything looks okay."

Devi slowed the van and they crawled down the street. Stella sighed with relief when she saw the kids playing in the front yard of Tabitha's mother's house. She resisted the urge to call out to them to make sure their grandmother was okay. After all, nothing good could come from a stranger in a van yelling to children.

Devi did a U-turn at the end of the block and they drove past the house one last time.

She almost missed it.

"Wait!" she exclaimed, and then her body slammed against her seatbelt when Devi pumped the brakes. "Back up!"

Instead, Devi pulled forward and parked alongside the curb. "What did you see?"

Her heart exploded, and unable to answer, she climbed out of the van and walked slowly toward Valerie's house. The door to the usually-immaculate structure was ajar, and cracks spider-webbed up from a corner of one of the front windows. It was so unlike Valerie that Stella broke into a run. She took the front steps two at a time and knocked sharply on the front door, causing it to swing completely open.

The front room was a mess: tables had been upended and a dark patch surrounded a broken vase where water had seeped into the carpet. Stella was about to step into the home when the TV above crashed to the floor right in front of her. She sucked in a sharp breath and froze, fighting her gut instinct to turn and run to safety. From behind, a hand brushed her shoulder.

"I'm rolling. What do you think is going on?" The camera was on Devi's shoulder and the sight filled her with a sense of purpose. They were there for a reason. She took the microphone out of her bag and turned it on.

"I don't know, but it doesn't look good, does it?" she said, finally taking the last step into the house.

"Hello?" she called into the home as she took another cautious step forward. "Valerie, are you here? Is everything okay?" She held out an arm to stop Devi from going any further, realizing belatedly that this was likely a crime scene. She didn't want to contaminate it more than they already had. "Valerie, I'm calling police right now. If you can hear me, please come out." She took out her cell phone, but instead of dialing 911, she called Sergeant Coyne.

"Not now, kid. Shit's hitting the fan," he said by way of greeting.

"Sergeant, I'm at Valerie Osmola's house—"

"Don't tell me she's dead, too?"

"I honestly don't know. I didn't want to—"

"I'm just a few blocks away, Stella. Just wait for me."

Her hand still rested on Devi's arm, and she gave it a squeeze and said, "Coyne is on his way. Let's wait for him outside." She started to turn when a rustling sound caught her attention. "Did you hear that?" she asked, scanning the inside of the home for the source of the noise.

"I can only hear the camera," he said with a frown.

The rustling sounded again, and this time Stella's eyes were drawn to the staircase just as a woman came flying down it with a colorful robe flapping behind her. It seemed like she had two sets of eyes, and Stella's hand clamped tighter around Devi's arm when a warrior's yell was issued from the woman's lips.

When the bird of prey finally got to the landing, she pivoted toward Stella and Devi, finally close enough for Stella to realize it was Valerie. Huge, Coke-bottle glasses covered half her face. As a relieved smile started to form on Stella's lips, Valerie raised a rifle and pointed it directly at Stella's chest.

"Definitely should have waited outside for Coyne," Devi said what had to be the understatement of the year.

Valerie had dark, almost-black circles underneath her eyes, and she was breathing hard, either from the exertion of running down the stairs, or from the adrenaline rush of defending her home. Stella held her hand up and said, "Valerie, it's me, Stella. I just wanted to make sure you were okay." Taking it as a good sign that Valerie didn't pull the trigger, Stella said, "There was another murder— someone else connected to one of the victims—

and I was worried about you. This is Devi, my photographer today. We came to check on you and saw that your front door was open. We were... we were worried," she repeated uncertainly.

The words finally seemed to cut through Valerie's mind. She slowly lowered the rifle until it hung at her side, but Stella noted that she didn't set the weapon down.

"What happened here?" she asked, motioning to the mess.

"She came for me," Valerie said, her voice barely more than a whisper.

"Who came for you?" Stella asked.

"I knew she was going to," Valerie said, talking to herself now more than Stella. "I knew she was coming, and I was right to hide. I haven't slept in days, keeping guard over my house. She came, though—I knew she would. She couldn't find me and got mad. Tore the house up and even sat on the couch, watching my TV, waiting for me to come home. I was home the whole time—she just didn't know it."

Stella and Devi traded alarmed glances, and then Stella turned back to Valerie. "Who was here, Valerie? Who was waiting for you?"

Valerie looked up at Stella as if just realizing she was there. "Tabitha. Tabitha was sitting right there on my couch, waiting for me. She knew I saw her kill Bobby, and she must've heard that I saw her kill Darren. I knew too much. She knew she had to get rid of me. It was Tabitha."

32

An hour later, Stella found herself sitting in the back of Sergeant Coyne's un-marked car. Much to her chagrin, she was officially a witness in what was now being called misdemeanor vandalism, although Stella thought that was just the tip of the iceberg.

Sergeant Coyne had asked her to go over what she'd seen several times. "So, then Ms. Osmola said Tabitha was the one who damaged her property?"

Stella nodded and added, "I told her it couldn't have been Tabitha, because Tabitha's in jail, but it was like she didn't even hear me."

"What happened after that?" Stella blew out a

sigh and gave Sergeant Coyne a look. "This is the last time, Stella, I promise."

"I told her I called the police, because we were worried about her, and she kind of freaked out again. She raised her rifle, pointed at the door, and said, if I tell the police what I know, they'll kill her. She actually said, 'She'll kill me. I know she'll kill me.'"

Stella looked out the window and saw Devi sitting in a nearly identical unmarked car on the other side of the street. A detective was interviewing him while Coyne was interviewing her.

"You'll need a subpoena, you know."

"What are you talking about?"

Stella turned from the window and met Coyne's eye. "Devi was rolling on the whole thing, but if you want a copy of that video, you'll need to subpoena. I can't just give it to you."

"I thought we were friends!" Coyne said with a tsk.

"We are, and that's why I'm telling you now: get a subpoena." She rolled the tension out of her neck and made eye contact with the sergeant in the rearview mirror. "That's the third time Val has identified Tabitha and the second time it couldn't have been Tabitha, since she was in jail. Any comment?"

"No comment. This investigation is ongoing."

"Did you see her glasses? They're an inch thick. I asked her if she wears contacts. Do you want to know the answer?"Coyne raised his eyebrows. "She doesn't. She has astigmatism in one eye, so contacts don't work for her. She is practically blind! It's why she wears such colorful clothes--so she can see herself better in the mirror."

"Are you done?"

"I'm just saying that your star eye-witness in Bobby's murder is blind."

Coyne blew out a sigh and got out of the car, opening her door a moment later. She stepped out and turned to squint at Valerie's house one last time, where an officer helped her board up the front window.

A car swerving down the center of the road made them both step quickly out of the way. "There shouldn't be any cars coming through here," Coyne said, picking up his radio. "How did they—"

"That's Eleanor Pochowski," Stella said, watching the agitated driver get out from behind the wheel. Stella and Coyne met her in the middle of the street.

"What happened? Are the kids okay?" Eleanor asked, looking in horror at Tabitha's parents' house. Her voice was high and breathy, her hair was windswept, she was missing one earring, and her outfit, impeccable just an hour earlier, was now wrinkled with sweat stains seeping from her armpits.

"Everyone here is fine," Sergeant Coyne answered, ushering Eleanor to the sidewalk closest to Tabitha's parents' house. "You can tell your client that her children are fine. The violence wasn't here at their house."

"What happened?" Eleanor asked, not calmed at all by Sergeant Coyne's explanation.

"It's an ongoing investigation—"

"What happened?" Eleanor shouted, cutting off the sergeant.

He gave her a withering look, and she remembered herself. She quickly smoothed her hair and cleared her throat. "Sergeant, my apologies. This has been a very stressful weekend for my client, as I'm sure you understand. Please just tell me what happened on the street. Why is everyone here?"

Coyne turned his beady eye onto Eleanor, but

after a moment, his look softened. "The woman who lives over there," he pointed at Valerie's home, "was burglarized. Items inside the home were damaged, and the suspect camped out on the couch for an hour or so. The victim believes she was waiting to ambush her when she got home."

"How did she escape unharmed?" Eleanor asked, still a bit breathless.

"She was home the whole time, hiding in an upstairs closet."

"My client's parents? The—the children?" she asked, pointing to the house where Tabitha's kids were living.

"All fine. Everyone's fine," Sergeant Coyne said, patting Eleanor on the shoulder.

Eleanor stared in shock at the house surrounded by caution tape. "Oh, thank God. Just... thank God."

Stella was struck by the genuine feeling in her voice. The woman was honestly relieved that Tabitha's parents and kids were all okay. Whatever thoughts she'd had about Eleanor during and after her interview were now at war with what was playing out in front of her.

Sergeant Coyne escorted Eleanor back to her car and told her he would call her with any updates on the situation. They watched her drive away.

"I've been waiting for that woman to break down for fifteen years, now," he said, shaking his head.

"Why's that?" Stella asked, looking at Coyne curiously.

"That's when the verdict came down in her daughter's case."

Stella nodded sadly. Eleanor had told her she'd lost a daughter to violence, but she hadn't said when.

"So sad," she agreed. "How do you recover from something like that?"

"Well, not to mention the guilt. I mean, should she have hired another lawyer? That's what I can't get past."

Stella's face scrunched up in confusion. "What... uh... what do you mean?"

"Eleanor represented her daughter in the murder trial and lost. The girl was convicted of first-degree murder. I always wonder if she wishes they'd hired another lawyer, instead of repre- senting her, herself. I really thought it would break her—it would have broken many. She came roaring back within years, but... I don't know, something seems off lately. That behavior right there," he pointed to where Eleanor had gotten out of the car and nearly collapsed, "that looks like a woman on the edge of insanity."

Stella shook her head. "No, no, no. Eleanor told me she lost her daughter to violent crime. Her daughter died!"

"Just the opposite, Stella! Her daughter killed someone. She was sentenced to ten years in a high-security prison. I lost track of her after she got out a number of years ago."

"Her daughter is still alive?" she asked, unable to make the jump to a new reality.

The two-way radio clipped to Coyne's shoulder strap came to life, and he held up a finger while he listened. After a moment, he pressed a button and answered whatever question had come his way. He then looked at Stella and said, "I've gotta head over to the homicide scene."

Stella walked with him toward his car. "So, what's going to happen here?" she asked, pointing to Valerie's house.

Coyne sighed. "Not much. Ms. Osmola doesn't want to press charges about whatever happened inside her house. Right now, the statements from you and Devi are the only ones we have to go on, and for a misdemeanor breaking and entering without assistance from the victim, it's not even worth filing."

"Misdemeanor?" Stella asked, thinking about the state of the house as she found it this morning.

"The damage looks to be less than five hundred bucks."

"What about the TV?"

"Yeah," Sergeant Coyne said with a barely-contained grin, "it sounds like you owe her a new TV."

Stella groaned, realizing he was right. The TV had been hanging on the wall until she had opened the door.

She watched him drive away, and Devi joined her on the sidewalk outside Valerie's house. "We've got to get you back to the station," he said, looking at his watch. "Beatrice has been calling for the last twenty minutes. She keeps saying, 'I need an anchor to anchor the newscast!' She's freaking out."

"So am I," Stella muttered. "So am I."

33

The following morning, Stella was waiting outside the courthouse, coffee in hand, when the doors opened at eight o'clock. She bypassed the elevator and took the stairs to the probation office on the third floor.

A young man sat behind a reception desk in an open, utilitarian office space. "Do you have an appointment?" he asked suspiciously, eyeing her over his computer screen.

"Not exactly," Stella said.

"You have to have an appointment. It's the rule," he said before swiveling in his seat to block further questions.

"Well, I'm here to visit a friend," she said. Even

to her ears, it sounded phony. She tried to smile winningly when he turned back around.

He snorted. "Is that right? Which friend, exactly?"

"Ed Jones—he's kind of my neighbor. Can you just let him know Stella is waiting?"

She turned her back on *him* this time and took a seat in one of the worn, faded, pleather couches in the room. She closed her eyes and took a sip of her coffee, now only lukewarm, and let the knowledge that caffeine would soon be coursing through her veins cheer her. She heard the receptionist pick up his phone, although he muttered so quietly into the handset that Stella couldn't make out what he said, and then he bustled out of the main office, leaving her alone.

Ten minutes passed and she was just wondering if the receptionist had only pretended to call Ed when her downstairs neighbor's boyfriend walked into the lobby.

His face broke out into an easy grin when he caught sight of Stella. "Well, they didn't tell me you were the one waiting—just some lady without an appointment."

Stella stood and they shook hands. "Do you

have a minute?" she asked. "I'm working on a story and I need some background information."

"Sure, come on back." She followed him through the door and down a short maze of hallways. Everything was painted the same pale yellow as the lobby and the dark gray carpet underfoot had likely been chosen for its ability to hide stains and dirt.

Jones opened the door to his office, and Stella saw he had attempted to make his space slightly cozier. Some framed poster prints hung on the walls and a sad-looking, nearly dead potted tree leaned against the corner, adding a splash of color to the space.

"That is not looking good," she said, pointing to the plant.

Jones grimaced. "I *was* under-watering it, but now I think I'm over-watering it. I need a cactus." They sat down in the only two seats in the room and Jones made a steeple with his fingers under his chin as he looked at her expectantly.

"Do you know anything about a murder case from fifteen years ago? The suspect was the daughter of a defense attorney still working in Columbus, Eleanor Pochowski."

324 | LIBBY KIRSCH

Jones nodded. "Oh, sure," he tilted his head back. "I think the defendant's name was Anne Pochowski—or was it Amy?" He tipped forward in his chair and typed something into his computer. After a moment, he said, "Ah, that's right: *Joanne* Pochowski. She was convicted of murder, let's see... looks like it'll be fifteen years ago this May. She served eight years on a twelve-year sentence. Looks like she's already done her five years of intensive probation, and now she's on a plan where she just has to check in if she's going to leave the state or country."

"Do you remember any details of the case?"

He shook his head before tapping more keys and scanning his computer screen. "Oh yeah, it was an ugly bar brawl. She was a bartender and ended up killing a customer."

"Whoa. Motive?"

"It was never really clear at the trial, if I remember. It's all public record—you can probably check your station's archives. I don't have any of that information in my system here."

"Can you tell me what Joanne is doing now?"

"Now that she's out of the criminal justice system, none of that is public record." Stella nodded. "What's this all about, anyway?"

"I'm not really sure," Stella said, feeling disappointed. She didn't know what she'd been expecting, but this seemed like a dead end. In all her digging and reporting on the murders over the last weeks, she'd never run across a Joanne Pochowski. "Thanks for your help, Ed."

As they walked back out to the lobby, they chatted about the store and Stella's apartment. She took the elevator down to the main level of the building and was about to concede defeat when she spotted the window for the clerk of courts office and had an idea.

After a few minutes of waiting, a woman walked up to the counter holding a can of soda.

"Oh, hi there," she said, opening the drink with a pop. "What can I do for you?"

"Is Mattie here?"

The woman shook her head and said, "Can I help you with something?"

Stella tried to hide her disappointment behind a smile. Mattie was a very kind older woman, and she never seemed to mind looking up files and paperwork for Stella. More than that, she'd worked in the clerk's office for nearly twenty-five years and generally seemed to know everything that had ever happened in the court system.

"Uhh..." Stella was trying to decide whether to

come back later when another woman walked up behind the window. Her coat was still on and her bag was slung over one shoulder.

"Lee, I've got this," the older woman said, unbuttoning her coat and hanging it on a hook behind them. Mattie had spiky, gray hair and wore brown lipstick and a green, button-down shirt.

"Mattie," Stella said with a smile, "it's so nice to see you."

"What are you working on today, Stella?" she asked, taking a toothpick from her breast pocket and sticking it in her mouth as she sat down at her computer station.

"It's a murder case from fifteen years ago."

"Lordy, you do like to make me work," Mattie said with a smile that matched Stella's. "Are you working on a sweeps piece?"

Stella realized the other reason she liked this woman so much--she really had her news jargon down. "I might be—May sweeps is right around the corner. I guess it depends on what you can tell me."

"What's the case?" Mattie asked, logging onto the computer and then looking up, alert. She chewed absently on the toothpick while she waited for the information.

Stella leaned over the counter. "I don't want to start any rumors, or anything—I know what a small world the justice system is." She lowered her voice. "It's the Joanne Pochowski case. She was convicted of murder fifteen years ago, but I wanted to know if anything else has come up for her since." Mattie's hands became still over her keyboard when Stella said the name. "Do you remember the case?"

"Uh," the older woman faltered, finally tapping on the keys again, "sure, I remember. It was kind of a big deal at the time. We all thought Eleanor was crazy to take the case—her own daughter—and it was a devastating blow when the verdict came in."

"I'm sure for the victim's family, too," Stella said. There was lots of talk about how Eleanor felt, but it was almost as if no one remembered someone had been killed.

Mattie stared at the computer screen in front of her, her mouth slightly open and the toothpick in real danger of falling out.

"Mattie?" Stella asked, leaning even closer. "Is everything okay?"

"Uh..." Mattie seemed to be at war with herself. She looked around quickly and then attacked the keyboard, her fingers moving fast. She scrunched up her nose and squinted first at her computer screen and then at Stella. "I'm going to trust you with this information. If it's important, use it. If it's not, don't."

"Okay," Stella said, looking with interest at the older woman.

"I told myself three years ago that, if anyone ever inquired, I'd share this. It wasn't done strictly by the books, but Eleanor asked for my help as a favor—mother to mother, you know? She didn't want me shouting about it, but I told myself, if it's okay to do it, it's okay to tell someone about it— but only if they ask, you know?"

Stella wanted to say, "No, I have no idea what you're talking about," but she nodded encouragingly at the other woman, instead. A printer came to life behind Mattie, and a moment later, she handed Stella a single sheet of paper.

"What is this?" she asked, scanning the document. It was some kind of form from the social security office.

"It's not supposed to be done for convicted felons, but she was having such a hard time getting a job and had a glowing recommendation from her probation officer, and with Eleanor's connections... I just didn't think it was fair, you know? It seemed like such an additional challenge. I'm not sure it was the right thing to do, but here we are."

Stella held the paper up, still confused. "What is this, exactly?"

"I filed the papers so Joanne could take a new name. Eleanor asked me to help as a personal favor, and you know, she'd been through so much, already. It didn't seem like that big of a deal." Mattie was now taking great interest in the keyboard in front of her. She scratched at a piece of dirt with her fingernail and then took a cleaning wipe from a container on the counter and rubbed the edges until they gleamed.

Stella's eyes flew back to the paper and read the new name at the bottom of the page, along with Joanne's new signature.

"It's not as simple as filling out a piece of paper, though, surely?"

"No, no, you have to go before a judge, but I think Eleanor took care of that."

"What does that mean?"

"She had some connection—saved poor Joanne the hassle of going into court again."

"Hm," Stella said, looking over the form again.

Someone had signed the bottom of the form, but she couldn't make out which judge's name was scrawled on the line. "Her new name is Felicia Andrews?"

"Yes, and she sent me a really nice thank you note not long ago telling me she had a great new job, and that it wouldn't have been possible without my help." Mattie drew herself up proudly, all guilty feelings gone.

"Which judge signed off on this?" Stella asked curiously, wondering just how far Eleanor's connections went.

"Well..." Once again, Mattie got busy fussing with a stack of papers to the side of her keyboard.

"Did a judge sign off on this?"

"Not... uh, no, not exactly."

"Mattie!" Stella said, shocked. "Did you forge the judge's signature?"

"I didn't..."

"Eleanor did?"

"Well..."

"Wow."

She looked down at the paper in her hand, now understanding exactly what she had: proof that Eleanor had broken the law. She bit her lip, feeling torn. Stella could imagine how difficult it could be for a convicted felon to get a job. Stella supposed that, with a new name, your felony history wouldn't be as easy to trace, making it far easier to find employment if you were willing to fudge the truth a bit. Apparently, Joanne and Eleanor were willing.

She put the paper into her briefcase and slung her bag over her shoulder. She had wasted too much time on this wild goose chase, already. Because Mattie was looking at her expectantly, she said, "It's okay, Mattie. I don't want to get you in trouble, and I don't think this matters much, anyway."

"Thanks, Stella. I'm glad. She's just the sweetest girl, and a really hard worker, too."

"I'm glad she got a job. I heard she left the state —a shame for her mother."

"Oh, no, she's here in town, working for some big-time communications company," Mattie answered proudly, as if it was her own daughter who was finally getting her life right.

Stella stopped mid-stride, her feet pointed toward the main entrance and her left hand still resting awkwardly on the countertop. "Felicia," she muttered under her breath, and all of a sudden the name seemed sticky, like she should be remembering something. "Wait—" Bobby and Rhonda had both worked at a communications company. "Was it Hieroglyphics Communications?"

"Oh yes, that's it exactly!" Mattie confirmed with a smile, plucking the toothpick out of her mouth. "She was even up for a promotion—that's how great she's doing these days!"

Stella walked slowly back to the parking lot, her mind racing. A convicted murderer was hiding her identity and working at the same company as two recent murder victims. Rhonda had told her someone was upset about Bobby getting the promotion to the point of leaving anonymous, threatening messages on his desk and on his phone.

The convicted murderer's mother, who didn't mind breaking the law to help her daughter get ahead, had volunteered to represent the person accused in Bobby's death. Was Eleanor working to make sure Tabitha took the fall for the crimes to keep her daughter out of the criminal justice system?

The conflict of interest was so strong—so egregious—that, should it ever come to light, Eleanor would be disbarred and likely charged with a crime, herself. If it didn't come to light, she had no doubt that Tabitha might spend the rest of her life behind bars.

Eleanor had been right about one thing in her office on Sunday: some light needed to be pointed on this entire situation. Now Stella just had to figure out how to do it.

34

"Stella?" Joy looked down at her computer in confusion. "What are you working on today?"

"I've got that Make-A-Wish story in the can. I just have to write it," she answered with a smile, slipping past the assignment desk and heading for her own. She logged onto her computer and called up the news program search function, where she typed in Joanne's name. Her finger hovered over the "enter" button for a moment before she pressed it.

A list of old stories started to appear as the computer searched through thousands of files in the database. She printed out her search results and scrolled through the story titles to the very end, looking for the first time Joanne Pochowski's name was mentioned on air.

"Joy?" she called, headed back to the assignment desk, "I need help."

Joy stopped typing and looked curiously at the printout trailing behind Stella.

She pointed to the last line. "Can you help me find this tape in the archives?"

"Hmm. Sixteen years ago, we were still shooting on BetaMax," Joy said, tapping her lip. "Joanne Pochowski... I'd forgotten about that case. Terribly sad. You should be able to find the stories in the archive room." Stella looked at the other woman hopefully. "Oh, okay," Joy said with a half-groan, half-laugh. "Follow me." She got up from the assignment desk and headed for the door. Stella followed her down a narrow hallway, past the studio, and into a rarely used room next to the makeup room.

Joy flicked on the switch as she walked into the cool, dark space, and Stella felt like Belle walking into the Beast's library for the first time. Instead of books, though, she was staring at row after row of old, dusty tapes. Multiple formats lined the shelves from giant BetaMax tapes the size of a textbook to smaller, VHS tapes and finally to the very small, light, compact DVC-Pro tapes they used today.

"All right," Joy said, looking at the list Stella had handed her. "You'll need to check the date in the book and then we should be able to find the tape number."

The more recent video clips were archived on-line, so a quick computer search would tell Stella the tape number she needed and the timecode for the video on that tape. This story was so old, how-ever, that she'd have to search through an archive tracker book manually.

Stella peered uncertainly around the room until Joy pointed to a shelf directly behind them. She blew out a sigh as she scanned the row of three-ring binders, finally finding the one with the right date range listed on its spine.

She pulled it off the shelf and flipped through hundreds of pages of hand-written spreadsheets, finally finding the one she was looking for. On the page, someone—some long-gone production as-sistant or intern, likely—had written down the entire list of stories that had been covered on the news that day sixteen years ago. Each story slug had a date, tape number, and timecode listed after it.

The first page Stella looked for had the story listed, but didn't have a corresponding tape number. She groaned. Someone hadn't finished filling out the form all those years ago. She went to the next line on her printout and flipped through a few more pages in the binder before finding the right one.

"Ah-ha!" she exclaimed, running her finger along the line in the book. "It says tape number 4,039."

Both women started scanning tape numbers along the shelves—mostly in numerical order— and Stella found it first. She pulled the ladder to the right section of the wall and climbed up. The tape was on the second shelf down from the ceiling, and she pulled it, along with the tapes on either side, figuring there might be additional stories on those tapes, as well.

Joy and Stella repeated the process four more times—twice getting all the way to looking for tape numbers 4,044 and 4,061, which weren't on the shelves. After a few more minutes of dedicated treasure hunting, though, Stella was satisfied that she'd have a few stories to watch.

Before they left the room, Joy admonished, "Make sure *you* put the tapes back when you're done. I'm sure the missing tapes have been sitting on someone's desk for years. People never clean up around here!"

Stella nodded as she backed out of the room, arms full of heavy, cumbersome tapes. Joy set the folded-up printout on top and carried the three-ring binders out of the room.

"Thanks, Joy. You saved me twenty minutes."

"No problem." She followed Stella to an editing suite and set the binders down before adding, "You will tell me what you're working on at some point?"

Stella nodded. "First, I need to figure it out, but then I'll let you know."

It was tedious work, looking up the story information in the binder, inserting the right tape, and scrolling backward or forward to find the correct timecode.

The first story she found gave her the details of the murder. The anchor back then was a man named Bill Brown, and he sounded like he was trying to channel Tom Brokaw as he intoned details of the then-recent murder.

"Tonight, police have placed one woman under arrest, seen here as detectives take her away from the scene of the crime. Joanne Pochowski is identified as a drifter, moving from one job to another after dropping out of high school. Police say she used excessive force to subdue an unruly customer. That customer, Jeremy Bagren, died from his injuries Saturday night. Pochowski's mother, well-known attorney Eleanor Pochowski, is telling our cameras she will work tirelessly to defend her offspring."

Offspring? Television reporting had certainly become more casual in the years since this broadcast was recorded. There was one positive, though--the woman shown being led away by police looked like a young Eleanor, albeit with light brown hair.

Stella ejected the tape and tried another. This one didn't have any new video—just some updated information on the victim. Again, Bill Brown glared seriously at the camera and spoke with studied authority. "The victim, by all accounts a stranger to Ms. Pochowski, will be laid to rest this weekend at Holden Funeral Home, thanks to generous donations from the community. Meanwhile, the woman accused of killing him learns that she will remain in prison until the time of her trial, after a judge in the case denied bail."

Stella tried the last two tapes, but didn't learn anything new about the case. She looked at her watch to find she'd wasted two hours.

She collected the tapes and brought them back to the archive room, putting each one away on the proper shelf. On her way back down the hall for the binders, though, she passed Russ, the college intern. He was balancing a dozen BetaMax tapes in his arms as he walked slowly past Stella toward the archive room.

"Busy day in here, huh?" Stella said, backtracking so she could hold the door open for him. She flipped on the lights and stood in the open doorway. "What do they have you working on?"

He looked up warily from the stack of tapes he'd just deposited onto the floor. "The anniversary show for sports. They want highlight clips from every season since 1977!" he exclaimed. "I think they're just trying to keep me out of the way, so I don't screw anything up," he added with a frown.

"Oh, I'm sure that's not true," Stella said, feeling bad for the kid. He turned to leave. "Hey! You have to actually put those tapes away on the shelf when you're done with them," she said indignantly. "You don't just leave them on the floor!"

"Nah, it's cool. I've just been stacking them over there." He pointed to the bottom shelf to the right of the door. Stella's eyes grew wide as she took in the haphazardly stacked tapes, mixed by date, tape number, and even format without regard to order.

"How long have you been working on this project?" Stella asked faintly.

"I don't know, a few weeks, I guess. Feels like a lifetime," he added, frowning at the long row of disordered plastic and metal.

Stella ignored him as she scanned the tape boxes, finally letting out a frustrated groan. The missing tape numbers she'd been looking for weren't there. "Do you have any more archive tapes anywhere?"

"Sure. I've got about twenty more stacked in the sports department."

"Thanks, Russ. I'll let Joy know you'll be MIA while you clean up."

"Oh," he said, looking at the mess with distaste. "Okay, right. Thanks."

She nearly broke out into a run in the hallway and didn't stop until she was panting by the sports office. After slipping inside, she made a beeline for a cluttered desk stacked high with tapes. She carefully shifted papers, wading through the leaning towers of tapes until she found it: tape 4061. There was still no sign of tape 4044, but she hoped it didn't matter.

She took the lost tape back to her editing suite and pushed it into the machine. It took a few minutes for the old spools to rewind to the right spot, but it was worth the wait. Here, finally, was a story with all the information Stella had been looking for.

Bill: Shocking indifference to a crime prosecutors say amounts to murder. Holly Jackson is live downtown with more from today's sentencing hearing for Joanne Pochowski.

Holly: Joanne Pochowski learned today

that she'll spend twelve years behind bars for murdering a man in cold blood, but her attorney—her own mother—hopes she'll be out in eight for good behavior.

Take Video
Jeremy Bagren was shot twice at the bar where Pochowski worked. No witnesses ever came forward to corroborate Pochowski's claim that he was harassing her and she shot him in self-defense, but the jury did convict her of the lesser second-degree murder...

Stella paused the video and leaned closer as a picture of the victim filled the screen. She stared at him for a beat. "No... what does this mean?" she asked the empty room. After another minute, she took her phone out of her pocket and scrolled through her pictures, finally coming to a stop on a picture of the same man—the picture Stella had snapped of the inside of Eleanor Pochowski's locket.

Why did Eleanor have a picture of the man her daughter murdered in a locket? This supposed stranger had been kept close at hand for the last fifteen years. There must have been some connection, but what?

Stella leaned back in the chair, unable to tear her eyes away from the screen in front of her. She shook her head. It was time to bring in Sergeant Coyne and her boss—and Parker. Yes, she would definitely need Parker for what she was thinking about doing.

35

The few days that had passed since Stella's shocking revelation felt like a lifetime. She knew she needed to act, but she also knew she might only get one shot at exposing Eleanor and her daughter. She wanted to make sure she did it right and caught it all on camera, not only for the news, but for Tabitha's trial, as well.

Not to mention the fact that she'd finally told Lucky that work would, yet again, get in the way of her visiting. He hadn't taken the news well. Actually, she was only guessing that, as he hadn't called her back since she left the voicemail days earlier.

And it was just as well, she tried to convince herself, because she had a lot on her plate just then.

As it stood, she had several fragments of information: Joanne was now living as Felicia, she likely knew the man she was convicted of killing years ago, two people she worked with had been recently killed, Eleanor had volunteered to represent Tabitha, despite a conflict of interest, and Tabitha was innocent. Taken all together, they amounted to intrigue and suspicion, but not quite guilt.

Stella needed to prove that Felicia had both motive and access in the murders, and that Eleanor not only knew Tabitha was innocent, but also that she suspected her daughter might be involved in the crimes. It was a tall order, and she would need to get Eleanor and her daughter in the same room for an epic confrontation. After conferencing with her boss and police, they all agreed that it was going to come down to Parker.

"You are asking for a miracle, Stella," Parker said. She had caught him at home and interrupted a celebration of the sudden influx of cash after a visit from Edie. In his excitement, he'd agreed to help Stella. Now, just hours from the main event, he was starting to panic. "There just isn't time, mmkay?"

"Parker, I have seen you take limp, lifeless, over-dyed, under-moisturized hair and turn it into beautiful locks that would make a supermodel jealous—and in less time than you've spent complaining to me today."

"That's right, you have, girl, and I'll do it again tomorrow. You're asking me to host a pretend makeover contest to catch a killer, though, and that sounds more difficult."

"Actually, it sounds like a good movie, doesn't it?"

"Stella Reynolds, I'm serious here. I'm starting to freak out! I cannot makeover a murderer!"

"There's the title," she said with a snicker. "Killer Makeover."

"Stella!" he yelped.

"Parker!" she snapped. "You're not handcuffing her—you're combing her hair. It's no big deal."

There was a beat of silence and then Parker yelled, "No big deal? What do you mean no big deal?"

Stella held the phone away from her face as Parker continued shouting. When he fell quiet, she said, "Everyone will be here in two hours. You'd better get over here, so you're ready."

"Of course I'll be ready. Parker is always ready, mmkay?"

Stella was smiling when they hung up, but it didn't last long. Harry stood by the assignment desk. He had changed all of the TV monitors from their regular stations to the feed from the weather department—a massive storm was bearing down on the Buckeye state. Was it possible that, after days of work, her exclusive story would be derailed by W3? She turned away from the monitors, as if not looking at them could keep the storm at bay.

Lou sat at an empty desk next to Stella. "I want to go over the plan one more time."

Stella nodded, happy that Lou was being so diligent in preparing for the story. "I've invited all the women at Hieroglyphics Communications to come to the station for a makeover. What Felicia doesn't know is that her mother, Eleanor, will also be here." Lou nodded. After a long pause, Stella said, "Any other questions?"

"What's the goal?" he asked, turning to her. "What's the point of it all?"

"The goal is to put Eleanor and her daughter together while talking about the case and see if anything shakes loose. If that doesn't work, we'll bring in the surprise guests and hope for the best."

"Is Parker freaking out?"

"Yes, but he's trying not to."

"Police will be standing by?"

"Yes, of course. Sergeant Coyne's got an undercover officer acting as another makeover winner and more officers will be out front, in case things start going south."

"By 'going south,' you mean Felicia opening fire on us?"

She glared at the photographer, who didn't look concerned by the thought. "Sergeant Coyne is in charge of the whole thing—we'll be just fine," Stella said with more conviction than she felt.

"You'll be right there in the thick of things?"

"Yes, like I told you, I'll be getting highlights. It's the only way Harry would agree to the plan."

"You really trust—"

"I wouldn't say I trust her, but she's who we have."

"Stella." She looked up as Harry's voice cut through the din in the newsroom, and she made her way to the assignment desk where he was standing by the monitors. "Looks like a whopper headed our way."

She nodded, watching the giant line of storms

marching eastward across the map. "Time?" she asked, her eyes glued to the screen.

"Bob says it's still a couple hours away, but it's picking up speed. I just want you to know that, no matter what happens, I won't pull you from your story today."

Stella looked up at her boss with surprise. Frankly, she'd expected him to say just the opposite. In fact, she had been ready to argue her case. Now that she didn't have to, she was speechless.

"At least, not right away," he added, daring her to object. "I know your story is important, but weather disasters trump everything else, especially in this newsroom. Let's just hope you don't run out of time."

Harry walked back to his office, leaving Stella staring at the storm system bearing down on Columbus.

Would she have time? The overhead speakers came to life and Bob James' voice rang through the office. "A quick update for everyone in the newsroom. The storm system has produced its first confirmed tornado touching down near Chicago. It appears to be picking up steam as it heads southeast. We expect the forward edge of the storm system to reach our viewing area shortly after one o'clock this afternoon. Be ready for wall-to-wall weather coverage."

There were several moments of silence at the conclusion of the announcement before the usual noise and activity of the newsroom came back. The producers all stared at each other, knowing they had to stack an entire rundown for their half-hour newscasts and fill it with news that likely would never see the light of day. W3 would push everything else aside.

Stella's eyes moved back to the monitors in the newsroom and she wondered which tornado would touch down first: one from the storm, or one from Felicia.

36

"I don't like this," Parker said, smashing his lips together into a straight line.

"I know, but we needed the extra hands. She was who we could get."

They were both standing in the doorway of the station, looking out into the parking lot, as Edie Hawthorne walked their way.

"Hi, guys," she said, sliding between them and into the building. "Wow. Houndstooth, huh?" she said, running her fingers down Parker's sleeve.

"Well, you couldn't pull this pattern off with your pale, pasty skin, but some of us—"

"You're probably right. Plus, I'm not quite

ready to relive the eighties. Some decades ought to stay in the past, am I right?"

"Parker, let's show Edie the space," Stella said, cutting him off at the pass. He looked like he'd been about to make a snide remark, and they didn't have time for a diva showdown just then.

He held his head high and marched past Stella, leading the way down the hall, past the studio, and into the makeup room, which had recently been transformed into a luxury spa.

"Ooh, nice," Edie said appreciatively as she looked around the space.

Parker had brought all of his equipment in and they'd spent the last two days fixing up the room to serve their purposes for the story. Harry had agreed to get a plumber in to connect the hair-washing sinks to a water source.

Everything was black, gray, and silver, and Stella had to admit it was fabulous. They'd raided Goodwill, and now dozens of old cameras hung on the walls and from the ceiling. Some were still-cameras and others were antique-looking video cameras.

"Did Lou get the—oh, there it is!" Stella exclaimed when she'd found the news camera hidden in the mix, sitting between leaves of a potted rubber tree in the corner. Another camera was set up in plain view near the wall closest to the door. As Stella walked by, she caught sight of herself in a large playback monitor. "Nice. No doubt about people being recorded," she said, stopping to watch herself inspect the video camera.

"You will be camera-ready when you leave this room every time," Parker said theatrically.

"Every mic is a hot mic, as well." She looked to Edie and Parker for confirmation that they'd heard her, but the two were locked in a silent glaring contest. She clapped. "Guys, focus. We have less than an hour until this goes down. Try to put your past behind you—just for the next hour—okay?"

"I just want to say that I'm only doing this because you're giving me the tape when it's done. I can't have that video hanging over my head." Edie spit the words out like bullets. The stylist couldn't wait to get the raw video Parker had recorded outside the football stadium the week before.

"Yes, we'd all hate for viewers to know how you really feel about them, wouldn't we?" Parker answered coolly, using his sleeve to wipe an invisible spot from the mirror closest to him.

"I'll have you know—"

"Seriously!" Stella exclaimed. "Police are going to be here any minute; please don't give them a reason to call this off. We all," she shot a pointed look at Edie, "need this to go off without a hitch."

Edie straightened her shoulders and bit back a retort. "You're right, Stella. Of course."

Stella turned her glare on Parker. "Can you handle it?"

"Of course," he said, standing even straighter than Edie.

She rolled her eyes, but started moving around the room as she spoke. "Paul said he'd bring all the ladies here just after the noon news is over. They think they've won a makeover contest that Paul entered them in. Attendance is mandatory." She stopped by Edie and leaned against the counter. "I'll be walking around with a photographer, interviewing the women, while you and Parker do your thing. We'll mostly be doing light makeup and maybe a quick blowout—nothing too time-consuming. The goal," she began walking around again, "is to make sure the women are here and comfortable when Eleanor walks in. The key is to have Eleanor and Felicia meet unexpectedly. We must capture their reaction on camera."

"Why?" Edie asked, unaware of any of the backstory in the case.

"We just do."

Edie looked unconcerned. "Just as long as I get that tape, that's all I care about."

Parker frowned, looking out the big picture windows on the far wall. "They won't cancel if it rains, will they?"

"Paul wouldn't miss all this free publicity," Stella said with a confidence she didn't feel. She scrutinized the sky: dark clouds were rolling in from the north and the wind was kicking up, but it was still dry. For that, Stella was thankful. She hoped the weather would hold.

"Are we ready?" Harry asked, walking into the room with Lou.

"Almost," Stella answered, still staring out the window.

"Parker, you know what to do?" Harry asked. Stella looked fondly at Parker, who nodded steadily at their boss. Harry said, "Stella, it really is the perfect time for those highlights we've been talking about. Everyone is here to get a makeover; it just makes sense for you to get one, too."

"Right," Stella said. Harry looked at her suspiciously and she grinned. "You're so right, Harry. It will only take a few minutes to get video of the makeovers, and so there will be plenty of time to take care of my hair, too." Harry nodded happily and Stella was left trying to wipe the grin off her face until her boss was gone. She'd worked something out with Parker about her hair, and couldn't be happier.

"Stella, your visitors are here," the tinny voice of the receptionist announced through the overhead speakers.

"Great. Let's do this!" Harry said with the same level of enthusiasm Stella had moments ago. They both left the makeup room. Harry peeled off toward his office, and she walked down the hall to the receptionist area.

Sergeant Coyne introduced her to the woman standing next to him.

"This is Detective Cindy Lao. She'll be in the room with you for the duration."

Stella nodded. She and Coyne had agreed upon a plan the day she'd learned about the connection between Eleanor, her daughter, Felicia, and Felicia's coworkers, Bobby and Rhonda. He didn't want to rely solely on hidden camera video, which is why they'd decided on having one camera in plain view, another hidden, and an undercover police officer with them.

She escorted the pair back to their respective spots. Lou worked on the live feed and taped down some last-minute wires that went between the studio and the new salon, and before anyone was ready, the overhead speakers came to life again. "Stella, your visitors are here," the receptionist said for the second time that day.

"Showtime," Parker said, and they all shared a meaningful look. "How will I know which one is Felicia?"

"We'll just have to play it by ear," she answered before leaving to collect the new arrivals.

She needn't have worried; as soon as she walked into the lobby, she spotted Eleanor's daughter. She realized, with a barely-concealed groan, that she'd actually recognized her during her very first visit to Hieroglyphics Communications. She had chalked it up to seeing one too many blonds in a row, though, instead of the similarities between her and her mother.

"I'm not sure a single one of these women needs a makeover, but we're excited just the same," Paul said with a lecherous smile on his lips.

Several of the women made faces at his remark, and Felicia looked longingly out the door to the parking lot. "Thanks, Paul. We'll take good care of them," she said, turning to lead the women out of the lobby.

"Well, I'm not going to miss the fun," he said, his words warm and his expression calculating.

"No men allowed," she said, still smiling, but with an edge to her voice that she couldn't disguise.

"I'll just—"

"We'll call you in for the big reveal, don't you worry, Paul."

His eyebrows drew together, and Stella smiled again, worried that her tone had exposed her true feelings for him. Her smile widened as she led the women down the hallway, away from their boss. He'd get what was coming to him—she'd be sure of *that.*

37

Stella hurried through the throng of women to the front of the line. "This way, ladies. We've set up a special room just up here. Only the best hairdresser and stylist will be working on you today." She pushed open the door to the salon.

"Congratulations, ladies!" Parker boomed with a gleaming smile, his arms open wide as the women filed in. "Everyone loves a makeover show, but don't worry, only the highlights will end up on TV—and oh, ladies, are we going to do some highlights!" Parker said, shooting Stella a nervous look. She motioned to Felicia with her chin and he moved toward her, picked up a lock of her bleached hair, and plunked her in front of the camera. "Now, who are you and what are we doing for you today?"

"I'm Felicia, and it's actually perfect timing," she said, looking at herself in the monitor. "I was just planning a complete do-over with my hair when Paul told us about the makeover day!"

"Tell me what you're thinking about."

"Well, I uh, I thought I'd go darker."

"Definitely. Your skin tone was never meant to go with blond hair," he said, nodding for emphasis.

Startled by his frank assessment, Felicia recovered quickly and said, "So, I was thinking of going really dark. Maybe black?"

"Black?" he gasped. "No, no, no—not with your coloring. I'm thinking warm chocolate to match your obvious roots with some subtle highlights by your face."

Felicia's face darkened at the dig, but Parker crowed, "Now, now. This is a safe space, and if you can't listen to your stylist, who can you listen to?"

Edie quipped, "Even a broken clock is right twice a day. Your skin tone couldn't handle black hair any more than it can handle blond."

Parker shot a dirty look at Edie and opened his

mouth to reply, but Stella beat him to it. "Okay, so Felicia's look is settled. Who's next?" She moved the next blond forward, but her mind was stuck on Felicia wanting to change her look. She had no doubt why: it would be a great way to conceal what she'd done, should anyone start questioning whether Tabitha was guilty. If police were going to be looking for another blond, Felicia would no longer fit the bill.

Edie welcomed another woman into her chair, "Good lord, what happened to your eyes..."

She trailed off at Stella's glare. "We're so lucky to have Edie helping us out today," she said to the woman, whose expression had gone from excited to shell-shocked with Edie's words. "She's going to very kindly show you some new techniques to apply mascara, isn't that right?" Edie was spared answering when the outer door opened again and a small, lithe woman entered the room.

"You must be Cindy," Parker said, welcoming the undercover officer into the room. He went through the same motions of making sure Cindy stood in front of the camera while they talked about her hair. "May I suggest some layers? They'd really soften your look—"

"No layers," she said without hesitation.

"This is a makeover," Parker said with sass. "I'll tell you what's gonna happen, mmkay?"

The cop looked appropriately chastened and said, "You're the boss."

"That's right, I am," Parker sat Cindy in a chair next to Felicia.

Another HC employee sat down with Edie, and Lou started making the rounds with the camera, capturing the initial consultations and the first sounds of the makeovers that would be the cover for their story. Capes went on, sinks came to life, and Stella's stomach started to clench. There was no going back now.

"Stella!" Parker said, pointing to another chair. "I've got your color ready!"

"Oh," she said, watching the chaos unfold in the small space. "I think we should probably wait on me. Let's get these women taken care of first!"

Parker nodded and started mixing ingredients together with a small paintbrush in a cone-shaped container when the door opened yet again and Harry walked in.

"My, it feels very crowded in here," Stella muttered, glaring at her boss. He was supposed to be waiting in the studio with Sergeant Coyne, watching everything on the live feed.

"Hello, ladies. Welcome to NBC News 5," he said, ignoring Stella's glare. "No, no, sit down!" he told the group when one woman started to stand in greeting. "We want you to relax and enjoy a little pampering. That includes you, Stella," he said, finally swinging around to face her. "*Everyone* gets a makeover today." Stella stood her ground and didn't move. "I mean literally everyone," he said, also standing firm.

She frowned. "Harry—"

"Parker, should Stella sit here for her highlights?" Harry motioned to an open chair next to Felicia.

"That's what I was planning, boss," Parker said, a grin threatening at the corners of his mouth.

Stella took a deep breath and reminded herself that it didn't matter if she looked silly on air—this story was much bigger than her. With as much grace as she could manage, she moved to the chair, continuing to glare at her boss. He was completely unaffected.

"Great! Can't wait for the final reveal!" Harry said, rubbing his hands together. He stood with his arms crossed and didn't leave the room until Parker painted the first brush strokes of color solution onto Stella's hair. Parker nodded encouragingly at her through the mirror, and Stella reminded herself that everything would work out fine in the end, even if she did have to suffer through a highlight reel of her getting highlights.

The stylists worked in silence for a few minutes, the only sounds from an occasional swish of a cape, scrape of a chair against the tile floor, or the swipe of a brush through someone's hair.

Once Stella was foiled, Parker turned to Felicia. "Before I can change *your* hair's color, I need to address the damage." He picked up a lock of her hair and bent it around his finger. "See how your hair doesn't ribbon around?" he asked, showing Felicia in the mirror how her hair stuck out at a right angle. "I'm going to give you a deep-conditioning, moisturizing rinse called a protein and hydrate treatment, and then we'll add the color." Felicia grimaced and Parker added, "This would cost you a fortune at a salon, so no arguing. It's our treat to you."

Lou came by with the camera and Stella made a face. He snickered and moved on to Felicia.

"Are you ready for this change?" he asked.

Felicia's forehead wrinkled. "Definitely. I need it. It's good to try something new, you know? Like a mini-escape."

Lou and Stella locked eyes for a beat before Parker tipped her chair back without warning. She yelped.

"Easy does it, Stella. Time to wash this out. Your transformation is almost complete!"

Parker washed the dye out of her hair and then combed out the tangles. She twisted her still-wet hair into a bun and started to move around the room with Lou while Parker worked on Felicia. He washed out the conditioning treatment and Stella looked nervously at the door. She felt the tension go up in the room and wondered if Felicia felt it, as well.

Edie was applying new makeup on two blonds from HC, Parker was mixing the dye for Felicia's brown hair, and Cindy and another woman were waiting on haircuts. Stella was waiting on something else, though—someone else.

Eleanor was late.

The lawyer would be the last person to walk in the door, but for all intents and purposes, her arrival would mark the real beginning of the show.

Parker made a point of telling Lou in great detail what he would be doing next, so he could capture it on camera, but Stella knew he was stalling. He knew that actually dyeing Felicia's hair could hamper the murder case against her. After all, police had an eyewitness identifying a blond woman pulling the trigger in two murders—not a brunette.

Parker rubbed Felicia's head briskly with a towel and then moved down to Cindy's chair and repeated the process. Just as Cindy's face started to take on a pained expression—he'd been rubbing her hair for several minutes by then—the door to the salon opened and Eleanor walked in.

"Stella? They said you'd be in—"

The lawyer stopped when she came face to face with her daughter. There was a moment of silence as the women locked eyes, neither able nor willing to speak. Parker stepped between them and welcomed Eleanor with false bravado.

"Congratulations on winning a makeover, Eleanor Pochowski! Let's get you in the chair, mmkay?"

Eleanor stood, frozen, in the open doorway, as if unsure whether she would take the final step inside or turn and run. "What is this?" she finally asked, her voice shaking. "What's going on here?"

Parker looked uncertainly at one of the hidden cameras before taking a stab at staying in character. "This is going to be a day full of excitement, that's what this is. You'll leave this room a changed woman!"

The words weren't as comforting as Parker might have intended, and Eleanor took a step back, stumbling as she encountered the uneven threshold at the doorway. "I—I'm not sure..."

Lou moved to capture Eleanor's reaction, and Stella was concerned to see that her eyebrows were drawn together seriously. The lawyer's lower lip trembled as she looked at her daughter with something akin to fear on her face. She took another step backward, stumbling again, and said, "I've made a terrible mistake. I've got to go!" With that, she turned and fled down the hall.

38

"There's nothing to be scared of, ladies, except peroxide!" Parker said to the remaining women. Stella would have laughed, except she was already halfway out the door after Eleanor.

Coyne's head popped out of the studio after Eleanor ran past, and Stella watched him speak quietly and calmly into the radio clipped to his shoulder. Just before Eleanor reached the door to the lobby, two uniformed officers walked into the hallway, chatting amiably with the station receptionist. Coyne must have radioed them to come in.

Eleanor stopped so suddenly that she practically left skid marks on the carpet. In a flash,

Coyne ducked back into the studio seconds before Eleanor spun on the spot, facing Stella.

"Eleanor?" she asked with concern. "Is everything all right?"

The lawyer glanced back at the officers and then double-timed it toward Stella. "Uh, it's... everything is... I just wasn't expecting such a crowd," Eleanor said, looking wildly around the hallway.

"We're giving the ladies at Hieroglyphics Communications a little special treatment, after... well, after all their recent losses. It seemed to be the least we could do," Stella explained as she steered Eleanor back down the hall.

The lawyer was so on-edge that the mere sight of the cops was driving her right back toward the makeup room—toward Felicia. Flustered, she looked over her shoulder nervously as the officers lingered in the hallway, only breathing out a sigh of relief when they were back in the makeup room. Eleanor backed along the wall of windows toward Parker. "Sorry. I'm not feeling like myself today," she explained with a nervous smile.

Parker smiled at her encouragingly. "That's why you're all here," he said, wrapping an arm around her and escorting her to the chair next to Felicia. "For a chance to start over."

Eleanor didn't sit, though. She stood, unblinking, as if she was seeing her daughter for the first time. "You're... *you're* here," she finally said with a tremor in her voice.

"I'm Felicia. It's so nice to meet you." Her voice was sickeningly sweet, yet firm, meant to both remind Eleanor that they weren't supposed to know each other and warn her not to say anything else.

Eleanor was close to a total meltdown, though, and she didn't seem able to stop herself. "What are you doing? What have you done?" she asked, her wide eyes slowly contracting to tiny slits.

Felicia barked out a mirthless laugh and then tried to soften it when Lou walked over with the camera pointed right at them. "I haven't done anything, *yet*, but I guess we're going to go hot chocolate with sugar—is that what you said, Parker?"

"Warm chocolate with honey highlights—" Parker corrected before Eleanor cut him off.

"I can't be a part of this, anymore. You have to know that. Not—not again..."

Felicia stood in a flash, and all pretense of civility was gone. Stella couldn't hear what she said, but the words were like a hot poker to Eleanor.

She stumbled back, tripped over the foot crank of the salon chair, and hit the ground hard.

Parker's hands started flapping and Cindy jumped out of her chair. To the rest of the room, she looked to be rushing to help the lawyer up, but Stella suspected the undercover cop was putting herself between the two women for Eleanor's safety.

"Ladies, there's enough makeup for everyone!" Parker said, his hands still flapping ineffectually at his sides. He looked from the hidden camera to Felicia and back again, and Stella wondered if he would crack under the pressure.

Eleanor stood slowly, never taking her eyes off of her daughter—it was like powerful magnets were connecting the two women. Even Stella couldn't look away.

"This cannot go on. I will not let it," Eleanor said, her back straight and her countenance suddenly sure and steady. "I'll go right to police. I won't let anyone else suffer at your hands."

"Get this woman a cup of tea," Felicia said. She attempted to smile, but Stella saw heat in her eyes. "She sounds like a crazy lady."

"I'm not kidding, Joanne," Eleanor said, her eyes never leaving her daughter's face. "It's over."

"Who's Joanne? There's no one here with that name," Felicia said, her eyes boring holes into her mother's.

"I can't—I can't be a part of this by staying silent."

"*Can't?*" Felicia asked, her carefully controlled rage simmering over. "Can't?" she repeated. The lawyer shook her head slowly as she backed toward the door, but Felicia rushed to block her path, her eyes wild and angry. "So you'll stand up *to* me, even though you never stood up *for* me, did you?"

Eleanor stopped as if she'd suffered a physical blow. "What are you—what do you—"

The reaction seemed to fuel Felicia, and now she was the one in control, her anger replaced by calm authority. "You know exactly what I mean. You could have protected me from him—that boyfriend of yours, Jeremy—but you believed *him* over *me,* and he took what he wanted." Eleanor blanched and Felicia stepped closer, not letting her mother look away. "Don't like to hear that, do you? Well, I won't ever forget, and I won't let you forget it, either." Although her voice was low, the fury was unmistakable.

Suddenly, everyone in the room was out of

their chairs, inching slowly away from the main event.

"I decided, when he died—" Eleanor flinched, but Felicia continued, "that I'd never let myself be taken advantage of again."

"To kill innocent people, Joanne? It doesn't make sense."

Felicia brushed off the sound of her real name. "No one is innocent. Don't you see? No one—not you, certainly not your precious boyfriend, Jeremy, and not Bobby. He stole that job! *It was supposed to be mine.* Paul promised it *to me!*"

One of the blonds by the window made a noise, but before Felicia could turn, Stella asked, "What about Darren? What did he do to you? And Rhonda? What were their crimes?"

Felicia pushed her wet hair away from her wild eyes. "Rhonda knew too much—she knew about the messages and the notes. Darren..." Felicia finally paused and shook her head, "that was a mistake." She looked imploringly at Stella. "Just a terrible mistake."

"Why were you even at Tabitha's house that day? Why were you back in her house?"

"I dropped my hat the day before, with Bobby. I worried police would find it and somehow know

I'd been there. I had to get it, and then before I could leave, the door was opening. I... I couldn't have someone find me there. I... I..."

She turned away from Stella—away from the questions—and instead faced Eleanor. "You know what? No one is completely innocent, mother, and no one was on my side." Felicia nodded frantically, "That *makes* them my enemy. That job should have been mine—MINE—but he took it from me."

The room fell silent and Stella broke in again, "What about Paul? Why didn't you get rid of him?"

Eleanor gasped, stunned, but the four other blonds in the room turned questioningly to Felicia. Hardly a second passed before she snarled, "He's next on my list, that self-important, woman-hating, abusive jerk." She sucked in a deep breath and looked around the room of women staring at her. "He was using all of us. He doesn't deserve to live." She stopped short, seeming to finally realize what she'd just said—what she'd just admitted. She stumbled back a step only to have her legs slam into a chair; she lost her balance and sat down hard.

No one moved for a beat as Felicia's confession sunk in.

"Knock, knock!" a voice called out seconds

before the door to the studio opened. Paul crossed the threshold and took in his employees with glee. "I just couldn't wait to see my girls in all their glory!" he said, stepping behind the nearest woman, Edie, and kneading her shoulders. She shrugged out of his grasp, but he immediately put his arm around her shoulders and pulled her close. "Looking good, ladies! Mmm."

For a moment, nobody spoke, and then Stella said, "Who here has been treated inappropriately by Paul Blackwell?"

The four HC employees looked nervously at each other and then slowly raised their hands. After a beat, Edie pushed away from Paul and raised her hand, too.

"Was anyone here promised the promotion *before* Bobby got it?" Only Edie's hand dropped. "Who was promised the promotion *after* Bobby died?" All the hands remained in the air.

Paul's smile was frozen on his pale, splotchy face. "I always said it was going to be a down-to-the-wire decision," he said with a sneer. "How can a man like me choose between so many wonderful candidates?"

"Unbelievable," the blond receptionist said.

"Ladies, ladies, we can work this out," Paul said heartily.

Stella nudged Lou. Felicia, using Paul's arrival as a distraction, was backing toward the door.

"Not yet," Cindy said, taking a pair of hand-cuffs out of her back pocket. She snapped them onto Felicia's wrists.

"What—"

"Felicia Andrews, a.k.a. Joanne Pochowski, you are under arrest for the murder of Bobby Herbert, the murder of Darren Lambern, the murder of Rhonda Leavy, and misdemeanor vandalism against Valerie Osmola. Anything you say can and will be used against you..."

As Cindy read the Miranda warning to Felicia, Sergeant Coyne walked into the room with additional officers. He slapped cuffs onto Eleanor's wrists, and she looked up in surprise, but didn't object or ask any questions.

"Eleanor Pochowski, you are under arrest for obstruction of justice, withholding information on a felony, and perjury."

Stella put a bracing hand on Parker's arm—he looked pale under his milk chocolate skin—and Coyne started reading Eleanor her rights as he walked her outside. Stella and Lou followed them, recording the entire walk from the building until Coyne handed the lawyer off to a uniformed cop waiting on the sidewalk.

"Good job in there, Stella," Coyne said, crossing his arms to watch as Eleanor lowered herself gingerly into the backseat of the police cruiser. "You helped us catch a killer, and you got highlights to boot."

"Well... thanks," she said under her breath as she tucked her wet hair—which had fallen loose, behind her ears.

"What?" Coyne asked.

"Err—What about Tabitha?"

"We'll talk to prosecutors tonight. She might be home tomorrow."

A clap of thunder sounded, followed almost immediately by a flash of lightning. Within seconds, huge drops of rain splashed down from the sky. Although she was just steps from the front door to the TV station, Stella's phone vibrated with an incoming call from the newsroom.

"W3 starts now, Stella. Harry wants you to take Lou and get a live shot up as soon as possible."

"We've got lightning," she said triumphantly, waving as Coyne climbed into his cruiser.

"Then get to a safer area. We'll need you live ASAP."

"Where, exactly, am I supposed to find a safe place in this storm?" Stella asked, looking up at the black skies and then at the cruisers pulling away from the curb. Each had their lights flashing as officers started the journey to the Franklin County Correctional Facility.

She heard mumbling away from the phone before the producer came back on the line. "Harry says sometimes you have to head through the storm to find safety."

Stella slipped her phone back into her pocket without answering. *Through the storm.* It was a surprisingly prescient statement from her boss—not only on W3, but also on life in general.

39

Stella slipped on her sunglasses as she walked out into the bright sunshine from the courthouse. Her newly lightened hair seemed to sparkle in the sun and she frowned as a wisp blew into her line of sight. It's not that she didn't *like* the highlights, because she did. Parker (and Harry, much to her chagrin) had been right, the change resulted in a sharper, more professional look on TV. She also knew she was making a lot of fuss about nothing, as Parker had only gone one shade lighter—many people probably didn't even notice a difference. But after a lifetime of one hair color she was finding it difficult to get used to something new.

She tucked the stray strands behind her ear, then squared her shoulders and headed for the news car, determined to stop thinking about something so trivial, especially when there were far more important topics to consider.

A few weeks had passed since the makeover madness, but fallout from her exclusive was still making headlines.

"Stella?" She smiled at the voice and turned to find Sergeant Coyne headed her way. "I was hoping to catch you here," he said. "Were you in there for Blackwell's hearing?"

"Yes. A grand jury approved three counts of sexual harassment against him, and all of his employees are prepared to testify. It's going to get ugly if it goes to trial."

"He'll plead out," Coyne said dismissively.

"I don't know. He seems pretty defiant."

"They all are, until their lawyers explain the process to them."

"Hmm," Stella said, unconvinced. Blackwell didn't seem to think he'd done anything wrong. "So, what's up?" Stella asked, looking at the cop curiously.

"Do you have a minute?" He motioned to a café across the street and she followed him inside.

When they were settled with coffee at an outside table, he began, "You know I can't go on the record about anything, but I wanted to fill in the blanks for you, off the record. You deserve it."

Stella leaned forward in anticipation. She'd been able to piece together much of what had happened, but she still had lingering questions—mostly about the murder from years earlier.

"Where should I start?" Sergeant Coyne asked.

"Jeremy Bagren," she said promptly, knowing there was more to the fifteen-year-old murder than prosecutors had ever discovered at the time of the crime.

"Jeremy Bagren," Coyne repeated with a sigh. "Well, you heard Felicia: he was no stranger."

"How is it even possible that prosecutors didn't know that back then?"

"According to Eleanor, she and Jeremy had only been dating for a couple of months. It was so new that she hadn't even introduced him to any of her friends, yet."

"Her daughter knew him, though," Stella said.

"Right," Coyne sighed again.

"I don't understand." Stella added more sugar to her coffee and stirred the drink with her spoon, never taking her eyes off Sergeant Coyne.

He reached for the sugar bowl and doctored up his cup before answering. "We have a two-hour-long confession from Eleanor. She said that when Joanne came to her years ago and told her Jeremy had forced himself on her, she just didn't believe her. She thought she was trying to get attention, like when she'd dropped out of high school and got some tattoos—"

"God, how terrible!" Stella said.

"Joanne told her Jeremy came to her bar and threatened to kill her if she went to police with her accusations. He was angry—shoved her—and she unloaded on him with an 8mm handgun."

"Why not go with the truth, then? Why hide it for all these years? Surely it would have made a difference to prosecutors as some kind of justified crime?"

He shook his head. "Eleanor said Joanne didn't want to be labeled as a victim."

"Better to be labeled a killer?" Stella asked incredulously. Coyne shrugged, and she tried to get back to the case. "Didn't Jeremy have a job—coworkers who would have known he was dating someone?"

"He had been living out of an extended stay hotel. Eleanor said he talked a lot about interviewing for positions, but never had a job in their six-week relationship. He didn't have any friends that police could find, and that's how Eleanor and Felicia were able to keep their secret during the trial."

"Wow." Stella set her cup down, unable to drink any more. So many years of Joanne's life had been wasted in prison, and if you believed Eleanor, she should never have been in prison. Did she believe Eleanor, though? "When exactly did Eleanor become aware that her daughter might be involved in Bobby's murder?" She remembered the lawyer wrapping an arm around Tabitha at her first court appearance. Had she been acting in good faith, or had she already suspected her daughter had killed again?

"She told us it wasn't until you showed her the video from the bus stop that she got suspicious."

Stella shook her head. "That can't be. The woman at the transit authority security office told me someone fitting Eleanor's description had already seen the video. She was sitting on Tabitha's alibi for at least a week before I found out about it. Plus, she only volunteered to represent Tabitha after she found out the victim had worked with her daughter. That's pretty fishy, don't you think?"

"Yes. Yes, I do, prosecutors do—we all do," Coyne said, lowering the volume on his police radio after it made a particularly loud beep. "I think, in the end, Eleanor was too concerned about her own reputation to care about her daughter's. I think she convinced Joanne to take the fall for Jeremy's murder, so no one would know she'd been dating a rapist. I also think she immediately suspected Joanne of killing Bobby and decided to keep close tabs on the case by volunteering to represent Tabitha. It will take a while to get all of our information lined up, but I think Eleanor's going to spend just as much time behind bars as Joanne." Sergeant Coyne finished the dregs of his coffee and stood. "Are you headed back to the station?"

"Not yet. I've got something to do first."

They headed in opposite directions, Coyne down the sidewalk toward the police department and Stella for her car. Fifteen minutes later, she parallel parked alongside the curb and waved to Jill DeMario, who was standing on her porch with her hands on her hips.

"Stella! Girl, I knew you'd be back!" Jill called.

Construction crews were in the process of replacing the storm sewer lines a block away, and

Stella saw red and blue utility flags planted in the grass along the sidewalk, as well as lines spray-painted on the street, marking off the existing underground utilities.

"Is your street next?" Stella asked, motioning to the orange barrels down the road.

"You know it is! They said it will take eight weeks total, but the project should be done before summer's over."

"I'm so glad!" Stella said, stepping onto the porch.

"Don't think your job is over, though. Girl, you ain't off the clock, yet. Don't get me started on why we don't got a supermarket on this side of town. Do you know I have to drive all the way to—"

"Is Cara home?" Stella interrupted.

Jill grinned. "I'm sorry, you're right. I'll give you a minute to breathe. She's not home—she's at debate practice." At Stella's raised eyebrows, Jill cackled. "She's like a new child, lately—really embracing her skills. No more card games and texting. She's all about truth and justice, my little Care Bear," she said fondly.

"When she gets home, give her this," Stella said, holding out a small paper bag.

"A notebook?" Jill asked, peeking inside.

"Not just any notebook—a reporter notebook and pen. Tell her she should keep it with her to write down anything important."

Jill nodded. "All right. I like it. A notebook for my girl."

Stella turned to leave, but stopped when the woman said, "No, no, no, you can't leave so quick. I gotta know what's the latest on the case? Cara will slay me if I tell her I saw you and didn't ask!"

"Well, you know Tabitha is home."

"Of course I know that. Ain't her kids running all over my house night and day again?"

She swallowed a laugh. Jill acted irritated, but Stella remembered the pantry packed with teen-favorite snacks in her kitchen and had a feeling the other woman loved keeping tabs on Cara and her friends. "Now prosecutors are deciding what to do with Eleanor and Felicia."

"I never did understand how that lawyer lady got involved in everything," Jill asked shrewdly, eyeing Stella over her sunglasses.

"It's complicated," she said, quoting Jill's daughter, "but the county prosecutor told me they'll ask for jail time for Eleanor for her role in covering up the crimes. Her daughter, Felicia, may never leave prison again."

"Mmm! That was some crazy stuff," Jill exclaimed, running her fingers over the notebook.

Stella nodded. "Oh, how is Valerie doing? I've tried calling a few times, but she didn't answer."

"Valerie? She's at the hospital—don't worry, she's fine—getting cataract surgery. She should be home by the end of the day. She said she couldn't stand the fact that she was a bad eye witness... finally pushed her over the edge to get the procedure."

Stella stifled another smile over the fact that her hypothesis was proven correct. "Tell Cara thanks," she finally said, backing away from the porch. "Tabitha would probably still be in jail if she hadn't spoken up."

"I'll tell her—and don't forget about us on Journey Street! These new sewer lines are just the beginning. We need groceries, Stella! I don't have time to drive across town every other day to feed my family! Why don't we have a local store that serves the neighborhood?"

It was another fifteen minutes before Stella managed to get away.

Back in the newsroom, she took a moment to savor the silence. The scanners were squawking and the phones were ringing, but it seemed muted, somehow, with all the other reporters and photographers out on stories. Stella had a few days to work on her stories that would air during May sweeps; Harry was giving her a half-hour special on the murder cases. They'd have the secretly recorded video, Tabitha and her family would join Stella live on set, and Stella had set up an exclusive interview with prosecutors about their cases against the Pochowski women.

"Stella!" Harry's voice floated over the empty desks, and she looked up inquisitively. He motioned her over.

"What's up?" she asked moments later as she walked into his office.

"I just got off the phone with NBC News in New York."

"Do they want more on the court case? The only new thing is that Paul Blackwell is facing multiple sexual harassment charges from his current and former employees from Hieroglyphics Communications. Felicia's public defender told me they'll likely use that to their advantage, if the case against her goes to trial—"

"No. No, it wasn't about Felicia or Paul or Eleanor or Tabitha," Harry said, straightening some papers on his desk before looking back up at

Stella. "It was about you. They need to get clearance from me to talk to you. It's just the right way to do business."

"What do you mean? I've been talking to them about this case for weeks, now."

"Not just *a* producer—the *executive producer* at NBC News. She wanted to know if they could buy out your contract here."

"Why would they do that?"

"They're very interested in having you work for them."

"In New York?"

"I'm not sure. They'll be calling you soon. I just wanted to give you a head's up."

"Wow," Stella said for the second time that day.

"Yeah, wow," Harry said, looking at her with pride.

"Do you think it was—"

"The highlights? Yes, I do."

She leveled a glare at her boss. "No. I was going to say the murders. Do you think that's why they're interested in me?"

"Well, there's no doubt you've proven yourself time and time again in your career, Stella. I would say this is only the latest example of your tenacity as a reporter and your ability to sniff out news wherever you are."

Silence stretched between them.

"Wow," Stella said again, suddenly feeling nervous. "When will they call?"

"I don't know, but I got the impression that it would be soon. Apparently, they have a national correspondent position to fill and they'd like to have someone in place for May sweeps."

"Well, I can't—"

"Yes, I told them we'd have to move your sweeps special up to the beginning of May, so you could be in New York by the end of the month." He smiled again and then swiveled away from her to face his computer. "Let me know how it goes when you talk to her—Rhee Parsons."

Stella nodded, even though Harry wasn't looking at her, and walked slowly back to her desk. Network? It was almost unimaginable. National correspondents flew around the country for different stories every week: one night, a flood in Texas and the next, a protest in California. You never knew where you'd be going, or what you'd be covering.

She was stressed out just thinking about taking such a huge job... but also excited. She sat at her desk in a trance. Would she keep her apartment in Columbus, or just live out of hotel rooms?

Would this Rhee Parsons person actually call? Although Harry said she'd sounded motivated, part of Stella didn't really believe it. Network interested in her? She didn't even have an agent to represent her!

Her cell phone rang and she felt her heartbeat thrum uncomfortably in her chest. Was she ready? She looked down at her screen and her heart surged for another reason: it was Lucky. They hadn't spoken in weeks. Not since she'd missed his race in Bristol.

With a slightly shaky hand, she answered the phone.

"I just heard you came to Knoxville to see me."

"Huh?" The greeting was so unexpected that it took her a moment to remember her failed attempt to surprise Lucky. "Oh, that."

"Why didn't you tell me? When we talked on the phone that day, why didn't you tell me you were there?"

"Oh... well, I guess I felt dumb. I should have told you before I made the drive. I wanted to surprise you, and instead, I was surprised. And not in a good way. How did you find out?"

"Ben just told me. "

"The gardener?"

"Yes, just today. I was... letting off some steam... and didn't realize he was just outside the garage. He mentioned that he'd seen you do the same."

"Were you yelling in your garage?" Stella asked, laughing as she thought of the gardener witnessing both of their frustrated breakdowns.

"It doesn't matter, but what does matter is that you made the effort. I didn't think you ever had."

"Of course I did, Lucky. You're important to me. I came to see you, but you weren't there, and I..." She still felt like an idiot about the trip.

"Stella, half the battle of dating from hundreds of miles apart is making the effort and showing up. I didn't think you were doing either."

"Well, I didn't come to your race," Stella said, not wanting to get too cozy before the other shoe dropped.

"No, you didn't," Lucky's voice was flat.

She swiveled away from her computer screen to focus on the conversation. She'd left him a half-dozen messages explaining the story, the arrests, and her need to see it through to the end, but he hadn't picked up a single time.

"It wasn't fair of me to ask you to," he finally said, his voice cracking with emotion.

"No—it was, Lucky. I just—"

"You freed that woman, didn't you?'

"Well, she's home now, yes."

"You found the real killer, too?"

"I did. Police were close to figuring it all out, but they just didn't have the whole story like I did."

"I just watched your stories online. The lawyer —the one who volunteered to help—she was actually guilty?"

"Eleanor? Well, she didn't know her daughter was the real killer at first, but when she heard that the victim had worked at the same place as Felicia, she knew she wanted to stay close to the case— that's why she volunteered to represent Tabitha. She then saw the bus stop video and knew her client was innocent, which is when she got suspicious of Felicia."

"Now Felicia and Eleanor are in jail, and that other woman is free?"

"Yeah, she is. Tabitha is home with her kids."

"You changed the course of her life—her kids' lives—with your story. Their whole lives changed because of what you did. I forget sometimes that it's not all races and trophies. I... I know your work is important."

"Oh—"

"Just—just let me finish," he interrupted. "I know your work is important, but so are we. *So are we*, Stella, and I need to know that you feel that way."

"I do, Lucky. I know we are—I know *you* are —but..."

"But," he agreed, and they didn't speak for a moment.

"I don't know how we can make this work," Stella said slowly.

"Don't. Don't say that. Don't give up."

"I'm not giving up. I don't know how we can make this work, but I know we can keep trying."

"Yes! Yes, that's all I wanted to hear from you. Because I'm all in, Stella. Are you?"

"Yes. All in, Lucky."

They ended their conversation and Stella lowered the phone with a small smile. Before she could set it down, though, it rang again in her hand.

She grinned and said, "I knew you wanted to say how much you loved me!"

"Ahem... is this Stella Reynolds?" a woman asked after a pause.

"Yes," she answered, cringing in embarrassment. It was not Lucky, and she really needed to start checking her phone screen before answering.

"Well, you're right," the woman said, "I really do love you—your work, at least. This is Rhee Parsons from NBC News in New York. I wanted to discuss an opening we have. Do you have time to talk?"

"Yes, I do," Stella said, her stomach clenching with nerves. "Thanks for calling."

She straightened her back and swiveled around to her desk, suddenly all business. She couldn't believe she was on the phone with an executive producer from network.

Was she ready?

Did she want to be?

She was about to find out.

###

LIBBY KIRSCH

The

Big

Job

A *Stella Reynolds* MYSTERY

THE BIG JOB

"Standby, Stella."

She'd heard photographers say the same thing to her in different states across the country for years, but nothing else about this day was familiar. Stella Reynolds blotted her forehead with her fingertips and smoothed a hand over her long, auburn hair. Her chest felt tight, her stomach fluttered, and she pressed her lips together. It was ridiculous, but she couldn't ignore the signs: she was *nervous*.

A nasal, confident, familiar voice behind her calmed her enough to take a deep breath. She listened to Vindi Vassa, a coworker from what felt like another lifetime, as she wrapped up a live shot for her station in San Diego to Stella's left.

"Preston Harrington has always maintained his innocence and has refused to cooperate with police or prosecutors..."

More reporters—some half-dozen—stood in front of the Palm Springs, California, courthouse, covering a whopper of a murder trial smack dab in the middle of paradise. Local stations from nearby San Diego and Los Angeles were there, along with CNN... and Stella.

The thought made her stomach flutter again and she gulped. Irritated at herself, she then shook her head hard.

"Hey. Are you okay?" Kelly Wozniack stuck his head out from behind the camera and looked at her over his glasses. "It's just a teaser—you know that, right? Five seconds—ten, max—and then we're done until three."

"Yeah, I know," Stella said, grimacing when her breath stuttered in three hops. She closed her mouth. Breathless for a pre-recorded tease! What was wrong with her?

"Okay, well, any time you're ready. I'm rolling." He didn't put his head behind the camera, though--just continued to stare, like he knew a car accident was about to happen and didn't want to miss it.

Woz was about her height at five-foot-nine but wider than a MAC truck and just as noisy. His loud breathing echoed through the parking lot, and in the desert heat, he had long ago sweat through his shirt. His messy, grey and black hair was curly and longish, sticking straight out from his head like he had a hand on one of those static electric balls at a science museum.

She squared her shoulders and took a cleansing breath. "Three, two—"

"Wait," Woz interrupted, "we don't do that countdown thing out loud. You just have to count in your head and then start."

Stella blinked. It was a small thing, really, but she'd been saying, "Three, two, one," before every pre-recorded standup for years. She'd been told long ago that the short countdown gave the editor enough tape to grab the edit. Now she felt tiny beads of sweat reform at her hairline. "Right, count to myself. No problem."

It was a problem, though. It took her three tries to say her six-second line correctly. Finally, she got it out. "A murder in paradise, and now the trial begins for the man accused of killing his business partner, all while the world waits for what could be a life-saving, game-changing drug." She looked up at him, her eyebrows raised.

Woz hit a button on the camera and said, "It's okay; they probably won't even use it."

She barked out a laugh at the absurdity of her day, which, although it was only noon in California, had started more than nine hours earlier in Ohio.

Lucky Haskins, her boyfriend of several years, had taken her to the Columbus airport for an early flight that morning. She had planned to fly to New York City for her new job as a network reporter for NBC News, where she would spend the week in training at their offices near Times Square, and then get her first assignment. Instead, she'd gotten a call from her new manager as she'd stood on the curb by Lucky's car.

"Change of plans, Stella. Can you rebook onto the five-ten flight to Palm Springs? Our reporter covering the Harrington trial fell ill."

"The five-ten to Palm Springs?" she'd repeated. "Uh..." Stella had scrunched her face together, wondering if she should head into the airport to make the change or call from her phone.

"If you can't do it," Sher Patrick had snapped,

"tell me now. We've got a storm system moving into the Plain states, though, and I don't want to pull my roaming reporters."

"Uh," she'd repeated. She hadn't been sure the logistics of switching her flight at this late hour, but before she could say as much, Lucky had held his phone in front of her face. She'd squinted to focus, and then said, "No problem, Sher. I'm headed that way now." Lucky had booked her onto the flight on the app on his phone.

After six hours on a plane and a quick introduction to the photographer she'd be working with that day, she was now taping a tease for the evening news and preparing for her first network live shot in the field.

"News starts at six thirty Eastern, three thirty Pacific," Woz said, "so you've got three hours to figure out what you're going to say."

"Do they just want a video wrap or a sound bite?" She had no idea what he had shot from opening arguments and didn't know how she was going to wade through hours of court video in time for the news.

Woz shrugged and Stella hid a grimace. Was he intentionally being difficult, or was he just unaware of how unhelpful he was? She let out a deep breath and squared her shoulders. After all, Woz was only going to be her partner for the day, not the year.

He lumbered up the steps to the satellite truck and opened the door, waving her in with a grunt.

As she stepped into the small room, Stella felt at home at last. News feeds from across the country played on the half-dozen monitors facing her. Rows of blinking, square buttons and lines of audio and video input and output jacks stared back at her. She rolled a wheeled desk chair to the editing computer, inserted the disc Woz handed her, took a notebook out of her briefcase, and sat back to listen.

The case had been making headlines since Dr. Drew Chambers, a founding member of the startup, Luna C Engineering, had been brutally murdered at their offices in Palm Springs. The company had designed a revolutionary new drug for anxiety and depression called Wondred, which was touted as a game-changer in the mental health industry. No side effects had been reported during years of trials. The company had been waiting on FDA approval and was on the verge of going public when the murder happened. Millions of dollars had already been lost and millions more were at stake as the company's future was tied up in the murder trial.

The camera locked on Preston Harrington, who sat stone-faced, staring straight ahead toward the judge. He was so tall that his long legs barely fit under the desk; he had wavy brown hair, an off-putting, seemingly permanent frown, and wore an unusual, fuzzy, green sweater.

Stella's lips crowded to one side of her face. It was ninety degrees outside and Preston Harrington was wearing a sweater? It was likely a last-minute idea by his lawyer to make him appear friendlier and more approachable, but the effort had been wasted. No amount of sweater-softening would reach the subconscious of the jury—not with a scowl etched across Preston's face.

The judge finally called court to order, and the prosecutor stood to address the jury. Gail Abingdon walked behind the defendant and reached out, as if to put her hands on his shoulders, but then she stopped theatrically and dropped her hands to her sides.

"Preston Harrington isn't like your neighbor. He's not like anyone you know. He's cold, he's calculating, and he's a killer. He couldn't take the insult of coming in second—of being constantly outshone by the victim. Dr. Drew Chambers not only designed the product industry insiders say will revolutionize the way doctors treat patients, but he was also the face of the company—the media darling. Who was Preston Harrington? He was a no one, a never was, a hanger-on, and in his jealousy, he finally snapped."

Harrington glared through the entire twenty-five-minute barrage of accusations.

The prosecutor's speech was methodical—scholarly, almost—as she laid out the state's case: Preston Harrington killed his business partner in a jealous rage the day before the company was to go public. Gail Abingdon sat down and Stella turned her eyes back to Preston Harrington, interested to hear how his lawyer would paint the same set of facts. Instead, the video went to black. She looked over at Woz in surprise. "Defense didn't speak?"

"Nah." He leaned against the counter and wiped his brow with a handkerchief. "The judge dismissed everyone after Abingdon spoke—said we'll start back up in the morning for the defense's opening arguments."

"That's weird," Stella said. "It's the first day of the trial and she only has the jury hear one side of the case?"

"I know. At this rate, we'll be here for weeks."

You'll be here for weeks, Stella thought, wondering when she could book her flight to New York.

The Big Job, book 5 in the *Stella Reynolds Mystery Series,* is available now.

ALSO BY LIBBY KIRSCH

The Stella Reynolds Mystery Series

The Big Lead

The Big Interview

The Big Overnight

The Big Weekend

The Big Job

The Janet Black Mystery Series

Last Call

Last Minute

Last Chance

For updates on new releases or to connect with the author, go to www.LibbyKirschBooks.com

ABOUT THE AUTHOR

Libby Kirsch is an Emmy award-winning television news journalist. She draws on her rich history of making embarrassing mistakes on live TV, and is happy to finally indulge her creative writing side, instead of always having to stick to the facts.

Libby grew up in Columbus, Ohio and now lives with her husband and children in Ann Arbor, Michigan. Yes, Thanksgiving weekend* is tense. For more information, check out her website at www.LibbyKirschBooks.com

*Also known as College Football Rivalry Weekend.

Connect with Libby:
www.LibbyKirschBooks.com
Libby@LibbyKirschBooks.com

facebook.com/libbykirschbooks

twitter.com/LibbyKirsch

amazon.com/author/libbykirsch

bookbub.com/authors/libby-kirsch

goodreads.com/libbykirsch

.

www.ingramcontent.com/pod-product-compliance
Lightning Source LLC
Chambersburg PA
CBHW051934240626

47153CB00005B/1484